EVA CHASE

A Study in Seduction

Book 1 in the Moriarty's Men series

First Digital Edition, 2019

Cover design: Deranged Doctor Design

Ebook ISBN: 978-1-989096-34-5

Paperback ISBN: 978-1-989096-35-2

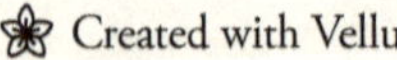 Created with Vellum

CHAPTER ONE

Jemma

I slipped into the reception hall crowd like a lover's hand easing up a skirt, half of my attention on the figures around me and half watching for the man I was going to ruin.

The finest investigative minds in the world filled the expansive room, all decked out in their cocktail best. The light from the crystal chandeliers shimmered off silk and satin. Voices bounced off the high molded ceiling, their tones bright thanks to the champagne that was flowing so freely I could taste the bubbles in the air.

The sequins on my violet evening gown whispered as I sidestepped between a few Australian sergeants and a couple of Peruvian detectives. I smiled demurely at the latter. One of the sergeants, who looked as though his suit was wearing him more than he the suit, took a surreptitious picture of the reception's finery with his phone. This gala was a pretty far cry from a normal day for a cop on the beat.

A waiter swept by with a platter of canapes, but I'd eaten before I arrived. The moment of action wasn't going to catch me with my hands full of poached pear on brioche. The wine glass in my hand served as a perfectly good prop—especially since I could transform it into a weapon with a quick smash, on the off-chance I needed one.

Even in distinguished company, you could never be sure. And not all of my company here was distinguished.

Ah, there was my man. If the cops and PIs around me had been half as good at their jobs as their being invited here should suggest, they'd have noted the recently released convict in their midst. The catering uniform fit the guy's stocky form just fine, but there were telltale signs a few months out of the clink could hardly come close to erasing. The marks on his shoes. The hang of his hair.

He'd been posted at the champagne table doling out glasses. That would make it easy to keep track of him.

The guy could have used some lessons in subtlety. I followed his gaze to the Glasgow commissioner. The woman was flicking back her fluffy blond bob as she chatted with a younger female officer who'd dabbed on enough face powder to turn an elephant Honey Beige. My convict was just barely restraining a glower at her.

The steady beat of my pulse picked up its pace in anticipation, but it wasn't time for either of us to make a move yet. I drifted in the commissioner's general direction. My mouth had gone a bit dry.

Everything was in place. There was no reason to get anxious, even if the consequences of failure would be devastating. Better to simply put that possibility out of my mind.

Another face caught my eye, this one from an interview I'd been perusing yesterday. I paused and turned toward it.

"Professor Charleston, isn't it?" I said, holding out my hand and beaming at the droopy-eyed man as if my life depended on this gambit. Which it very well might. "I've been following your work on trace evidence retrieval for years. It's an honor to be in the same room as you."

The professor made a pleased sound, with a twitch of his suit jacket like a bird ruffling its feathers to show off its plumage. As he shook my hand with a brisk pump, he peered at me, from my face down to the narrow but precipitous dip of my neckline, and then jerked his gaze back up. A little skin could make a large impression if you picked the right part of the landscape.

"I considered it an honor to be asked to lead one of the seminars here," he said. "It's good to know I have some wisdom worth imparting on the next generation."

"Absolutely! I'm dying to hear more about your recent strategies regarding gunshot residue. We'll see if I can't score a front row seat tomorrow."

My enthusiasm brought a flush to the professor's cheeks. "I'd save you one if I could."

I waggled a finger at him. "I'll just have to be resourceful. I'd better give the rest of the attendees a chance to talk to you before I embarrass myself with my gushing."

Professor Charleston chuckled as I gave him a little wave and glided onward. I continued smiling, now to myself. He might as well be tied up in a gift box with a bow on top.

Skirting a cluster of Japanese officers who'd gotten into a hushed debate, I checked that my convict had remained at his table. Indeed he had, with a little tug of his pants that told me in an instant where he'd hidden the pistol. Excellent. Every part of this plan was flowing along smoothly, except… where was the most important part of my audience?

A twinge of impatience had only just passed through me when the three I'd been waiting for strode into the reception hall. Half the heads in the room turned their way, which meant I could observe without looking unusually interested. This time I smiled only inwardly.

The trio of men who'd been selected for this conference from right here in London made odd companions. On the left, Garrett Lestrade was a little fox terrier of a man with dark eyes and boyishly angular features—the youngest detective inspector in Scotland Yard. On the right, John Watson, surgeon turned army medical officer turned forensics specialist, sported the bright hair and upbeat demeanor of a golden retriever. And looming tall between the two of them, his lean face as sharply alert as a deerhound, walked Sherlock Holmes, consulting detective, all of twenty-eight and already hailed in some circles as one of the greatest analytical minds of the century.

It might have been that reputation that drew so many gazes their way, but even an objective observer had to admit that the three of them were easy enough on the eyes in their differing ways. Watson bounded forward, a gleaming wooden walking stick offsetting his slight limp, already offering cheerful greetings and grasps of arms. Lestrade sauntered behind him, his hands slung in the pockets of his trousers and his chin raised at an angle that looked like a dare.

Holmes proceeded at a more leisurely pace, studying the room from beneath the messy dark waves of his hair, his stance aloof but a pleased smile curling his lips when a couple of lieutenants from Cardiff came over to compliment him on this or that brilliantly solved case. With the great height of his slender frame and that detached attitude, he might as well have been a king accepting the reverence of his subjects.

He had a dazzling mind to back up that confidence, absolutely, but even the mighty could falter. My heart thumped a little faster with a giddy shiver through my nerves.

I *would* have him, one way or another. The great Holmes hadn't yet tangled with the great Moriarty. Barely anyone even knew the great Moriarty existed, which was exactly how I liked it.

Possibly by design, the trio had timed their entrance perfectly. As the initial round of fawning wrapped itself up, a burly man with a pinstriped suit and a head like a turnip walked up to the podium at the head of the room and leaned toward the mounted microphone.

"Distinguished colleagues," he said with a faint whine of mic feedback. The conversations around the room quieted. "I'm overjoyed to welcome you all to London for our first International Conference of Investigative Skills."

I veered toward the fluffy-haired commissioner as we all moved closer to the podium. As if by chance, I came to a stop just a couple feet to her left. A quick glance toward the wine table told me that my convict was on the move too. I adjusted my weight on my feet, ready to spring.

Turnip-head at the podium went on with his speech. "I pride myself in thinking we've managed to assemble the top minds in criminal investigation from all across the world. You were invited because you're at the top of your field, but I'm sure you made it to those heights through the understanding that there's always more you can absorb. For the next ten days, you'll be able to learn from other investigators as skilled as yourself in their specific areas of expertise."

A flicker in the light over his head caught my eye. When I glanced up, the glow streaming down from the chandelier shimmered with a texture like a filmy piece of gauze. I didn't let myself visibly react, but inside my stomach tightened.

The shrouded one had already tracked me here. What was it doing, playing with light effects?

No one else appeared to have noticed anything off. It only wanted me to know it was here. Watching. Waiting.

My fingers curled toward my palm, not quite a fist. I

wasn't letting that piece of supernatural excrement distract me from my mission.

Turnip-Head rambled on about how lucky, dedicated, and wise we all were—I could claim the latter two out of three; not bad—and the catering convict edged into view through the crowd. He had his hand tucked close to his waist, close to his pistol. Well, technically *my* pistol, since I'd contrived to get it into his hands. And to get him in here. And to give him this opening.

Fifteen years ago, Ms. Commissioner had been a sergeant who'd gotten him put away for killing a father of two in a bar brawl. The guy's long-time girlfriend had left him. He'd lost a job he liked to brag about. He'd been happy to take an opportunity to get revenge.

I couldn't really take credit for ruining him. That honor belonged to his poor life choices.

He could have ignored my offer. He could have walked away even now. But he didn't. Instead, he lunged, whipping the pistol forward at the same time.

All his attention had been focused on the commissioner, and none of it on me. Another poor choice.

A shout of warning rang out. The commissioner spun around, her face blanching. I sprang between the convict and her in one smooth movement guided by years of physical training.

Knee to the groin. Elbow to the ribs. My heel to his hand, kicking the gun out of his grasp.

I giveth, and I taketh away.

I pinned the convict to the ground, braced against his back. The flexible fabric of my violet evening gown pooled against his white catering shirt. Quite a few people were yelling. A security officer hustled through the throng and knelt down to snap a pair of handcuffs around the guy's wrists. We were in a room stuffed with cops, but this one night they'd all left their equipment behind.

"Oh my God," the commissioner said, holding out her hand to help me up, the other pressed to her chest. "Thank you so much—you moved so fast. He came out of nowhere."

I'd give too much away if I looked around to check, but I hoped the London trio had gotten a good view. I stood and squeezed the commissioner's hand with a small smile. "I saw the gun, and I just reacted. I'm glad you're okay."

After toasts and exclamations over my heroics, I welcomed the stillness of my hotel room. The grand establishment hosting the conference boasted worn historic limestone and ornate arched lintels on the outside, but the innards had been tastefully modernized. Ivory walls, thick slate-gray carpeting, a sleek ebony desk against one wall, a king-sized bed with matching ebony frame against the other, a little table in the corner near the window.

The window looked out over the back courtyard, dark now other than a few pools of light from the security lamps. I'd arranged a suite at the end of the hall on the second floor. The broad limestone sill outside would serve Bash just fine when he needed to drop in.

I turned away from the view, and all my satisfaction drained away.

A translucent white figure wavered in the glow of the bedside light. It formed a lumpy but vaguely humanoid shape beneath overlapping strips of ragged white fabric—at least, they looked like fabric. Sometimes I wondered if they weren't swaths of dead skin.

The only part the strips didn't totally cover was the area that should have been a face. There, amid the folds of cloth, a haze of mist stared back at me, so deep that if I looked at it for long, I'd feel I were staring clear across the continent into a realm where no human had ever ventured.

A chill raced over my skin, but I meandered across the room to the mirror over the desk as if I had no qualms about my visitor. "Hello, Bog," I said. "What brings you here?"

Bog wasn't really the thing's name. The shrouded folk had their own language that human ears couldn't properly decipher. Bog sounded somewhat right, and it gave me a tiny shred of amusement to call the monster after something repellant, if I had to address it at all.

I could still see it at the side of the mirror while I unpinned my hair. As the red waves spilled down over my narrow shoulders, the folds around Bog's face quivered.

"You are playing games," it said in a voice as dry as desert-bleached bone and as distant as the mist it came from. "I thought you might need reminding of our agreement."

A pinching sensation emanated from the spot on the

back of my neck just below my hairline where the magic of our contract had marked me.

"Oh, I'm hardly going to forget that," I said. "I have a month longer. Why shouldn't I play during the time I have left?"

"Why play *here*, bloodling? You are no 'investigator'."

"Oh, I don't know. I think I've investigated plenty in my time."

"If that is what pleases you. Perhaps I will find something of interest in it too."

The shrouded one's tone stayed perfectly even, like mine had. We were playing a game right now—the game where I pretended I didn't plan to do everything in my power to escape the deal I'd made, and it pretended not to suspect me of that scheming. But those last words had been a warning.

I shrugged and picked up my brush. "You can spend your time however you want."

The mist stirred. I could almost have said I caught a glint of a smirk.

"Think more about how you wish to spend yours, bloodling. You received your ten years. In thirty days, your life is mine."

I smiled back at it through the mirror despite the tremor that ran through my chest. *We'll see about that.*

CHAPTER TWO

Sherlock

Halfway through the first morning of the International Conference of Investigative Skills, I had yet to be convinced that this wasn't an utter waste of my time. I wouldn't deny that it had been a badge of honor for the selection committee to have recognized my contributions despite my lack of formal credentials. They'd extended an invitation to John no doubt mainly in deference to how closely we worked together, and there was no denying *he* was enjoying the experience.

Nevertheless, so far the seminars had done nothing to alleviate my feeling that modern police work was woefully behind the times. I could have pointed out a dozen errors mentioned by the lecturer for our session on toxins—and would have, if John hadn't given me a pained look as if I were poisoning him with my initial clarifications. So far, our current session on the identification and analysis of trace evidence had revealed nothing I hadn't determined through my own work.

The trouble was, being permitted to solve crimes alongside the police required keeping the good will of the police. I could only imagine the offense that various parties would take if I removed myself, regardless of how much good I might do elsewhere during this time.

So, for now, I remained in the hard wooden chair in the fourth row of the bland beige room, letting Professor Charleston's baritone roll over me and resisting the urge to recommend to the woman sitting in front of me that she apply approximately thirty percent less of her jasmine-and-patchouli perfume out of consideration for the lungs of her colleagues.

From the worried strip of skin around her left ring finger, anyone should have been able to tell that she was recently and unhappily divorced. I probably ought to be considerate of her mental state. For John's sake, in any case.

As Charleston flipped through several crime scene photographs on a projector screen at the front of the room, Garrett shifted in his chair at my other side. This session might be of some use to my Scotland Yard associate, as loath as he'd be to admit it. He had his hands clamped together in his lap to keep from fidgeting. Sitting still and waiting for information to come to him had never been Detective Inspector Lestrade's forte.

"All right," Charleston said, rubbing his hands together. "I've laid out the scenario. Now why don't I give the rest of you a chance to weigh in? Would anyone like to volunteer what they would glean from the evidence offered so far?"

A hand shot up in the front row. I couldn't see the woman's face, and her casual blouse and slacks set a very different tone from her dress at the reception last night, but her flame-red hair and delicate build made her easy to identify. Yesterday's events had proven she wasn't as delicate as she looked. She'd thrown and pinned a man who had to weigh nearly twice what she did.

The reception had been all astir after that, even John and Garrett, as if they'd never witnessed an example of excellent physical conditioning before. You wouldn't think training in martial arts would be all that uncommon among the enforcers of justice. When dealing with criminals, it was careless not to be prepared for a situation to come to blows.

Several other hands lifted in the audience, but Charleston's face lit up when his gaze rested on the young woman in the front. He motioned for her to speak.

"What you were saying about the tire marks," she said in a voice that was soft yet precise enough to carry through the room. Her American-esque English was faintly accented with what sounded like a variety of mild influences rather than a single source I could pinpoint. "The obvious conclusion from the depth of the impressions and the drops of oil is that the perpetrator sat in the car for several hours waiting for the victim—not knowing her well enough to guess when she'd arrive."

I suppressed a sigh. Yes, that was the obvious

conclusion, and the one almost anyone here could have drawn. It took *real* observation and insight to—

"I'd suggest that answer is misleadingly easy," the woman went on, to my surprise. She motioned to the photos. "In my opinion, it's more likely that the perp *did* know the victim and had parked there to visit her many times in the past, resulting in deepened impressions."

Charleston's eyebrows leapt up. "How would you support that conclusion?" he asked.

I found myself tilting forward slightly to make sure I caught every word of the woman's response.

"It's a very narrow turn into the driveway," she said confidently. "You can see the post has been scraped often —but there's no fresh marking, as though any recent visitors were practiced at avoiding it. The treads themselves look like the type to support an older car that might leak a few drops of oil in a short time. If I were investigating, I'd take soil samples to determine if the same oil lingered deeper in the earth and check the victim's friends and associates for anyone owning a leaky older car."

"Well." The professor blinked, and his lips twitched with amusement. "I'll have to give that take some thought. Anyone have another angle to offer?"

He called on some fellow farther down our row, but I was still watching the woman ahead of us. Her attention to detail and the swift leaps of her deductions—they almost reminded me of my own line of reasoning with...

I turned to John. "Did you write up any public accounts of the Yardsley murder?" Perhaps she wasn't particularly swift but merely remembering past investigations not her own.

John shook his head. His puzzled expression faded after a moment. "Her approach *was* quite a bit like yours there, wasn't it? She couldn't have read about it through any public channel that I know of."

The police records wouldn't have laid out my process either. She'd followed a similar train of thought through the adeptness of her own mind.

My gaze settled back on her bright hair. This conference might turn out to be more than mundane after all.

"You know," our little detective inspector said, trailing behind me as I strode into the hotel's library, "some people might call this stalking."

I dismissed Garrett's comment with a wave of my hand. "I'm merely looking to talk with a colleague of sorts. We're at a conference meant for the sharing of ideas. And I think *you* are just as interested to learn more about her as I am."

He didn't argue that point. John nodded toward a table at the back of the room just as I spotted that head of flaming red hair. We made our way over, past gleaming modern bookcases that held mostly recent volumes and none of the scent of stale binding glue and aged paper that belonged in a proper library.

The woman was poring over the contents of a folder,

several photographs on one side and what looked like a police report on the other, glancing up only briefly to tap a few notes on a propped tablet. She was so absorbed in her study that she didn't notice our approach immediately, which gave me a moment to study *her*.

Other than that stark red hair, her eyes were her most striking feature: deep-set and the irises darkly ringed in a hue I couldn't determine at a distance. The rest of her pale face contained a mix of contradictory features. Her upturned nose and sharp chin gave an almost childlike impression that contrasted with those eyes and full lips and her overall bearing, which spoke of maturity beyond her apparent years. The set of her shoulders said they'd carried a lot but were prepared for more, as the chips fell.

Not a countenance one would soon forget.

Beyond her bearing, everything about her spoke of care and exactness. She kept her fingernails neatly trimmed and clean. Her clothes showed not the slightest stain or tear. She wore no accessories other than a simple but elegant silver ladies watch, not designed to draw attention but to keep time impeccably.

The entire effect revealed little about her history. She was unmarried and, to the best of my judgment, unattached. There were difficulties in her past she'd risen above—but what precisely I couldn't determine. Intriguing.

We were only a few feet from the table when she registered our footsteps. Her head jerked up, her slim hand automatically moving to flip the folder closed. Ah, that response I could read. She wasn't supposed to have brought the file here.

"My apologies for interrupting your work," I said, coming to a stop beside the table. "I'm Sherlock Holmes, and these are my colleagues, Dr. John Watson and Detective Inspector Garrett Lestrade. We were quite impressed by your analysis in the trace evidence seminar this morning. I was hoping we might get to know each other a little better."

The woman considered me for a moment, her hand still resting protectively on her folder. Her eyes were gray —the pale shade of a frozen lake bleeding into an outer ring that was dark as a thunderstorm. I'd imagine many men found them difficult to look away from.

After a few seconds, her shoulders eased down a smidgeon. "Jemma Moriarty," she said. "You… want to get to know *me*?"

She clearly recognized me, or at least my name. Whatever fame I'd earned could perhaps have its downsides if it intimidated her.

I propped myself against the table. John took the seat across from her, and Garrett stayed on his feet, gripping the back of the next chair over.

"I'll be honest," I said. "Even the experts assembled here tend to fall into the same tired patterns of thinking. You have a rare ingenuity. I like to cultivate as many inspired associates as I can."

"You were pretty impressive giving that gunman the smackdown," Garrett put in. "A bit of a firecracker, aren't you?"

"I guess you could say that." She flashed a smile. "I do my best."

"What made you focus on those details in the scene Professor Charleston laid out?" I asked.

"They were the details that were there," Jemma said matter-of-factly. "I've never believed in accepting the obvious answer from the most obvious evidence. You get to the truth faster if you take every available factor into account."

A spark of electricity raced through my nerves like it had when I'd listened to her speak in the seminar. She did have a mind, all right.

"I couldn't have said it much better myself." I dropped my gaze to her file folder, an itch of curiosity chasing the eager spark. I'd developed numerous strategies for coping with boredom in recent years, so no danger lurked in that area now, but I found it vastly more satisfying to avoid the sensation altogether.

It would be the perfect irony if the most stimulating part of this conference had nothing to do with the conference at all.

"What are you working on?" I asked.

Jemma tucked the folder a little closer to her. "Just a case from back home that's basically closed."

I judged her reaction. "But not solved."

She shrugged awkwardly. "We—*I*—ran out of leads. I thought being here in this atmosphere, something might click. No luck so far."

Her hesitation only made me more intrigued. I nodded to the folder. "I've yet to meet a case I couldn't crack. Why don't you let me put my mind to it and see if I can't shake something loose?"

"Well, I…" A bit of color rose in her pale cheeks. "I'm not actually supposed to have printed off the documents or brought them with me."

"I can manage discretion," I said.

"He isn't just full of himself, as much as he might sound like it," John said with a warm grin. "If there's a problem in existence Sherlock can't work out, I haven't seen it."

"Those of us at Scotland Yard have started to rely on him for our most complicated cases," Garrett added, more grudgingly.

Her hand stayed tensed on the folder. "We only just met. I couldn't ask you for a favor like that."

I waved off her concern. "You'd be doing *me* a favor. Alleviate the boredom of this humdrum symposium. What could it hurt? I swear I won't mention it to your superior officers back in…?"

"Freising," Jemma said. "It's a small city just outside of—"

"Munich," I filled in. "Are you German, then?" That could explain the softness of her Rs, but not much else in her accent.

In that moment, her smile looked almost sly. "For the time being. I wasn't born there."

The woman was a puzzle, but I could unravel that mystery soon enough. For now, I wanted to keep my primary goal in sight. I tapped the edge of the folder. "Five minutes. You can kick me off the case if I don't find anything."

Her eyebrows rose. She hesitated a second longer, and then she released the file to me. As I opened it, she crossed her arms over her chest, tension lingering in her shoulders. Garrett leaned over and John got up to peer at the folder's contents with me.

A city councilor had been found dead from a head wound on the side of a road on the outskirts of Freising— but one glimpse at the photo told me it hadn't been an encounter with a car. The side of the poor fellow's skull had been bashed open with a blunt rectangular instrument, the rest of him uninjured.

John grimaced. "With a hit like that, he'd have been gone so fast he wouldn't have suffered much."

"He was moved there," I said, glancing over the surroundings. "The murder happened at another site."

"We determined that," Jemma said quietly. "But not where."

Following that trail would be rather difficult at this distance. I considered the photograph again. "The assailant knew him—it was personal."

"How can you tell *that* from one picture?" Garrett said.

I pointed at the wound. "I expect John could follow my reasoning."

My friend considered the photograph. He'd struggled to piece together the blatant clues when he'd first begun assisting with my investigations, but in the past two years he'd proven himself a quick study.

"It was a crime of passion," he said. "You don't bludgeon someone that close up and that hard unless you're in the grip of strong emotion."

"Rage, most likely," I said with a satisfied nod.

Garrett grimaced. "Maybe this councilor was such an arsehole he could provoke rage in a stranger."

I ignored the off-the-cuff remark and flipped through the other photos from the scene. My fingers stilled around one near the back that showed what appeared to be a torn fragment of another photo.

"What's this?" I asked, setting it on the table.

Jemma peered at it and frowned. "We found that in his jacket pocket. Chances are it had nothing to do with his murder. Even if it does, it's impossible to determine what it was a picture of from just that piece."

A smile curled my lips. "Not at all," I said. "I can tell you exactly where you'd find that bit of stonework. It's just a quick jog across town. The real question is, why was your murdered councilor carrying a torn photo taken in London when he died?"

CHAPTER THREE

Jemma

It was a thrill to watch Sherlock Holmes at work—even more so because he clearly didn't suspect how much I'd engineered his current quest. I had to admit I hadn't expected him to identify the location in the scrap of photograph so quickly and from memory.

Now he strode briskly along the posh West London street without any concern that he was leaving John and me at his heels, taking the buildings and people around us in with his sharp gaze from beneath the fall of his dark hair. The crisp early spring breeze stirred the messy waves, and his trench coat billowed behind his lanky frame.

He thought he saw everything, picked up on every clue. He had no idea how much horror lurked at the edges of this world, hungry and conscienceless. Would he and his regular companions have believed that the things I knew even existed? Doubtful.

"From the way you handled the gunman at the reception, you've obviously done some combat training," John said to me, managing to keep up a pretty good pace and to still look relaxed about it despite his mild limp. His walking stick tapped against the pavement in an upbeat patter that fit his whole demeanor. "Do you have a preferred style?"

"I wanted to learn a variety of methods so I could apply whichever works best in any given situation," I said. "I started with Judo and Muay Thai and worked up to Krav Maga."

Holmes—well, Sherlock; we were all on a first name basis now—hummed to himself. He glanced back at me for a second before leading us across the street. "I'd have said there was some American military influence in your form as well."

Oh, he did see a lot, didn't he? An eager prickling ran through me at the thought of all those wits at my disposal.

"Funny you should mention that," I said, as if surprised. "While I was training, I'd often do some sparring with a friend of mine who served in the American army. I guess a few tics rubbed off on me."

A smile curled the corners of Sherlock's lips. That was how he got off: noticing and interpreting details other people didn't or couldn't. Every moment I spent in his presence was further confirmation of what I'd guessed— that his greatest point of weakness was his pride in his intellectual strengths. Did he care about my stakes in this supposed investigation? Not a chance. He'd come this far because of his need to show off his abilities at every turn.

He had an ego as big as an anaconda and equally difficult to shake. Play to that, and he'd dance, thinking it was all his idea. Like he was right now.

Arrogance aside, he *had* recognized exactly where that photo had been taken. He drew up short and pointed farther down the street to a stately bank building with a textured arc of stone along its top.

"This isn't the only building in the world or even this city designed in that style," he said. "But the combination of the texturing and the wear and the quality of the stone told the story clearly enough. Your dead councilor's photograph was taken within a foot of where we're standing right now."

Delight at the problem solved rang through his firm tenor. We'd only made it to the start of the trail, though. I peered at the bank building, choosing my words with care. If I gave him too large a shove in the right direction, he'd pick up on my intent, and then I'd be nowhere near getting him to the real goal.

"I can see it," I said. "But there's no way to tell what was in the rest of the photo—or whether it was something that led to the murder."

"We can tease out the possibilities and test our hypotheses." Sherlock steepled his hands together in front of him as if to hold his enthusiasm in check. "If it *did* prompt the murder, we have to assume it contained some sort of incriminating material, most likely as a point of blackmail. A photograph taken from this angle would have caught some of the neighboring buildings. Which of these do you think would be most likely to produce illicit behavior?"

I had to make it sound as if I were working through the options right now. "I suppose a bank robbery would be too convenient—and conventional. I don't notice anything particularly provocative about the boutique next door. And then…" I tipped forward to peer at the next sign. "Cavalier's. What kind of business is that?"

"I believe it's a gentlemen's club," John said in a wry tone.

"Indeed," Sherlock said. "One of the old-fashioned ones that still doesn't allow any gentle*women* as members."

"Exclusive clubs can be a hotbed for activity that skirts the law," I said. "I suppose if I were investigating I'd start there."

Sherlock's smile grew. "As would I. So, let us investigate. I'd like to get a look at their membership file to determine if any of those 'gentlemen' have recently been in the vicinity of Munich."

"Hold on," I said. "I don't have any jurisdiction here, and you're not even supposed to know about the crime. They aren't going to hand over their members' names to anyone who asks."

"Who says we're going to ask?" Sherlock said. "Sometimes bringing about justice requires a little bending of the law."

I'd already known he held that philosophy—no doubt it was another reason that Garrett Lestrade of Scotland Yard had begged off this little expedition, citing an appearance he was expected to make. But it wouldn't do to sound eager myself.

"Oh?" I said. "But if we're caught…"

A flicker of disappointment and maybe a little wariness crossed the detective's handsome face. His gaze turned downright piercing. He'd expected me to be committed enough to solving this crime to jump right in.

"If we play our cards right, we won't be caught," he said. "Unless you're not willing to take that gamble to find the answers you've been searching for?"

The question had the feel of a test. I had to walk a fine line between hiding my true motivations and keeping his good will. He'd be even *more* wary if I suddenly charged ahead after my initial hesitation.

"It's just not my usual approach," I hedged, buying myself a little time.

John grinned at his friend, his hazel eyes lit with fondness. It wasn't really me he was here to support—for him, this was all about his friend. "Sherlock's methods may not be entirely conventional, but he's never dragged me into danger we couldn't get out of. If you're not comfortable coming along, we can handle it between the two of us."

I pretended to waver for a moment longer. Then I exhaled in a sigh. "No. It's my case. If we're taking risks for it, I should be a part of that. What exactly is your plan, Sherlock?"

The detective studied me as if judging whether to accept my involvement after all. Then he shifted his attention to John. "Do you have a flash drive on you?"

At the other man's nod, Sherlock rubbed his hands together. "You'll be a gentleman interested in joining the club. His long-term girlfriend has her doubts. The management will bring you into the offices to see about registering, and then an unfortunate incident will draw them out of the room to make sure nothing jeopardizes the club's reputation in the eyes of the young lady. Simple as anything."

Exactly what I wanted to hear. And once he had the membership file, I could hope that it would be simple enough for him to identify my mark and dredge up one crime or another to pin him with. All I needed was the guy in custody for a day or two, and that would be enough of a window to make my real move, no further tactics necessary.

John set his broad hand on the small of my back. "Just follow my lead, and we'll be in and out in a matter of minutes," he said, so warmly confident I expected anyone would have gone along with him, a shrouded one's claim hanging over their heads or not.

I dragged in a breath as if from nerves. My actual nerves were tingling with exhilaration. In a matter of minutes, I might be nearly through with this mission. It'd be bye-bye to Bog without him or the men I'd used being any wiser.

Then I could get on with my real work. When I was finished with the shrouded folk, those ghostly creeps would never hurt another innocent soul like my sister again.

"All right," I said. "Let's do it."

Sherlock hung back as we started across the street. John whipped a strip of hair that matched the golden-blond stuff on his head out of his jacket pocket and patted it onto the skin beneath his nose. I arched an eyebrow at him with honest amusement.

"Do you always keep a fake moustache on you?"

He turned his grin on me. "Sometimes two or three. It has to be the right one for the occasion. Shall I take your arm? We'd better look the part."

I let him tuck his free hand around my elbow and dug into my purse so I could pop a sugar cube into my mouth. The pure sweetness dissolving over my tongue sharpened my concentration—and I wanted to be doubly sharp for this encounter.

We sauntered up the steps outside the club. Even from the door, the place stank of rich men: cigar smoke and fine scotch. The doorman held up his hand to stop us at the edge of the thick crimson carpet.

"I'm sorry, sir," he said, "but the lady may not enter."

"Well, now," John said in a snooty voice that matched the awful moustache. "I understand that she won't be joining me on regular occasions, but I've come to ask about acquiring a membership, and my darling has a few questions to set her mind at ease. Surely she can't harm anything by merely stepping over the threshold. We wished to speak to the manager—she won't stray beyond his office."

The doorman frowned, but he ducked inside. When he returned a moment later with a gaunt man in a full suit, presumably the manager, John pulled his considerable frame taller with a raise of his chin.

"Is this how you treat all interested parties—leaving them to catch a chill on the doorstep? My cousin owns half the newspapers in this city, you know. I'm sure *he'd* like to hear about—"

"Sir, sir, no need for distress," the manager broke in, a hair shy of wringing his hands. He beckoned us in with a nervous glance around as if he thought my feminine presence in the front hall might bring the building collapsing down around our ears. "Cavalier's is pleased that you're considering joining our establishment. I'd be happy to address any concerns your charming partner has."

I stroked my hand down the side of John's arm as if in a loving caress. Whoa there. He might have looked like a sweet golden retriever of a man, but he was hiding a good bit of muscle under the softness.

He still had that pompous look pasted on his face, but I thought a glimmer of heat sparked in his eyes at my touch. An excellent start in case I did need to resort to my more complicated alternate plan.

"I just don't see how a place like this can be anything other than backwards when you have such outdated policies about women," I said, giving the manager a tight smile. "It's like you must be getting up to antics you wouldn't want us knowing about."

The manager smiled back just as tightly. He ushered us into his office where a laptop and various papers sat on a mahogany desk, surrounded by built-in bookshelves lined with leather-bound volumes I'd have bet half my accumulated fortune he'd never even opened. We sat on leather chairs that based on their patina were only slightly less old.

"I assure you, miss, that nothing at all inappropriate goes on within these walls," the manager said, sinking down across from us. "Our policy is simply a tradition that we've found many members enjoy keeping up. A sort of bonding within our gender. I'm sure you can understand that."

I rubbed my hand against my mouth. "I suppose. What sort of activities do you host here, then?"

"Most of our members simply stop by for a short span of relaxation—a drink, a smoke, a browse through the day's papers. We offer all the local publications as well as several international ones." His gaze flicked to John in memory of the comment about his supposed cousin. "We have a room for card games and another for watching sports matches. Our focus is the comfort of our clientele while they're with us."

"See, darling," John said, patting my hand. "There's nothing to worry about."

"Well, all right. Why don't you go ahead and do this registration—but I might think of more questions I want to ask."

The manager looked both relieved and horrified at the same time. He opened up his laptop and tapped on the keyboard. "Have you already been apprised of the fees, Mr...?"

"Yes," John said. "And it's Eric—Eric Freeman."

"Right. I'll need to see some ID, and then we'll go over the requirements. You may need to send in documentation of—"

A hoarse voice carried through the door, bellowing out a raunchy song that within its first few lines managed to describe a woman's genitalia and the uses the singer felt they might be put to solely through nautical metaphors. It was actually rather creative.

That had to be Sherlock providing our distraction. I made myself stiffen in my seat, and the manager blanched.

"What on Earth is *that*?" I demanded.

The manager shot out of his chair. "I assure you that cannot be anyone who ought to be in this building. I'll see that the disturbance is removed immediately."

I caught John's eye as the other man fled the room. He looked as if he was suppressing a laugh. The second the door had thumped shut behind the manager, he leapt around the desk so smoothly you could hardly tell he needed a cane. He whipped out a silver flash drive and plugged it in.

"Membership file… Bingo!" He beamed at me around the laptop. "You were perfect. Are you sure you haven't done this sort of thing before?"

I let myself offer a small smirk. "Not in the line of *duty* I haven't…"

He chuckled and clicked on the trackpad. The hoarse singer was still caterwauling away, but his voice was getting fainter. The club's security must be managing to oust him. We didn't have much more time.

"Have you got it?" I asked, with an urgency I didn't need to feign. If we were caught, he and Sherlock might give up on this line of inquiry. He *had* to get that list.

"There we go. But here's a folder of minutes from meetings of the board as well..." He dragged it over.

"John," I protested. "We didn't come here for that. The manager will be back any second."

John glanced up again, his face lit up in a way I hadn't seen before. For an instant, he had the look of a junkie who'd just shot up his favorite drug. Then it was gone, and he was his regular grinning self again.

Interesting. Despite the jangling of my nerves, I filed that moment away for future reference.

"There could be something useful in there," he said. "I don't want to leave until we have everything Sherlock needs to break open this case for you."

The floor creaked on the other side of the door. John sprang up. He yanked the drive from the computer and dropped into his chair beside me a second before the manager stalked inside.

"I do apologize for the disruption," the manager started, but John was already pushing back to his feet. I followed suit.

"I apologize too," John said, with a respectful bob of his head. "I may have wasted your time. I have to say I'm having doubts now about whether this establishment is quite the right fit. Good day to you."

As we hustled out, I could still see the excited light dancing in his eyes, bright as his hair.

Maybe his participation in this scheme wasn't just about his devotion to Sherlock. Maybe Dr. John Watson got off on investigations like this in ways all his own.

CHAPTER FOUR

Jemma

I didn't have to wait long for results. The London trio caught up with me in the hotel dining room the next morning just as I'd reached the pastry table.

"You slept well enough," Sherlock said without preamble —not a question but a statement of fact. "Grab something quick for your breakfast. We have a lot to discuss."

That gave me an excuse to indulge my sweet tooth. Banana muffin? Raspberry sweet roll? Cinnamon-pecan bun? Yes, yes, yes, please.

I balanced my plate in one hand and gripped my mug of coffee with the other as the detective led the way out of the dining room and into a lounge area down the hall. There, a linen loveseat and armchairs surrounded a broad oak coffee table.

Sherlock dropped a bulging file folder onto the

polished table top and paced from one end of the loveseat to the other. John propped himself against the loveseat's arm. Garrett took the nearest chair, sipping his own coffee and setting a small notepad on one knee.

I sank into one of the armchairs too, taking a bite of my raspberry roll. Fuck, that was good—the perfect balance of doughy and fruitily sweet. Would it draw unwanted attention if I ate nothing but these for every meal?

"What's that?" I asked with a nod to the folder.

Sherlock set off on another pace back and forth, his hands clasped behind his back and his lean face solemn, though his cool blue eyes were starkly alert. "I went over the membership records for Cavalier's as soon as I had the chance. It took barely any time at all to narrow down the list to one name. A Stefan Richter has been a member there for twenty-three years. He also recently spent a few weeks in Munich, departing on the same night as your councilor was murdered."

Oh, good work, good work—all the applause. I restrained my smile and cocked my head. "That is a pretty big coincidence. Is there any other reason to suspect he'd commit a murder?"

Garrett motioned to the file folder with the pen he was holding. "Only the stack of reports I was able to dig up through police channels." He hadn't relaxed into the chair but sat there tensed. Something about this situation unsettled him. "This Richter has been on a lot of people's radar."

I widened my eyes. "If he's got that thick a record, why is he still walking free?"

"It's not a real record," Sherlock said. "No police department aware of his various exploits across Europe has ever been able to make a charge stick. I supplemented Garrett's findings with my own private research. The man has many hobbies—women, gambling, historic art and artifacts—and he tends to take first and make amends later if someone complains. Generally with a large pay-off to ensure no one presses charges."

Disgust colored his voice. Good to see we had similar feelings about our target.

Garrett gave Sherlock a disgruntled look as if he felt he'd been interrupted. He ran his hand—and the pen in it —through his short fawn-brown hair. "There have been investigations both here in London and in various cities abroad. He's been under suspicion of theft and extortion, but no one's been able to gather enough proof to really pin something on him. Evidence disappears, witnesses refuse to talk… He even sued the Paris police department once for supposed harassment to get them to back off."

"All that said, this is a little unusual, isn't it?" John said. "For a long-time criminal to suddenly leap from mainly property crimes to a violent act like murder?"

"Perhaps," Sherlock said, "but from what I gathered, there are plenty of women across the continent who could testify that he has no shortage of violent urges. If he was backed into a corner, he'd lash out however he could."

"Or he might not have committed the crime himself," Garrett pointed out. "It could have been a lackey."

The consulting detective made a dismissive sound. "As John pointed out so succinctly on examining the body, it was a crime of passion. A lackey with no personal stakes carrying out a premeditated murder would have used a method other than bludgeoning. Richter was provoked in some way and responded with a burst of rage. That much should be obvious to anyone."

John's posture pulled a little straighter at the recognition. Garrett's grew stiffer. He scribbled something in his notepad with terse jerks of his pen.

Watching the three of them, their working dynamic came into even sharper focus. Sherlock strode ahead in the lead with his arrogant certainty, John tagged along performing for scraps of praise, and Garrett trailed behind, not fully part of the team, always knowing that when he solved one of his cases, he couldn't take the full credit for the job well done.

The knowledge that Sherlock continually stayed a few steps ahead ate at him, didn't it? It wasn't enough for him to solve the crime and bring the perpetrator to justice—he wanted to have been the one with the right answers. I took that in with a stirring of uncomfortable memories.

I knew what it was like to feel every interaction with your peers was a competition. To be driven by the need to prove yourself better than all of them.

That need had nearly gotten me eaten alive.

I wet my lips. I might still find myself eaten alive if I didn't keep this trio on track. "Whatever Richter's reasons, is there any real chance of bringing him to justice for the murder while he's in London? I don't have any authorization to pursue him—and all the evidence of the murder is back in Freising."

Sherlock waved his hand dismissively and resumed his pacing. "Richter has had his fingers in enough corrupt pies right here that there must be some angle we can use to solidify a case. Bring him in on a local charge, and then 'discover' his connection to your case and reach out to your department. Nothing simpler."

"Sure," Garrett said. "And where are you going to start this incredibly simple process?"

Sherlock cocked his head. "I'd like to have a look inside his private offices. The police may not have managed to get access, but I'm sure it can be arranged with the right approach." He smiled like he had when he'd talked about conning Cavalier's to get their member list.

I clasped my hands together on my lap with a nervous twitch. "Are you sure that would be worth the risk? He's apparently killed one man who messed with him already."

"I know how to handle myself," Sherlock said.

"It's not just him… It sounds like you're talking about breaking the law."

His breath came out in a faint huff. "I take the chances I need to. Obtaining the facts is more important than any emotional concepts of morality."

A man after my own heart—or rather, my mind.

Sherlock cast his gaze toward Garrett. "No need for you to worry about that aspect, of course—your participation won't be necessary."

Garrett took a gulp of his coffee, his fingers gripping the handle tight. "I'm not completely seeing why *you* should be participating that far." He glanced at me. "The murder happened hundreds of miles away. Why are we getting so wrapped up in solving this woman's case for her?"

"Garrett," John said in a pacifying tone, but Sherlock had already raised his chin imperiously.

"The situation goes far beyond Miss Moriarty's case. This man has gotten away with innumerable crimes, and we have a chance to shut him down once and for all. You of all people should be concerned with that. If your police force had conducted itself more effectively, he wouldn't have been walking around Freising ready to murder a man in the first place."

A flush flooded Garrett's face. He slammed his mug down on the table so hard a little of the liquid sloshed over the sides. Shoving his notepad into his pocket, he sprang to his feet.

"Then I'll check in with you when you're in a less needling mood," he said, and stalked toward the doorway.

He would have marched right through it if a filmy white figure hadn't flickered into sight at exactly that moment. My heart lurched as a prickle ran down the back of my neck from my contract mark. Garrett stopped dead, staring. He rubbed his eyes.

"What is it?" John said, looking over. Bog's form was already fading. I blinked, and the shrouded one was gone.

What the hell was it doing? The shrouded folk had laws about their interactions with human society. To appear before the unknowing…

"I just—it must have been a trick of the light," Garrett

said. "I thought I saw a flash of something in the doorway." He shook himself and marched on out.

I willed myself to relax in my chair. *I'd* seen Bog in full clarity, but my senses were attuned to its kind. It hadn't fully manifested on this plane. Toeing the line without quite crossing it.

Reminding me that it was still watching me, and that it could interfere in certain ways if it wanted to.

Sherlock and John didn't appear to have noticed anything at all. Sherlock was eyeing *me*.

Shit. I hadn't been able to completely control my reaction. This called for some redirection. Thankfully, I had an obvious route to restore my grip on the conversation.

"Detective Lestrade is a little prickly, isn't he?" I said with a shaky laugh, as if it were his abrupt exit that had unsettled me.

"He's very committed to his job," John said diplomatically.

"He has a temper, but he always sees reason quickly enough," Sherlock said. He swept up his file folder. "Now, I have work to do. I'll keep you apprised of my progress, Miss Moriarty."

Dusk fell early in London at this time of year. As the sun sank below the tops of the buildings across the courtyard, I tugged my window open and slid the gauzy curtain across it. A gust of cool air washed over me, but I could tolerate that for the moment. I turned on my reading lamp and set it on the little table where it would be visible through the curtain.

While I waited, I worked through a couple rounds of push-ups, sit-ups, and lunges, and then shifted into practicing some of the combat sequences from my training. I didn't get into physical altercations very often, and you lost your precision if you let your practice slide. Besides, keeping the body fit invigorated the mind as well.

I was halfway through a set of jab-cross-hook combos when the curtain whispered. I continued through the motions, snapping out my right fist, swiveling on my left leg. My visitor approached with a shift in the air and a wisp of warmth over my skin.

"This elbow could stand to be a little higher, Majesty," Bash said in his low smooth voice. He tapped my arm, bringing with him the familiar scent of gun oil mingled with a light tang of musk. After seven years in my service, Sebastian Moran trusted that I knew when he'd arrived even if I didn't let on—and that I wouldn't break his nose with one of these fists in a startled reflex.

I made a face at the wry nickname, nudged my elbow up, and threw another punch. "Better?" I asked with an arch of my eyebrow.

"Perfect." Bash offered his usual subtle smile. He'd worn a black turtleneck and black jeans for his foray up the hotel wall, setting off his tan skin and light green eyes. A little scruff had accumulated on his jaw since I'd seen him last week, nearly as thick as the wiry black hair he kept cropped close to his skull.

I'd asked him once about his background, and he'd told me he was a bit of this and a bit of that. *A Venezuelan lady on one side, a Turk on the other, and my grandma insists that if you go back a few generations there was a Kenyan prince in the mix somewhere. It makes it easy to blend in wherever I want to go. Although in my experience, people usually choose to see me as whatever option gives them the most excuse to be an asshole.*

He'd said that last bit with a hint of a smirk. If Bash wanted to, he could make any person regret being an asshole before they could so much as blink.

When he was standing this close to me, a part of me wanted to lean into him, to drink in his scent right up against his solidly muscled chest. But I had no shortage of practice at leashing that urge and sending it off to its kennel. Only an idiot would ruin the formidable partnership Bash and I had with a tumble between the sheets. He was the only person in the world *I* trusted. I wanted to keep him standing right here beside me.

I threw myself into the combination again with a little more force.

"And though she be but little, she is fierce," Bash said dryly.

I snorted at the Shakespearean quote and his pretense at irony. I'd somehow found myself with a hitman who was a sucker for historical dramas, no matter how much he made fun of them.

He stepped back, and I let my body fall out of the fighting stance. His gaze traveled to the dresser beneath the TV. The corner of his mouth quirked up, but he didn't comment on the odd arrangement of cosmetics bottles, notepapers, and TV remote spread out across it. My little Fibonacci sequence. It wouldn't stop Bog from dropping in if the shrouded one really wanted to, but it worked as a casual deterrent.

"I checked in with your local forgers and the new auto ring," he said. "The latest payments should be arriving shortly."

"Perfect. And I got out some more funds for you." I reached for my purse. Bash accepted the wad of cash without a word and tucked it into his wallet. I sat down on the edge of the bed. "Are you settling into the new place all right?"

I wasn't sure he'd have complained even if he wasn't, but he definitely wouldn't say a peep if I didn't ask. I'd have set him up right here in the hotel if there wouldn't have been so much risk of one of the trio bumping into him at the wrong time.

"It's not bad." Bash glanced toward the window. "Heat, decent water pressure, a TV—that's about all I need. Now if only there was any place in London that could deliver a proper pizza."

I laughed. "You survived years in Afghanistan without your beloved New York-style slices—I think you'll make it through a few more weeks here."

"Only in intense agony," Bash said, completely deadpan. "Where are we at with your plans, Mori?"

That nickname I didn't mind at all. He'd started using it after a couple years of working together, saying that "Moriarty" was starting to feel ridiculously formal.

"Everything's moving along even faster than I'd hoped," I said. "They're investigating Richter's local crimes already. But the way Sherlock is, I'm sure the murder mystery will keep niggling at him. He's going to do some more digging into that chain of events sooner or later."

"I'll be ready for your alert, then."

I nodded. "Let's make sure he doesn't end up going down any roads I'd rather leave closed."

CHAPTER FIVE

Garrett

My fingers twisted over the notepad I was gripping, pulling the pen in a winding line that made a caricature of the woman sitting rigidly behind her desk between stacks of framed paintings. At this point, it seemed incredibly unlikely that I was going to get any information from her worth writing down. The smell of oil and varnish that hung in the art dealership's back room seeped farther into my lungs, and my stomach turned.

"I hope you understand that any additional insight you can provide may help us stop an on-going series of crimes that have affected far more than just this dealership," I said, leaning on guilt as a last-ditch effort. "What you tell us could protect so many more people in the future."

"I really can't think of anything I didn't tell the police

during the original investigation," the woman said. "I'm so sorry."

She didn't sound sorry at all. I restrained a sigh and flipped my notepad closed. The officers who'd been on this case had been almost certain that Stefan Richter had extorted early looks at and insanely cheap prices on valuable new acquisitions. Unfortunately, with the original tip anonymous, the sales records of any transactions with Richter mysteriously missing, and everyone at the dealership all clammed up, my colleagues hadn't been able to push the investigation very far.

Either this woman really didn't know anything, or she was a lot more afraid of Richter than she was of injustice going unpunished.

"Thank you for your time," I said, and left the place with gritted teeth. I'd set off yesterday morning determined to find just *one* fresh lead in all of the cases the department had on file—to come to Sherlock holding the key that would bring the villain to his knees, just this once. I'd skipped a seminar on interrogation techniques that I'd been looking forward to so I could hit the streets. All I'd come away with after two days' work was a notepad full of doodles.

This was ridiculous. We'd known Jemma Moriarty for all of ten minutes before Sherlock had been chomping at the bit to take on her problems. Weren't there enough crimes in London that needed solving?

The problem was I couldn't keep up that indignation for very long before I admitted that what I'd said to the dealership woman, as Sherlock himself had pointed out, was true. Richter was a menace. Why had I worked my arse off rising through the ranks if I didn't rise to an occasion like this? We had to put him out of commission. It would feel so satisfying when we did, like one huge piece of the balance had tipped in the right direction.

I couldn't rewrite my past, but I could do real good now. Had it been so much to ask that I turned up something remotely useful toward accomplishing that today?

Evening was setting in outside under the dreary sky. If I legged it, I could be back at the hotel in time for dinner.

I flagged a taxi. As it wove through traffic to where I was standing on the curb, an elderly woman walked by with a little Yorkie on a leash.

My skin tightened. I stepped as close to the road as I felt I could without risking the toes of my shoes, giving them plenty of space to pass, and trained my attention on following the taxi's path. The click of the dog's nails against the concrete made my nerves itch. When the taxi reached me, I hopped into the backseat and yanked shut the door, away from memories I'd rather not have dredged up.

Back at the hotel, I hustled into the lobby and spotted a bunch of the conference goers heading to the dining room. Maybe some good food would spark the inspiration I needed.

John was at the buffet table when I reached it. He ladled some buttered baby potatoes onto his plate and glanced over at me. "How was your day?"

"Not particularly productive," I admitted. My mouth

watered at the smell of the roast beef. I carved myself off a piece. "I suppose your partner has already tied the whole Richter thing up."

John knit his brow as he turned toward the white-clothed tables. "Far from it, actually. He's been in one of his dark moods since around lunch time. I let him skip that meal, but I told him I was going to cart him down here on a luggage trolley if he didn't come get some kind of nourishment into him."

Sherlock was stumped? A twinge of victory that really should have been beneath me shivered through my chest. Not that I'd been victorious in any way myself. *I'd* been stumped too.

I followed John's gaze to where our renowned consulting detective was sitting. His thin form loomed over the table, one elbow propped on the edge, while he prodded his plate noncommittally with his fork. Even if he hadn't been frowning, I'd have known he was in that mood from the atmosphere of melancholy that had come over his whole demeanor. Sherlock in a funk might as well have his own personal storm cloud casting a shadow on him wherever he went.

"He'll come out of it," John said with typical optimism. "He always does." His gaze twitched to the side. "Jemma! Why don't you join us?"

He waved the young officer over. Wonderful—now dinner would definitely revolve around her unresolved case. Although I supposed it probably would have anyway.

Jemma's plate was already full—a bit of meat, a bit of vegetables, and the rest offerings from the dessert table she was still perusing. She snatched up a lemon tart to add to her collection and swept her bright red hair back behind one ear as she joined us.

"Are we having our own little conference again?" she asked with a soft smile she aimed at John. I wouldn't have thought she was all that pretty just to glance over her in a room, but with the confident way she moved and that clear measured voice, something about her shone a little brighter. If I hadn't known Sherlock disdained anything to do with romance, I'd have thought we'd ended up on this crusade because he had a crush.

I certainly wasn't going to catch one. Even if, as we headed to the table, my gaze couldn't help straying just for a moment to the subtle sway of her slim hips in her tastefully fitted slacks.

"It seems that way," John said to her. "Although I'm not sure how much any of us have to contribute beyond what we discussed yesterday. I'm no detective in my own right—I fully accept my role as sidekick."

He grinned at her, she laughed, and I tried not to resent his easy good-naturedness. I benefitted from it often enough myself.

Sherlock barely stirred from his glum lethargy as we sat down around him. His blue eyes were always cool, but when they got this distant, they were outright chilly. He seemed to be looking a long way away through the centerpiece.

Some generous impulse compelled me to say, "I didn't have any luck either. That Richter fellow has every part of the city he's touched under lockdown."

Sherlock's lips pursed. His gaze didn't lift.

Jemma glanced from me to him. "You haven't been able to find enough grounds to arrest him for anything?"

"Not on my end," I said. "I dug into every old case I could. They couldn't be any colder."

"There will be a way," Sherlock said slowly. He blinked, and his eyes started to clear. "The man can't be clever enough to sow so much turmoil and cover his tracks successfully everywhere. But he has made it quite difficult. I'm not sure how long I'd have to stay on his trail to find a misstep."

Jemma bit her lip with obvious disappointment. "I can't ask you to put your other responsibilities aside to keep after him."

"Of course not." Sherlock tapped the tabletop, his energy coming back to him. "The answer is obvious. We follow the trail that's still warm—the murder he just committed. It may require some careful maneuvering of questions of jurisdiction and so forth, but we'll have our man much faster that way."

"Oh," Jemma said. "If you think that's our best option."

She wasn't fawning over him in adoring gratitude like the consulting detective's many professional fans tended to. Maybe I should cut her more slack—we'd come to her, after all.

On the other hand, who wouldn't jump for joy to have Sherlock Holmes personally investigating on their behalf?

I watched her as Sherlock poked at his already mangled green beans. "I think it's by far our best chance of putting him away for close to as long as he deserves," he said.

The smile she gave him looked genuine. "In that case, I can't thank you enough." She reached out and touched John's wrist where he was sitting next to Sherlock. "It means a lot to me that you'd both put your minds to this case."

Did John ease his arm a little closer to hers as he beamed back at her? Was it a little coy, the way she lowered her eyelids under his gaze?

Which one of us had been out there pounding the streets for her the last two days?

"I'll stay on the case too," I found myself blurting out. "I can get in touch with your local department over in Germany, see about setting up an exchange of information, and work through some of those jurisdiction concerns. Tomorrow, when they're out of bed."

"Of course," Jemma said. "I can get you their number. I have a card on me…" She opened her purse.

"That's all right," I said. "We've got a database at the department with the best contacts for international coordination."

"Right, of course you do." Jemma shook her head ruefully. "Maybe it would be helpful if I initiated the call?"

There was nothing about her tone or her expression that I could have pinpointed as disconcerting. All the same, while I knew I didn't have the same talent for quick analysis that Sherlock did, the impression prickled over me that for whatever reason, Jemma Moriarty was uneasy about me contacting her colleagues on my own.

Strange. Maybe I was reading too much into the exchange because I'd already been frustrated with how involved we'd gotten in her work. But my instincts had served me well before.

"I don't think that's necessary," I said. "It might even go over better for them to hear directly from us from the start, to reassure them that we're fully on board." Or, at least, that I was. I'd have to find out tomorrow what the chief was going to say about this.

Jemma leaned toward me, her distinctive gray eyes more intent than they'd been a moment ago. "You'll have a better idea than I do. I don't want you to think I'm ungrateful for the efforts you've already made, Garrett. Thank you so much for your dedication in following up on all those old cases—I know it must have been tedious. I never meant to derail anyone's plans by bringing that file here with me."

Under her gaze, with her that little bit closer to me, a flicker of heat raced over my skin. I couldn't deny that she cared a lot about the case, poring over it even during what should have been an escape from her regular work. Maybe she'd gotten the invitation to this conference thanks to her close-to-Sherlockian brilliance, but she had a sense of commitment I couldn't say very many of my colleagues in Scotland Yard shared.

I swallowed thickly. "We volunteered to pitch in. The man needs to be caught. I'm happy to contribute to the cause."

How true was that last comment? I couldn't have said. In that moment, I was happy to have her looking at me with so much appreciation… and possibly something more than that?

I tugged my gaze away and gave myself a mental smack upside the head. *Sherlock* would never have been distracted by a striking pair of eyes. I speared a piece of roast beef for something to do. My thoughts returned to the odd impression I'd had about her reaction.

"So, how long have you worked with the Freising police, Firecracker?" I asked, keeping my tone casual. We'd barely asked her anything about herself so far. Although maybe Sherlock had already catalogued her entire life history from the shape of her fingernails and the angle at which she tipped her head, so he hadn't felt the need to.

Jemma answered easily enough. "Coming up on three years—since I finished school. I've been based in Germany for five years altogether."

"And before that?"

She shrugged, swirling a chuck of potato in a pool of melted butter. "A little while here in the UK, in various parts of America, Portugal, Thailand, New Zealand… I've gotten around. My parents were roamers. I expect at some point I'll get restless and continue the tradition. It's useful having picked up the different languages and so on."

Being born and bred in London, I had trouble imagining a life that chaotic. How did you ever feel at home? Jemma didn't look fazed, though, and that hardly seemed like an appropriate question to ask a woman I was only just getting to know.

Before I could decide on a different angle from which to prod her, she glanced around the table. "I'm curious about the three of you. You seem to work together so well. How did you end up collaborating like this?"

"I found myself in London a couple years back, after my stint in the army ended for obvious reasons." John motioned to his leg. "I couldn't afford a place of my own, and a friend of mine knew this lunatic who was constantly over at the university experimenting with everything from poisons to bruising but who happened to need a roommate…" He raised his eyebrows at Sherlock.

"Oh, dear," Jemma said with a grin, brushing her fingers against his forearm again. "I suppose we should be glad you're still here and not dissected."

"I assure you, I have never dissected anyone who wasn't already dead," Sherlock said, straight-faced. "John proved a decent living companion and an excellent partner in the field. I can achieve a lot on my own, but I can't be everywhere, and some gambits are better pulled off with company."

I jumped in before they could continue their mutual adoration fest. "Sherlock has been offering Scotland Yard help with difficult cases for a few years. He… occasionally rubs some of the detectives the wrong way. He and I found we could cooperate without my wanting to strangle him—at least not very often. So, the commissioner often pairs us up."

"Garrett is the best of the lot over there," Sherlock said. "The police force truly is in a sorry state."

That was a backhanded compliment if I ever heard one. But Jemma was shaking her head at Sherlock and turning back to me. "Investigating can be a lot more difficult with the sorts of red tape we have to deal with. You must have quite the success rate with your own cases, or you wouldn't be here."

She wasn't even touching me, her hand lingering over the handle of her knife. I couldn't have called the blouse and slacks she was wearing anything but modest. So, why was my attention drawn more than before to the subtle curves beneath those clothes, to the fullness of her lips?

It'd been too long since I'd last had a shag, clearly.

I had to just ignore those impulses. And at the same time I desperately wanted to stop her from shifting her attention away from me again.

A couple of officers from one of the other tables sidled over, their hands twisted nervously in front of them. "Mr. Holmes?" the man said. "It's amazing to meet you in person. I've followed all of Dr. Watson's accounts of your investigations."

"They should have *you* giving all the talks here," the woman gushed. "Would you—is it too silly to ask you to autograph our program booklets?"

"I suppose I might as well," Sherlock said, bemused. As he brought pen to paper without a word of thanks for their compliments, John gave Jemma a nudge and rolled his eyes in mock exasperation.

"Poor you," she said, looking at him through her eyelashes. "The permanent bridesmaid?"

John chuckled, his face bright as he gazed back at her, and my stomach twisted the way it had right before I'd slammed my coffee mug on the table yesterday morning. Like a fool.

"Well," Sherlock said when his admirers had wandered off, "should we convene to discuss our next steps somewhere more private? Garrett, your room is the closest."

"It is," I agreed before I could think about whether I was being foolish now. "Why not? Let's go back to mine."

CHAPTER SIX

Jemma

After the four of us had talked for a while in Garrett's room, I'd flopped down on my back at the foot of the bed—not in a provocative pose, just as if the change in position and view might jog some new ideas loose. But when I propped myself up on one elbow as the conversation wound down, John's gaze lingered on the slope of my body for long enough to tell me the evening had been a success.

"All right then," the doctor said. "I'll see if there's anyone I know in the Munich area who could weigh in, and I guess we can make a final decision about how to proceed after we've slept on it." He stifled a yawn, his fingers clenching the handle of his walking stick a little tighter than usual. Even his grin looked a bit weary, though it was barely ten at night.

I knew from the medical records I'd dug up that he'd

left his military service with more than just a limp. The infection he'd gotten while recovering from his initial wounds had left his whole body weakened. This was the first sign of that larger infirmity I'd seen in person. He held himself together rather well.

"Until tomorrow," Sherlock said in his lofty way, as if he thought he might have the whole case tied up by then. *His* gaze didn't linger on me at all, but I hadn't expected it to. He was above emotion, after all.

Imagine what I might find beneath that cool exterior if I managed to wake up a feeling or two.

That wasn't tonight's plan, though, as appealing as the idea was. As the two men left, I pushed myself upright and rolled my shoulders. Garrett glanced over at me with a flash of hunger in his eyes.

It didn't take much to generate that kind of reaction if you knew how to handle yourself. The slightest arch of my back, the angle of my face, the way I trailed my fingers here or there—I could have been dressed like a nun and still brought lust into a man's mind when I wanted to. Both John and Garrett were aware of me as a woman now in ways they hadn't quite been before. And I'd made sure Garrett had noticed John's awareness as much as his own.

I didn't think the detective inspector wanted to come in second place yet again.

Now that taking Richter down for his past crimes was off the table, I had to shift focus from the short con I'd hoped for to the long con I'd prepared. All three of the trio had to be totally invested if I was going to pull this off.

Garrett appeared to be the best place to start, especially since I had another ruse I needed to carry out here.

"I suppose I should get going too," I said, standing up. To stay in the game, I was going to have to engage his sympathies as well as his desires. Not the easiest maneuver when he still seemed wary about the three of them being involved in my affairs at all.

I ambled toward the door and paused as if grappling with the question. "When do you think you'll put that call in to Freising?" I asked without quite meeting his eyes.

"First thing in the morning, I was planning," Garrett said.

I nodded stiffly, and that was enough, now that we were alone, to prompt the question he'd really wanted to ask.

He closed the notepad he'd been alternately scrawling and sketching in. "You don't like the idea of me talking to them, do you?"

I jerked around to face him. "Why would you say that?"

He tipped his head toward me. "Because you reacted like that to me saying it, Firecracker. Because you seem nervous about the subject every time it's come up." He folded his arms over his lean chest, drawing himself up a little taller. "What's going on?"

The woman he thought I was wouldn't give in that easily. My mouth twisted. "I don't know what you're talking about."

"You're hiding something. Don't you think it's going to come out, and sooner rather than later? Do you really think *Sherlock* won't figure out the whole story in five seconds flat?"

That last sentence held a touch of bitterness. Oh, yes, this man's competitive streak and the insecurities that fed it ran deep.

I stiffened as if the possibility hadn't occurred to me before and then sank into the chair at the desk, dropping my face into my hands. "It's nothing he'd even be concerned about. It's just embarrassing. It won't affect how you handle the case—I can promise you that."

"I'd be a lot more willing to believe that if you'd say what the problem is," Garrett said.

I took a deep breath and let my mind slip back to old childhood memories. All the jockeying for favor, the glares and the vicious sabotage, the desperation that had wrenched through me on the rare occasions I'd faltered and met my parents' glowers of disappointment. The fear that I'd also let down my little sister who couldn't quite keep up. The looming presence of the shrouded folk always watching, judging. Those tangled, fraught emotions prickled up to color my voice.

"It's been kind of tense at the department. I was at the top of my class, and I got a good position right out of the gate. A lot of the other officers resent that, I think. They hassle me and make sure the hardest cases end up on my desk. I work twice as hard as anyone there just to make sure I don't look like I'm falling behind."

"Go on," Garrett said—firmly but softer.

I let my head dip lower. "This case, the murder—I totally botched it. I ran down a lead I thought was good, and it went nowhere, and then the trail was getting cold. I couldn't get a foothold anywhere else… Everyone there has been sneering at me like I'm a failure, mocking the fact that I was picked for this conference, taking potshots at me every chance they get."

"That's ridiculous. No one solves every case."

"I was so sure with this one, though. I can handle the potshots. I'll survive. But I know when you call and tell them you're picking up the case, they're going to assume I went running to Scotland Yard to beg for help, and even my boss is going to lose all respect for me."

I tightened my voice on the last sentence, mastering the emotions I'd let leak out. When I raised my eyes, Garrett was staring at me. His jaw twitched as he grappled with the emotions my "confession" had stirred in him.

"I suppose I'm being as pathetic as they'd think I am if I let my worries affect how you handle the case," I said. "Forget I said anything. It's my problem to deal with. I'm sorry you had to listen to all that."

I got up from the chair and made for the door again, but Garrett reached for my arm.

"Hey." He eased me back around to face him. Whatever else he'd been feeling, compassion had won. It shone in his dark brown eyes, even if the rest of his expression had stayed tense.

"You don't have to apologize," he said. "I know what it's like to feel that no matter what you do, you can't quite earn the respect you want. I rose in the ranks quickly like you did, and it's a lot of weight knowing everyone's watching for proof that you didn't deserve the things you worked so hard for. Of course you're nervous. I'm sorry I pushed you into talking about it."

I gave him a pained smile. "Well, maybe it's better that you know. That way you won't be surprised about the attitude they might have about me when you call."

Garrett's fingers adjusted against my arm, but he didn't let go. The warmth of his hand bled through the thin cotton of my blouse. "What if… What if I didn't mention you at all?" he said. "Richter came here. We have every reason to be keeping an eye on him regardless. I can simply say that we heard about the murder and noticed that the timing of his visit to your area matched up, and we'd like to investigate further on our end."

My body relaxed. "That—that would be such a relief." Especially because if he did happen to mention an Officer Moriarty to any of the actual police in Freising, they'd have no clue who he was talking about. Bash had been meant to handle that call if it happened, but since Garrett had thwarted my earlier attempts to control the direction of the call, this was the most elegant possible solution. And he thought it was his idea.

He might not even have minded the deception if he'd known he was actually protecting me from a fate worse than death.

"It's easy enough," Garrett said with a rare smile. "Why should I let them think you came running to us when really it's that Sherlock badgered you into letting us on the case?"

"There is that too," I said, and laughed.

Garrett laughed too, looking more at ease in that

moment than I'd ever seen him. He really was a rather good-looking man when he wasn't scowling or narrowing his eyes in skepticism. Which meant tonight's finale might be particularly enjoyable.

It was too bad the trio hadn't found a way to get Richter locked up quickly on some unrelated charge. That would have made saving my life so much easier. Now, to see the larger plan through, they were going to have to cross a lot more lines than a little play-acting in a gentleman's club. They were going to have to *want* to.

And the simplest way to get them invested in my case was to get them invested in *me*.

"Thank you," I said softly. "Really. You're a good man." I leaned in and brushed a kiss to his cheek.

As I eased back, Garrett swallowed audibly. I wet my lips, holding his gaze, as clear a come-on as I could make after the subtle tension I'd spent all evening building without outright jumping his bones. But he stayed where he was, frozen, his mouth slanting with indecision.

All right. There were ways I could make the decision even simpler for him.

I slipped my arm from his grasp and gave him a regretful smile. "It seems like I really should go. I'll drop in on John on my way up and see if he's gotten anywhere with his possible local connections."

I said John's name with an affectionate lilt, and a possessive spark lit in Garrett's eyes. He caught my arm again with a sudden intensity that set off a flare of heat right through me.

"You don't have to leave," he said in a low hoarse voice, and tugged me into a kiss.

He tasted like the sweet brandy John had passed around while we'd brainstormed, his mouth hot enough to burn. I slipped my arm around his neck and kissed him back hard, not wanting to leave any doubt that I was completely on board with wherever he wanted to take this next.

My body swayed against his. With a rough sound, he turned us and lifted me onto the desk, never breaking the kiss. My legs splayed around his hips. I gave myself over to the pulse of need spreading from my core.

It was the best kind of ploy, really. I got one step closer to freeing my soul and ridding the world of a much greater evil than I could ever claim to be. He got to feel he'd won the prize. We both got our rocks off, well. Wins all around.

Our mouths crashed even more urgently together. Garrett tangled his fingers in my hair, his other hand stroking up and down my side over my blouse. His scent filled my nose, as singeing sharp as a live wire.

Mmm, I liked that.

I scooted closer on the desk, bringing my body completely in line with his, shivering eagerly at the feel of him already hard behind the zipper of his slacks. Garrett let out a choked sort of groan and eased back from the kiss, but when I raised my chin to offer him access to my neck, he couldn't resist. He pressed his mouth to the sensitive skin along my throat. The flick of his hot tongue brought a pleased sigh to my lips.

"So you do have it in you after all," I murmured.

His mouth trailed down to my collarbone. His hand was working its way up under my blouse, stroking bare skin now. A shaky breath spilled over my flesh. "I don't normally think it's a good idea to mix work with —with, ah—"

"Pleasure?" I ran my fingertips down his chest, tracing the taut muscles there. "I find it's good to burn off the tensions of the job every now and then if I can find the right partner. Which isn't always easy, I'll admit. I was starting to think you weren't game."

He captured my mouth again, kissing me so intently and thoroughly that I lost my breath despite myself. Maybe he was aiming to top every man who'd ever kissed me before. I wasn't going to argue with that ambition.

"Are you convinced now?" he muttered against my skin. At the same moment, he unhooked my bra. As his hand cupped my breast, his thumb swiveling over the nipple, I leaned into his touch.

"I wouldn't mind if you convinced me a whole lot more."

He let out a ragged laugh and resumed his plunder of my mouth. I rocked against him, wanting even more than this.

Garrett took the hint. He tipped my head back, his tongue tangling with mine, and fingered the clasp on my dress pants until he'd dislodged it. I lifted my hips, he jerked, and my slacks slipped off to pool on the floor.

He pressed his fingers to my panties, but not to dislodge them yet. A hungry rumble escaped him at the dampness already forming there. He teased his thumb over my clit and down to my opening, forcing a whimper out of me.

I grasped the front of his slacks and popped the button free. At the yank of the zipper, he tore his lips from mine just for a second. "Do you have—?"

"My purse." I reached for the bag where I'd dropped it on the desk beside me and fished out a foil packet.

There'd been men in the past who'd balked for a second at how readily I'd produced protection, who'd even sneered a bit. Garrett didn't so much as blink. With a few tugs of fabric, my panties were dangling from one ankle and his pants and boxers were at his feet. He sheathed himself in an instant. I arched toward him, and he plunged into me with a blissful groan.

And then he stayed there. Balls deep inside me, he eased his head back just far enough to meet my eyes. A strange tenderness had come over his face. My gut twisted.

That kind of look didn't have any place here. There was nothing like a hint of sappiness to ruin the mood.

I tilted forward, bringing my lips to his ear. "Fuck me," I said. "Fuck me until I can't see straight."

He exhaled with a stutter and started thrusting, harder and faster as I bucked to meet him. Oh, yes, this was what I needed. His thumb worked over my stiffened nipple, and his mouth crashed against mine, and for a few fleeting minutes everything in the world fell away except the swell of ecstasy building between my thighs.

He was awfully good at the whole fucking thing. Maybe we'd get the chance to take a second spin at it.

The pleasure sang through my nerves. I dug my fingers into Garrett's muscled back as my vision blurred. Then the searing sensation burst with a blissful shudder.

As I clenched around Garrett, he groaned and pounded into me a few more times. His breath hitched out of him as he came. I touched his cheek and drew him in for one more kiss.

Mine, I thought as my lips branded his. *From now until I'm done here, you're mine.*

CHAPTER SEVEN

Jemma

The smell dragged me out of sleep—a parched scent carrying a taint of sickly decay, like bones flecked with flesh so ancient it'd rotted right into dust. I opened my eyes with the side of my face still burrowed into the pillow.

Bog's depthless mist of a face was hovering beside the bed just a few feet away. My pulse lurched. If I'd been anyone other than Jemma Moriarty, I would have screamed. As it was, I had to clamp my jaw tight.

The shrouded one would probably have liked it if I'd screamed. There wasn't any good reason for Bog to be lurking around watching me sleep.

I pushed myself upright in the hotel bed—my own, since staying in Garrett's would have skewed the feelings I was encouraging him to develop too far in the wrong direction. "Good morning to you too, Bog," I said flatly.

"Get a good eyeful of my bedhead?" I fluffed my rumpled hair and resisted the urge to scratch at the mark on the back of my neck, which was itching at the shrouded one's presence.

Bog shifted. The floating swaths of white that shrouded it stirred as if in an underwater current. "In case you were starting to forget," it said in its husk of a voice. "Twenty-six days."

"Thank you so much for the reminder."

The shrouded one didn't answer, just faded from sight, leaving only that repulsive smell. I rubbed my nose. It was hard to imagine that I'd lived fourteen years immersed in the stink of the shrouded folk, barely noticing it.

The human body could adapt to an awful lot.

So much for my Fibonacci deterrent. I fiddled with the papers and bottles and added a handful of spare change to the sequence on the dresser, but who was I kidding? Bog had waited ten years to claim his reward. He was chomping at the bit to gobble me up. A little discomfort wasn't going to hold him back from his gloating.

Laying out the pattern did make me feel a little more in control, though, so I finished tweaking it anyway. Then I dug a sugar cube out of the baggie I kept in my purse and sucked on its clarifying sweetness while I got dressed.

Alerts on one of my phones informed me that the payments Bash had mentioned had gone through. Good —I wouldn't have to send him to crack any heads. My business was simple: I gave select criminal collectives a leg up with the insight and connections I'd cultivated over the years, helped keep the cops off their back as need be, and in thanks they passed on a nice percentage of their earnings. The arrangement worked out well for both sides as long as they held up their end.

Breakfast beckoned. Because Bog had woken me up earlier than usual, I was already through two cinnamon buns and one cup of coffee when my trio drifted into the dining room.

Sherlock came first, with an energetic stride and a brisk nod to me, emanating the air of a man about to get things done. As he shoveled eggs and ham onto his plate to join his toast, John ambled over and filled a bowl with cereal. They fell into step together as they approached my table, John grinning and giving his walking stick a quick flourish when he saw me watching. If yesterday's work had run him down, he appeared to have fully recovered.

The sweetness of the pastries lingered in my mouth. I smiled at both of them with nothing but genuine good will in my heart for that brief moment.

Garrett hustled in a minute later. His shoulders were already a little high, but they twitched up even more the second he glanced toward the table the three of us were sharing. I pretended to be absorbed in the last bite of my cinnamon bun so he wouldn't feel any need to make an immediate gesture of acknowledgement.

As he moved along the buffet, he appeared to get control of himself. He sauntered over to join us with a casual bob of his head and only the faintest flush in his cheeks. With extreme care, he didn't let his gaze linger on me any longer than on my companions.

"Good morning," he said evenly, and busied himself with his hash browns.

I licked sugar glaze off my fingers, suppressing my amusement. I'd had a feeling Garrett Lestrade was the type to get awkward the morning after. Did he think his colleagues would be able to sense what had happened between us? Was he afraid he'd overstepped some unspoken boundary?

It actually was somewhat possible that Sherlock would deduce what we'd gotten up to after he and John had left last night. He studied Garrett as the shorter man gulped his coffee. I didn't imagine he'd be particularly disturbed by that development, but Garrett might be by him knowing. The easiest way to redirect the one detective and reassure the other was to leap back into the case as if nothing at all had changed.

"Any responses to last night's inquiries?" I asked the table at large.

Of course, Sherlock was the one with a ready answer. "A contact of mine confirmed that Richter left by plane on the night of the murder from a private airfield near Freising, with a few crates of artistic artifacts as cargo. It seems he likes to show off his collection. He arranged an exhibit of the more valuable historic pieces in a gallery in Munich, like the one he's set up here in London."

Oh, excellent. I'd carefully nudged Sherlock toward that angle last night with an off-hand comment here and there.

"Were there any witnesses who could vouch for what

time he got to the airfield and when the plane left?" I asked.

"I believe so," Sherlock said. "Richter has a manager who handles most of the logistics for his showings. It appears they both normally travel alongside the art when it's transported."

"You have the whole case wrapped up already, don't you?" Garrett said, but his tone was more wry than bitter. He was still avoiding looking too long in my direction, but perhaps the fun we'd had last night had loosened him up all the same now that he could see I wasn't going to make a big thing of it.

"The course of justice is rarely so smooth," Sherlock said, flexing his lithe hands. He sounded as if he enjoyed the prospect of a longer chase now that he felt he was on the right trail. "To speak to this manager, I need to track the man down, and he keeps himself rather incognito. But I managed to procure a photograph, and my Irregulars are on the look-out. I'd be surprised if they don't locate him before the end of the day."

"Irregulars?" I said.

John motioned to Sherlock with an amused look. "He's got a squad of delinquent youth who are happy to be his eyes and ears for a couple tenners when he needs them. The kinds of people we're often tracking down might dodge us, but they aren't so cautious around a kid shooting hoops or rambling around the streets."

"Over time I've narrowed them down to quite an effective force," Sherlock added.

Garrett glanced up at the ceiling. "I'm definitely not hearing any of this."

No, I supposed Scotland Yard might not approve of paying off street kids to act as unofficial informants. I'd gleaned some hints of that practice in my prep work, but I hadn't realized how organized Sherlock was in his marshalling of the resource. It really was a brilliant strategy, I'd give him that. And useful to know for my various other business endeavors.

Sherlock leaned his elbows onto the table. "In the meantime, I'll delve further into Richter's other recent dealings. Who knows what fruit that will bear?" A delighted smile crossed his face at the prospect.

"How historic are the artifacts he includes in his exhibit?" I asked. Best if Sherlock kept the art aspect at the front of his mind. "Does he even have the right to own all of them?"

"I'd bet he acquired some of those through questionable methods," Garrett put in. "He just always produces convincing enough papers if anyone questions him. We won't get far with that angle if no one involved in the acquisition is willing to talk."

Sherlock waved his fork in the air, his eyes lit with enthusiasm. "It's disappointing, really, that collectors focus on the aesthetic side of history when the antiquities are rife with real innovations. Take the Rama Empire, for example—when do they get credit for their civil engineering that in many ways puts our own to shame? Perfectly ordered roads, and plumbing all through every building. Do you know, there are archeologists who claim they had no concept of social class?"

He chattered on in a smooth and lively tone, the total opposite of the distant sullen mood I'd first found him in at dinner last night. The great Sherlock Holmes was a study in contrasts. Who would have thought he'd have read up on obscure ancient civilizations? I supposed he absorbed whatever struck his fancy—and once absorbed, facts stuck in that mind of his forever.

Imagine how quickly we could have conquered everything ahead of us working together if we really had the same goals. Instead I had to guide the knife of his mind indirectly, always a hair away from slicing my own fingers off.

John nodded along and interjected a question now and then to encourage his friend onward. A person would have had to be blind not to see the admiration that practically shone off him as he watched Sherlock. I almost wondered if it was more than admiration. Not that I'd seen any reason to believe the two had a more intimate relationship... but that didn't mean the desire wasn't there, admitted or not. For all his brilliance, I didn't think Sherlock had picked up on *that*.

A rising murmur in the dining room broke through Sherlock's sparkling commentary. He trailed off at the same moment as I glanced around. The people at the tables around us were peering up over our heads with puzzled expressions that ranged between awed and frightened. I jerked my gaze upward.

Fucking hell. The light between the two fixtures on

either side of us was flowing in a stream across the ceiling like a strip of cloth blown by the wind. Like several strips, actually, weaving together and fraying apart with an eerie shuddering. My skin crawled at the sight, and I at least knew where it came from. The mark on my neck pinched.

Stalking me in my sleep hadn't been enough for Bog this morning. The shrouded one had decided to put on a light show for the whole conference.

My trio was staring up at the display too, Garrett paling, John wide-eyed, Sherlock frowning. The last thing I needed was them wondering whether their new colleague had brought some sort of unearthly influence down on them.

A ghost of an impression whispered through my nerves, taking me back to the wrenching moment of pure icy panic when I'd discovered where all my childhood ambitions had been leading me and where they'd lead my sister too if I couldn't find a way out. When I'd seen that our parents and all the other adults in the cult of the shrouded folk were whipping us toward earning not some exhilarating honor but our deaths. We were sacrificial lambs vying for the slaughter.

It'd felt as if my whole life were slipping from my fingers too fast for me to catch it—but I had caught it. I'd bent circumstances to my control, and I'd kept doing that, over and over, to get to this moment right now. The shrouded folk might have won more than I could ever accept, but they'd lose in the end.

I clamped down on the panicked sensation with an iron grip. "It's ridiculous, isn't it?" I said, aiming for the dismissive attitude I'd seen Sherlock take on more than once. "The electrical systems act up for a minute, and the whole room devolves into a tizzy. The greatest analytical minds in the world, huh?"

"Indeed." Sherlock looked a bit distracted, but he drew his gaze away with a shake of his head. "The undisciplined human mind does love to leap to fantastical assumptions about the most mundane phenomena." His gaze fell on me for a moment as if considering my expression. I kept it as bland as possible.

To my relief, the light show was petering out as if to support my dismissal. Bog was *really* pushing the limits creating an effect that visible.

The shrouded one knew I was up to something. It *hated* the thought that I might slip from its grasp after all the time spent waiting, after the wrath it'd risked making the deal with me in the first place. So now Bog was pulling out all the stops to throw me off.

Too bad for it I was already three steps ahead.

My pulse beat a little faster as I caught John's eye across the table. He shot me a smile. "Apparently we needed some more excitement around here. The organizers should consider fireworks next year."

Or we could make a few of our own. I smiled back, grazing my fingers over my cheek.

John Watson might already be hooked on Sherlock, but I intended to hook him too. And after that little display, I meant to lock him down fast.

CHAPTER EIGHT

John

I'd had to accept, living and working with Sherlock, that he only revealed his plan and prep-work on a need to know basis. Unless he was fully confident that he was on the right track and that sharing the information wouldn't jeopardize his mission, even I wouldn't hear a peep.

I suspected he also enjoyed seeing the looks on people's faces when he unraveled an entire scheme with one grand flourish.

In any case, he hadn't needed me for whatever he was up to this morning, so I figured I might as well make the most of the conference we'd meant to attend. I was studying the schedule in the program booklet when an unassuming fellow with dark dreadlocks and startlingly blue eyes stopped beside me. He cleared his throat apologetically.

"Could you point me in the direction of Banquet Room B, mate?" he said with a mild Australian accent. "I seem to keep getting turned around."

"Let me have a look." I flipped to the map and tapped the right spot. "I was in there for a talk a couple days ago. It's just down this hall here and to your left around the corner."

"Thank you so much! I don't want to miss a word of Dr. Tanaka's talk—she's always leaps and bounds ahead of the rest when it comes to anything DNA."

He saluted me and loped off down the hall. I watched him go and grabbed my walking stick from where I'd leaned it against the wall. The bodily side of forensics was the one area where I could occasionally offer more insight than Sherlock. With a recommendation like that, how could I skip this talk?

Plenty of other attendees had felt the same way. When I reached the hall, one minute before the presentation was due to start, it took me a moment to spot an open seat in the rows of chairs. My gaze snagged on a now-familiar fall of ruddy hair halfway down. Jemma had decided to sit in on this session too—and no one had claimed the seat at the end of the row next to her.

I hustled over just fast enough to provoke a faint twinge in my hip and sank into the chair. "Brushing up on the forensic sciences too?" I said teasingly. "Are you working toward the day when you can run circles around even Sherlock?"

Jemma laughed. "I'm not quite that ambitious. But it seems to me I'm better off filling in the gaps in my knowledge than listening to people explain what I already know."

I wondered if she realized what a Sherlockian thing that was to say. My heart beat a little faster just sitting next to her, for reasons I didn't see any need to examine too closely. She was a pretty woman. She was an intelligent woman. There'd have been something wrong with me if I hadn't felt a brief crackle of attraction.

I might have asked more about what experience she did have on the forensic side, limited or no, but our speaker stepped up to the podium.

The Australian fellow hadn't steered me wrong. Dr. Tanaka breezed through several recent developments in DNA collection and testing—most of which I hadn't understood in a great deal of depth and a couple of which I hadn't been aware of at all—with crisp enthusiasm and a knack for translating the concepts into laymen's terms. The non-experts in the crowd should have been able to follow along without any trouble.

Jemma leaned forward, watching the doctor avidly. She wasn't taking notes like many of the attendees around us, but I had the feeling that sharp mind of hers was absorbing everything.

Sherlock didn't like to take notes either. He said it distracted from really hearing what a person was saying, with both their words and their behavior.

My memory wasn't quite on par with his, so when Dr. Tanaka launched into her top tips for officers on the scene, I jotted those down in my case journal. Anything I could contribute to wrapping up our cases faster, *I* wanted to absorb.

I left the seminar with Jemma a little lighter on my feet, eager to put the new techniques to the test. Too bad in our current case the victim and all available concrete evidence lay hundreds of miles away.

"That was inspiring, wasn't it?" Jemma said. "The intersection of science and policing—it's getting harder for criminals to cover their tracks all the time."

"Yes!" I said with a grin. "And it gives medical professionals a way to be useful on the crime-solving side of things. Although I can't see the kind of detective work Sherlock and Garrett do ever becoming less valuable."

"Oh, definitely not. After all, finding the right source to test in the first place is such a key factor. There was this one case, while I was still in training..." She paused with a rueful smile. "Never mind. You don't want to hear me ramble on about my minor victories as a cadet."

"Ramble away." I waved my walking stick at her encouragingly. Sherlock could be rather intimidating, especially when you weren't used to his attitudes and moods. The last thing I wanted was for Jemma to feel diminished by the time she'd spent around us. "You were already closer to being professional law enforcement back then than I am right now, so I'm hardly anyone to judge."

"Oh, well—we were investigating a murder with a few possible suspects but no clear evidence in any of the usual places. I happened to notice one guy had a fresh looking mud stain on the golf shoes he'd tucked away by the back door. It hadn't rained for days before the night of the murder, and he hadn't mentioned golfing in his account of where he'd been around the time of the crime. The senior officers thought I was bonkers, but they took the shoes in, and even though he'd tried to wash them, they found traces of the victim's blood in the cleats."

"Well done!" I said, clapping my hands. "There you go. You were running circles around those officers even then."

"I just follow what makes sense to me," Jemma said with a shrug, her cheeks slightly pink from the praise. "It doesn't seem all that extraordinary when I'm thinking about it."

Did she not see how extraordinary *she* was? My God.

"You know, I wasn't exaggerating comparing you to Sherlock," I said. "I never thought I'd meet anyone who came close to his analytical abilities, but here you are. He sees it too—that's the whole reason he wanted to approach you."

Jemma's mouth twitched into a smile. "And now I've given him a perfectly complicated case to relieve him of his boredom. I hope it won't be too much of a let-down when he solves it. I get the impression it's not going to take him long."

"You didn't have that one bit of key information. How could you be expected to have memorized every bit of architecture in London?" I shook my head.

She had the same crystalline intelligence Sherlock did, sharp as a scalpel, but with a much more charming disposition. I'd never fault my friend his moods—he could hardly help them—but he could be pretty callous without realizing it. Jemma obviously had more sensitivity to her than that.

In a few moments now and then, when I'd seen her standing apart from our group, I thought I'd caught a bit of sadness in her expression. I'd be willing to bet that she'd had a painful loss in her life, either recently or major or both. The impression resonated with my own various losses, even though most of them were long healed over.

We drifted down the hall, other conference attendees streaming past us in more of a hurry. I wasn't sure what sessions were running now, but having Jemma to myself for the first time, I couldn't think of anything I'd rather do than chat with her at least a little longer.

She swept her hair back over her shoulder in a careless gesture, and my gaze followed the graze of her fingers across the pale skin at the edge of her shirt's neckline. Interest stirred in other parts of me. No, it wasn't just her mind I found appealing. Who could blame me?

"You and Sherlock are very close, aren't you?" she said. "You seem rather attached at the hip."

"A fair observation." I rubbed my mouth, the question pricking at me despite the lightness of her tone. "It means a lot to me that he trusts me so much as a friend and colleague. He gave me a new life when I was starved for direction, you know. I was a surgeon, and now I can't trust my body to stay as steady as it'd need to be for that kind of work… This way I can still save lives by applying my knowledge from a different angle."

It would have been hard to put into words my gloomy state fresh off of my tour of duty—my body even weaker than it was now, the work I loved torn from me—or how collaborating with Sherlock had shone a light through that darkness. I wasn't sure I'd have wanted to express all that to Jemma anyway. I wasn't exactly proud of my first few useless months in London.

"I can see how he'd inspire devotion," she said.

"Well, I'm not sure I'd call it that, but—loyalty, certainly." I hesitated and decided I might as well mention this little fact and see what she made of it. I could determine in an instant whether there was any point in indulging the sparks I'd felt. "Not everyone understands our partnership. I had to break it off with a girlfriend I quite liked a few months ago. The longer we were together, the more critical Mary got of the time I spent with Sherlock. I don't think she'd have been happy unless I'd ended my collaboration with him completely."

"That's ridiculous," Jemma said without any thought at all. "The work you do with him makes you happy—I've only known you a few days, and I can see that. How much could she have cared about you if she'd ask you to give that up?"

Her answer sent a sharper rush of relief through me than I'd expected. "Exactly what I thought," I said.

We'd almost reached the dining room, but there was an hour left to go before lunch. Jemma looked around and wrinkled her nose. "It's a nice hotel, but I have to admit I'm starting to find it a bit stuffy."

"Why don't we get some fresh air?" I motioned her toward the lobby. "I could use some of that myself."

It was difficult to call any of the air in central London

exactly *fresh*. The cool spring breeze we stepped out into carried a whiff of car exhaust and a waft of hot buttery grease from the Indian restaurant down the road. I did find it a little easier to breathe out there all the same. Restricting one's self to a hotel for days on end couldn't be good for the spirit.

"Should we take a turn around the corner and see where that leads us?" I said.

"Sounds good to me." Jemma tucked her hand around my elbow the way she had when we'd been putting on a show of being lovers, as if it were perfectly natural. Heat flowed through me from that point of contact.

I made an effort to walk as steadily as possible and lean on my walking stick as little as possible, not that Jemma had ever appeared bothered by my irregular gait. She peered through the window of the restaurant, sniffing the tang of curry that colored the air there, and commented that we should skip the hotel buffet to grab a bite there some evening. I was about to suggest that we do it tonight when we came around the corner to a clang and a muttered string of curses.

We jerked to a halt. A big guy, taller than me and with muscles flexing beneath his stained Henley, smacked the side of the newspaper box he was scuffling with farther down the road. His ragged blond hair shadowed his dark eyes.

He jammed a metal tool into the coin slot, trying to break it open. Here, in broad daylight—well, clouded dim daylight—without seeming to care who saw him. Figuring no one would dare challenge a guy who looked as tough as he did? I'd been around enough soldiers during my tour to know you couldn't judge fighting strength solely by appearances. A fact that applied to me as much as the man in front of me.

A tingle of adrenaline shot through my veins. I took a step toward him, and Jemma's grip on my arm tightened.

"We'll call the cops," she said. "He doesn't look like he's going to respond to a little friendly conversation. For all we know, he's armed."

Calling the police would be the wise thing to do. My pistol was back in my hotel room. Even if I'd had it on me, engaging with an already violent criminal could quickly cross the line from brave to brainless.

The guy glanced up and saw us watching him. He wrenched at the box, slammed it with his fist, and leered at Jemma. "Why don't you gawk a little closer, sweet stuff? Donate those tits to the cause."

Jemma's jaw clenched, but she turned away. "It's not worth it."

The fire that had flared up inside me said it was, though. No one should be allowed to talk to this woman like that.

I squeezed her hand. "I'll be fine," I said, and strode forward.

The guy straightened up as I approached. He took me in, and his leer turned into a sneer. He cracked his knuckles. "Think today is the day to prove yourself, huh?" he said.

"I think you'd better step away from that newspaper box and get going," I replied. The words tumbled out of my mouth automatically, propelled by the rush of adrenaline.

The guy guffawed. "That would be a no. Maybe I can break it open with that thick skull of yours."

I shifted my weight onto my good leg and adjusted my grip on my walking stick. When the guy swung a meaty fist at me, exactly as I'd expected him too, I dodged and jabbed my stick into the middle of his gut.

I knew how to deliver a good blow. The guy winced and stumbled, doubling over for a second before he lunged at me again, with a snarl this time. I couldn't yank myself out of the way fast enough.

His knuckles clipped the side of my head, sending my thoughts spinning. I gritted my teeth with a fresh flare of determination and whacked my stick across the guy's throat.

He sputtered and reeled back. The angry flush that had darkened his face faded. He spat out some incoherent insult, turned tail, and ran.

"John!" Jemma came to a stop beside me. She glanced me over as if checking for wounds. "You really didn't have to do that."

"I know," I said with a grin I couldn't restrain, my heart still thumping from the scuffle. It nearly drowned out the ache where the hooligan's fist had met my temple. "But so many of those guys are cowards. Show you can give them a proper fight, and they decide it's not worth the trouble."

From the look she gave me, she wasn't sure whether to thank me or keep berating me. I might have been fine with both. My pulse kicked up another notch as I gazed down into her cloud-gray eyes. A hint of her scent reached me, sweetly floral with a temptingly dark undertone. The impulse shot through me to trace my fingers along her delicate jaw and kiss her.

I balked, giving my passions a moment to cool. We were colleagues. She hadn't shown any definite signs of interest. She'd probably think I was taking advantage of the opportunity to play hero.

Before I could completely collect myself, my phone vibrated in my pocket. I fished it out, raising it faster when I saw the name on the text.

"Is that Sherlock?" Jemma asked.

I could give her news that I expected would be much more welcome than a kiss. "He's tracked down Richter's collection manager," I said with a nod. "We can talk to him this afternoon."

CHAPTER NINE

Jemma

My favorite kind of con hit two birds with one stone. Conveniently, John Watson had a complimentary pair of weaknesses.

As the four of us headed across the hotel's underground parking garage to John's car, I positioned myself at his side. Then I pressed my right heel into the concrete with slightly more pressure than before.

The heel snapped loose. I stumbled, and John caught my arm with his free hand. Savior impulse engaged.

"Whoa there," he said. "Are you all right?"

"Damned shoe." I examined the low heel dangling from the back of my practical black pump and sighed. "This brand usually holds up."

"We'll match," John said with his easy grin. "It's not so bad being a bit lopsided. On the other hand, I'm sure we've got time for you to run back to your room if you have another pair."

Sherlock made a disgruntled sound at the suggestion, already shifting his weight impatiently as if the interview he'd planned were a chemical reaction that would explode if the timing changed by a matter of seconds.

I patted my purse. "I always carry a little shoe glue just in case. I'll be lopsided the rest of the way to the car, and then I'll fix it up well enough to get through the day."

"Prepared for everything, hmm?" John said, with the admiring glint in his hazel eyes that I'd wanted to inspire. He liked saving me, but I got the impression he enjoyed watching my unwavering competence even more. Might as well appeal to both inclinations.

"Says the guy who carries multiple fake moustaches in his jacket pocket," I returned, and he chuckled.

He had another one on today, bushier than the one he'd used for the gentlemen's club, and a hat that hid his sandy blond hair. Sherlock had applied a full beard and dappled his messy waves with believable flecks of gray. They'd both dressed in scruffier clothes than usual too.

Only Garrett looked like his usual boyish self, but he was going to hang back in the car, both to stay out of any potentially illegal maneuvering we had to do and to be ready to call for back-up if Sherlock's plan went wrong.

I took the offending shoe off and walked with that foot on tiptoe, the pavement cold and unpleasantly damp through my sock. John kept his hand on my arm, more a touch than a hold, ready if I teetered. It was rather odd, really, to find a human being who both got off on coming to the rescue and applauded self-sufficiency. Most White Knight types preferred that their wounded birds stayed wounded.

You'd almost think the man was really as kind-hearted as he presented himself. But I'd seen how eagerly he'd leapt at the newspaper box guy this morning. Throw a reckless hankering for danger into the mix, and you got quite the stew.

At the silver Ford, John had to let go of me to head to the driver's seat. Garrett's glower followed him, one he wasn't making much effort to hide. Hmm. I should probably temper that jealousy before it sparked more of a fire. They did need to work *together*.

With his long legs, Sherlock naturally took the other front seat. I slid into the back next to Garrett. His expression stayed gloomy as he did up his seatbelt, but he didn't look at me.

John revved the Ford's engine and backed out of the spot with a smooth turn of the wheel and a burst of speed. I was glad for my own seatbelt as we zipped toward the exit. Apparently the good doctor enjoyed tempting danger on the road as well.

He and Sherlock fell into a conversation about another recent case a client had brought them. I dabbed the gummy glue onto my shoe, pressed the heel on tight, and turned toward Garrett. He wasn't so stoic that he could ignore my direct gaze. After a second, he glanced over at me, his mouth set at an angle that was tense but not hostile.

I brushed my fingers lightly over his forearm. "Hey," I

said, softly enough to speak under the front seat chatter. "We're all right, aren't we? If things went farther than you'd have wanted— I know I can get carried away."

My touch brought a glimmer of hunger into Garrett's eyes. He appeared to gather himself. "We're fine. It was— ah, it was very nice. But you and John have something going now…?" His voice stayed carefully terse.

"Not at the moment," I said. "But I can't say it won't happen. I'm only here until the end of the week. It's not as if I could be looking to make any kind of commitment."

"Of course not. It isn't even my business."

"I do like you," I said. Sure, I could summon some appreciation for the man's dogged ambition. And for the competitive passion he'd unleashed last night. "If things were different, I wouldn't see any need to play the field."

A bit of light came into his face under the grimness. *You won*, I was telling him. *I'd want you more*. Which was exactly what he wanted to hear. From now through to the end, I needed all three of these men both invested and away from each other's throats. We had bigger villains to tackle—bigger than any of them knew.

Richter was just the gateway to a horde of monsters that ate children's souls.

When we parked a couple of blocks from the warehouse where Sherlock was sure we'd find Richter's manager, Garrett leaned back in his seat, setting his police radio on his knee and taking out his ever-present notepad. He looked far more relaxed than he had when we'd gotten in. Good. My work here was done.

"I'll be watching for your signal," he said.

"I don't expect I'll need to give it," Sherlock said. "But in a case this volatile, it's worth taking the precaution." Both he and John were carrying pistols, just in case.

We set off past the dingy buildings toward the warehouse in question. This wasn't the sort of area where you'd expect a wealthy gent to have his lackeys working, but Richter had plenty of activities he'd rather keep far from curious eyes. My shoes tapped against the sidewalk. I dug my hands into the pockets of the worn jacket Sherlock had procured for my own "costume."

It was fascinating watching how the detective transformed. John had left his walking stick behind to move with a more definite hitch, and he slumped his shoulders a bit to change his posture, but I'd still have recognized him with a close glance. Sherlock, on the other hand, became an utterly different person.

Somehow with the bend of his legs, he affected a bowlegged gait and shaved a few inches off his considerable height. The swagger of his movements and the puff of his chest gave the impression of a much broader frame than he actually possessed. As we drove, he'd slicked back his hair with oil. Between all that and the beard, I had to peer to make out any hint of the man underneath.

Was that level of subterfuge really necessary for this lackey? I couldn't have said I was convinced, but Sherlock took pride in his disguise, and I enjoyed watching it, so I wasn't going to badger him about it.

At the warehouse, he shoved open the door, and we all marched in as if we belonged there. That was the core of his plan. Richter's manager wasn't likely to say much to strangers with detective airs. He'd be less on his guard with people he took to be colleagues.

As Sherlock had assured us, the slight man with a hawkish nose was puttering around by stacks of boxes at the far end of the main warehouse room. His ponytail, as much gray as it was dun brown, hissed against his shoulders when he spun around. His eyes narrowed.

"This is private property."

"Of course it is," Sherlock said in a boisterous voice that held no trace of his usual clear even tone. "You're Lenny, yeah? Richter passed on word for us to check that everything's in order for the new shipment."

Lenny frowned and reached for a clipboard he'd left on one of the boxes. "How new? I'm not expecting anything else until next week."

John's eyebrows leapt up. "Did you miss the message, then?" he asked, roughening his own voice. "Last-minute bid on some item that must be pretty special from how urgent he sounded about it. That's why he wanted everything double-checked."

Sherlock neatly picked up the thread. "Good thing we came by. Imagine how unhappy he'd be with you if he showed up tomorrow and you had no idea."

Lenny's skepticism hadn't totally faded, but he couldn't help paling at that suggestion. Richter didn't go easy on his employees.

"It's possible the manifest didn't come through," he said. "Do you have it?"

"We thought you'd have it. For fuck's sake, don't let on

you missed this one. We can sort it out. You'll know the thing when it turns up."

That was my opening. I rolled my eyes. "If it even does. I wouldn't put it past him to back out on the bid after all this. The boss's moods have been all over the place lately."

"Tell me about it," Lenny muttered.

"That's true." Sherlock grimaced. "Ever since the guy got back from Germany, he's been on kind of a tear."

We were improvising now. If I let him keep going, no doubt Sherlock would have spun a good tale to lead Lenny down the right path. But if I wanted to keep the consulting detective invested in me and this case, I'd better appeal to him the right way too. Show I could play at the same level. Excite that intellectual ego of his.

"It started *before* he left Munich," I said. "He rang the office while I was in—I had to field the call. He asked some strange questions and sounded kind of odd too." I cocked my head at Lenny. "You were over there with him, weren't you?"

I knew he had been, and I knew Richter had been edgy, even if it hadn't been because he'd just committed a murder, which was what the guys would think I was extrapolating from.

Lenny nodded. It was always easier to get someone to simply confirm rather than to volunteer information outright. "He was a little... restless. He came by to check on the shipment a bunch of times before we flew out."

Sherlock waggled a finger. "Right. Do you have the

crates from that lot around? We should take a look at their condition."

"They're right over there." Lenny pointed. "They were new ones for this trip—they should have at least a few more uses in them."

Several plywood boxes nearly as tall as me stood in one corner of the warehouse. A piney smell tickled my nose as we walked over.

Sherlock circled them and stopped by the third. He tapped one corner. "There's extra wear here compared to the others."

John considered it. "He must have opened it again at that end to pop something in last minute, don't you figure?"

A shade of Sherlock's usual knowing smile crossed his lips. "I think you've hit the nail on the head."

John's chin rose at the praise. Lenny sauntered over to see what we were talking about. Now was my chance to steer the great detective straight to our ultimate target.

"He *knew* he was going to stick something in at the last minute," I added. "Now the stuff he was talking about makes sense. He was carrying one of the pieces around with him until right before the plane was supposed to leave. One of the really valuable ones he was worried about getting nicked, I guess?"

Sherlock glanced at me, both wary and curious. Lenny stared at me for a few seconds, long enough to provoke a flicker of worry in me that I'd pushed too far. Then he let out a short ragged laugh.

"I don't know about the value, but you're right, he

held onto the one thing until it was time to head out. Had it in an inside pocket on his jacket and kept his arm tucked over that spot the whole time. I'd never seen him that protective of one of the pieces before."

"Huh," Sherlock said with a casual air. "What, was it the Hope Diamond?"

"He'd wish. I don't know. He kept it so close I didn't even see it."

The detective snapped his fingers. "Maybe it was something about—I overheard him mentioning a call he sounded upset about."

Good man. He was following the assumption that something must have brought Richter and the murdered councilor together that night, throwing out a possibility so the manager had the opportunity to confirm or correct him. Leading him straight to the other clue I'd wanted him to stumble on.

"I don't know about a call," Lenny said. "He was only in the hangar briefly here and there. But there was—this messenger came in with a note. The boss left the airfield for a while after that. Who knows?"

He shrugged, his mouth flattening as if he'd realized he might have gotten talking a tad carelessly. That was fine. He'd delivered all the information I could have hoped for.

Sherlock veered back toward the topic of the supposed new shipment that might or might not arrive tomorrow, and after a quick back and forth, we were on our way again. The detective kept up his bowlegged gait all the way back to the car.

"Well, you all made it back in one piece," Garrett said as we climbed in. "Did the plan pan out?"

"I'm increasingly convinced that the situation was some sort of blackmail," Sherlock said. "A photograph that was torn up, a note that disturbed Richter and sent him running presumably to confront the man who sent it, all the crimes he's managed to suppress proof of..." He swiveled in his seat to peer at me, his gaze as sharp as ever within his disguise. "How did you make that leap about Richter carrying one particular item around with him?"

I wasn't going to tell him I'd seen it with my own eyes.

"The crate," I said. "The scrapes on the corner suggested it'd been opened at least three times. Something was packed and then removed and then put back in, I guessed. The marks of the nails supported that conclusion —it was only fully sealed once. He didn't close the lid tight right away because he knew he was going to be returning something there. If he was worried enough not to leave that artifact in the crate, why would he leave it somewhere else? It had to be on him."

"Yes," Sherlock said. "I came to the same conclusions myself, just not quite as quickly. You're a swift one with your observations." He sounded impressed, but at the same time his gaze felt more analytical than awed, as if he was searching for more to my answer.

"I do my best," I said, smiling innocently back at him. "I wasn't sure—it was only a possibility that seemed worth pursuing."

"Indeed." He eased back in his seat. "I would be highly surprised if all of Richter's unusual behavior isn't tied to the murder. I believe our next order of business should be getting our hands on a manifest listing the contents of that particular crate."

And that would lead him straight to the final, perilous prize.

CHAPTER TEN

Jemma

A few sofas sat around the edges of the hotel lobby, and I'd positioned myself on the one that would be right in John's line of sight when he left the evening seminar he was attending. Tucking my legs up in front of me and resting my tablet on my knees, I nibbled on the sweet creaminess of a custard tart and checked the latest coded emails and bank transfers.

This chunk of money could go off to my account in Sweden, that one to the Cayman Islands. This contractor I'd send a little bonus to for a job well done. That one was going to need a visit from Bash if she strayed any farther.

Some people were just that stupid. As if they didn't realize I was paying enough attention to make sure they never got to make the actual attempt to screw me over. I hadn't built the most finely tuned network of illegal activity in the world by looking the other way.

For a few minutes, I skimmed through my database of contacts. This operation would be a lot more straightforward if I hadn't needed to keep my trio of crimefighters engaged but unaware. The trouble was, Stefan Richter had plenty of contacts and plenty of sway in the criminal underworld too.

The guy who'd been meant to pave the way to my score in Munich had flipped and gone to tattle to Richter at the last minute. Bash had gotten to him before he'd been able to say much, but I couldn't be completely sure of any of the lowlifes here either. Especially when Richter might have already spread the word that someone was out to steal from him.

I needed connections from the other side of the divide between criminal and crime-fighter. Sherlock and his friends were going to handle that for me as long as I played this right. I'd worked for nearly ten years to get to this point. I could be patient.

I switched to one of the local news sites in case I'd find something useful to riff off in the stories I was spinning. I'd made it through twelve pages of corrupt politicians, corporate negligence, and mass layoffs—who were the real villains in this world, exactly?—before the tap of John's walking stick reached my ears.

Keeping my gaze on the screen, I ran a hand through my hair so the waves rippled. The movement would catch his eye.

Sure enough, here came that soft tapping across the floor to my seat.

I glanced up when he was five feet away. John smiled

down at me with the warmth that always made me feel he was actually glad to see me. Only because he didn't know what I really was, of course.

"What are you doing out here at this hour, Jemma?" he asked.

I rubbed my eyes. "I guess I lost track of time."

"Good book?"

"Something like that." I looked toward the elevators and hesitated, letting my mouth slant downward just slightly.

John caught even that small sign of discomfort, as I'd expected he would. He propped himself against the arm of the sofa. "Is something the matter?"

I produced an awkward laugh and waved off the question. "It's nothing. I'm being silly." I pushed myself to my feet, paused, and set off toward the elevators.

John kept pace with me. "I have trouble imagining you getting caught up in anything 'silly.' Maybe I can help. I promise I don't judge—and I've certainly gotten myself worried about plenty of things that seemed silly in the aftermath."

I stopped in front of the elevators and pushed the button. Then I exhaled as if overcoming my reluctance. "After going out and talking to that Lenny guy today, knowing that we're dealing with a murderer and a rapist who's very good at covering his tracks… I started feeling a little nervous about being in my room alone. If I were at home, the situation wouldn't get to me like this, but in an unfamiliar place—like I said, it's silly. This building is *more* secure than my apartment."

"Nope," John said with a playfully definitive air. "Definitely not silly. As a doctor, I declare that a totally reasonable worry considering the circumstances."

The elevator arrived with a ding. As we stepped on, I lowered my head with a swipe at my mouth.

"I feel guilty, too," I said. "I got the three of you wrapped up in the case. You're probably in danger because of me. The more we keep investigating, the more danger it'll be. This is my *job*; I'm supposed to face those threats. But you—"

"Hey." John set his hand on my shoulder with a gentle squeeze. "I carry out the work I do knowing there'll be threats along the way. Sherlock and I have tackled some pretty horrible characters before. I'm glad I got the chance to contribute to a case this big."

"We'll see how glad you are by the end of it," I muttered, but I gave him a hint of a smile at the same time.

The elevator whirred to a stop at the second floor. John's room was on the fourth. I tensed as the door slid open and then squared my shoulders.

"Why don't you come back to my room, just for a bit?" John said abruptly. He wet his lips. "A little friendly conversation might help settle your nerves. I mean, if you'd rather just get back to yours, that's completely fine—"

"You know, I think that would be just what I need," I said before he could stumble any further in clarifying his invitation. "Thank you."

He beamed at me, but he obviously wasn't sure of

where this night might lead. I'd better make my interest a little more clear.

He jabbed the button to close the doors. As his hand dropped back to his side, I caught it in mine. My fingers tucked against his warm skin, and I stroked my thumb over his knuckles in a gentle caress.

John didn't say anything, but the air in the space between us warmed just a little. He adjusted his hand to twine his fingers with mine, like an answer to my proposition.

I suspected Garrett in the same situation would have tossed me on the bed—or maybe on the desk again—the second we walked into the room. John let go of me to amble over to his dresser.

"I picked up a bottle of sherry so I wouldn't be tempted by the mini bar. Would you like a drink?"

He couldn't help playing the gentleman, could he? I smiled in amusement and perched on the end of the bed. "Why not? I trust you chose good stuff."

John poured us each a dollop of amber liquid in the room's tumblers and handed one to me. Instead of sitting next to me on the bed, he turned the desk chair around to face me and sank onto that.

"You said before that you thought you might travel around like your parents did," he said in a casual conversational tone. "Where do you think you'd go first if you uprooted?"

A little more "getting to know you" before we got down to the fucking? His earnestness about this whole process was almost endearing. I could humor him.

"I'd like to spend more time in Iceland at some point," I said, somewhat at random. "And Peru—the little bit I saw of it was lovely."

"You really have been all over, huh?"

"I did tell you." I took a sip of the sherry, absorbing the rich nutty flavor. "What about you? Did the military take you many places?"

John's hand dropped instinctively to his hip. "I was only stationed in Iraq," he said. "A couple different bases. I'm sure if I'd been able to complete my tour, I'd have moved around more, but…" He shrugged. "These things happen."

He sounded genuinely regretful that he hadn't spent more time around bazookas and mines. "And now you have this," I said, gesturing at him to indicate his new career.

"Yes. It's hard to say I'd trade this life for another one. Maybe I missed my real calling until now."

He brought his glass to his lips, considering me. My gaze lingered on the ripple of his throat as he swallowed. How lucky I was to have my trio of crime-fighters made up of three such physically appealing men, as different as they were from each other.

"What drew *you* to this calling?" he asked. "Every police officer I've talked to has some kind of defining moment or urge they can point to."

I'd locked eyes with a lot of men over the years. I'd told lies to nearly all of them. But something about this man, in this moment, brought out an impulse to offer him an answer as close to the truth as I was capable of. I took a gulp of sherry to see if it would burn away the whim, but the sensation only prickled deeper.

Why not? It wouldn't hurt anything. He'd probably like the simplified version at least as well as anything I could make up.

"Someone who was very important to me died a long time ago," I said. "I've always felt like I should have been able to prevent it. I don't want anyone else to meet the fate she did if I can help it. So, here I am."

I held the memories at a distance where they couldn't hit me with more than a muted ache behind my sternum.

"I'm sorry," John said.

"*You've* got nothing to be sorry for." I drained the last of my sherry and set the glass down on the carpet. "Like I said, it was a long time ago."

"Still, that's the sort of experience that stays with you. And the sort no one should have to go through."

"And yet so many of us do." I leaned back on my hands, studying him, the alcohol having left me with a faint but pleasant tingling in my head. "Can I ask you a question now?"

The corners of his lips quirked up. "That seems only fair."

"The three of you have worked together all this time," I said. "And then suddenly you have this woman you hardly know tagging along everywhere you go. Sherlock is focused on the case, and Garrett has obviously had some concerns about some interloper crashing your party, but you've been nothing but welcoming right from the start. Why is that?"

John's smile turned uncharacteristically mysterious. "Maybe I recognized a kindred spirit."

If he'd known anything about the real Jemma Moriarty, he'd be aware that we couldn't have had less in common. I'd been more jaded than John Watson since the day I was born. I guessed his perceptions meant I'd done my job well.

I held out my hand. "If that's the case, kindred spirit, what are you doing all the way over there?"

Desire lit in his eyes. He set his glass, the sherry only half drunk, down on the desk and crossed the short distance to the bed without bothering with his walking stick. He stopped in front of me. Gazing down at me, he brought his hands to my face and teased them over my hair.

"Jemma," he said. "You are a gem. A brilliant jewel."

I trailed my fingers up his broad chest over his dress shirt. "You're pretty shiny yourself."

John laughed and lowered his head. His mouth found mine, careful and tender. So different from Garrett in this too, and yet with its own little thrill.

I gripped his shirt, urging him closer, and he deepened the kiss with a probe of his tongue. As we kissed and came up for air and kissed some more, one of his hands trailed down to trace the curve of my shoulder.

I yanked his shirt from his trousers. This position was perfect to get him panting with need.

When I unzipped his fly, his breath stuttered against my mouth. He kissed me harder, his fingers dipping to stroke over my breast, but I didn't miss the quiver of his thighs at the same time.

This wasn't the best position for *him* with that injured leg.

No need for that to stop me. I scooted back on the bed, tugging John with me, and he followed. He broke the kiss to ease my blouse up over my head. Then he was freeing my breasts from my bra, tipping one up to meet his descending mouth. His tongue swiped over my nipple, searing hot. I ran my fingers over his soft hair and hummed encouragingly.

His hands started to travel lower, reminding me of my earlier intentions. I nudged him down on his back on the fluffy bedspread and delved into the path I'd opened in his trousers.

"Fuck," John murmured as I closed my hand around his rigid cock. He was thick and silky and already beading precum at the tip. I flicked my thumb over the head and was rewarded with a groan.

Working him free from his boxers, I bent down at his side. I set my other hand carefully to avoid the jagged scar on his hip. A rough sound reverberated through his chest when my mouth closed over his cock.

His skin smelled clean and fresh like a light spring rain shower, with a hint of salt on my tongue as I swirled it around his cock. Alongside the bob of my head, I cupped his balls. John's hips bucked up encouragingly. Oh, yes, he liked that.

He was the kind of guy I could enjoy giving a blowjob too—responsive and eager but polite about it. He kept those hips in check while I sucked him down again, rocking with my motions but not jamming his dick down my throat. The panting I'd wanted to provoke rasped over his lips. The sound of it made me wet.

In this moment, you are mine. Mine, mine, mine. Just for this moment, this bright golden man wanted me more than anything else in the world.

John touched my waist and pulled at my body. It took me a few seconds to realize what he was after. I swiveled around, barely breaking my rhythm, until I straddled his shoulders. He eased my slacks and panties down and then pushed himself up to slick his tongue over my clit.

Oh, God Almighty. The number of guys who'd offer this generosity when I was already working them over was vanishingly slim. With my legs splayed over him, every part of my core felt doubly exposed and sensitive. The gentle pressure of his lips made me tremble. I wasn't going to last long like this.

I teased my teeth against the underside of his cock. John's hips jerked. He groaned against my core, the sound flooding me with pleasure. He was close too, but the throb of need inside me demanded more than this.

I slipped off of him and grabbed my purse to retrieve a condom. When I swung around to meet him face to face, John was waiting to draw me in for a kiss. Our breath mingled and our tongues collided as we kicked our pants and undergarments the rest of the way off. He slipped his hand between my thighs, one finger and then another slicking deep inside me until I couldn't have been readier.

At my tug, he rolled on top of me, bracing his weight

on one elbow as he prepped himself. His mouth found mine for another kiss. I lifted my knees to his sides, and he slid right in, filling me with that perfect blissful pressure.

John's breath washed over my neck. He nibbled my clavicle, gripping my thigh at the same time, easing back and plunging even deeper. My head tipped back with a whimper.

"Your mouth felt fantastic, but this is even better," he mumbled against my bare skin.

A giggle escaped me. "My sentiments exactly."

I wouldn't have needed it, but he tucked his hand between us anyway. His thumb grazed over my clit and then pressed harder. His thrusts picked up speed. Pleasure flared from that little nub and seared along every nerve around my core, surging high and fast with the combined stimulation. I dug my fingers into the folds of his shirt and held on as ecstasy split me down the middle.

I came shaking and moaning, clinging on to him so tight my knuckles ached. John bucked into me faster still, sending another swell of sensation through me. Then he was biting down on my shoulder with a strangled sound.

He drove deep a few more times and swayed to a stop with a ragged exhalation. And in the aftermath as he sank down beside me, his arm looping around my waist, my mind leapt to the moment, soon, when I'd have to make my excuses and leave.

CHAPTER ELEVEN

Bash

The moment I ducked through the window of Jemma's hotel room, I knew she'd just hooked up with one of her marks. I'd seen her post-seduction enough times to recognize the signs. Her hair hung straighter and darker than usual, damp from a recent shower, and her pose where she was sitting at the little table next to the window had the languid air of physical satisfaction.

She perked up in an instant at the sight of me, leaning her arms on the tabletop. The white hotel bathrobe she'd thrown on over her pajamas looked a little bulky on her slim figure, but the understated authority of her presence filled it out just fine.

"You got it?" she said.

I dropped into the chair across from her and pulled out the package I'd been carrying. "Exactly as you requested, Majesty."

Jemma gave me a mock grimace at the nickname and unwrapped the thin slab of metal. She ran her fingers over the etching on its surface, tracing the pattern of embedded gems.

"I doubt it'll fool the owner for more than a second," I said. "The forger said he needed to improvise some since you couldn't give him a visual reference."

She shrugged without any sign of concern. "I don't need to fool the owner. I just need to know my three do-gooders won't realize there's been a theft until I've had a chance to leave the building. They won't be paying attention to the details of this piece." She looked up at me with a sly smile. "Thank you. This is perfect."

Her damp hair made her deep-set eyes look even larger. That and the familiar smile took me back seven years to when I'd first met her. She'd been as scrawny as she was now and way too young to drink, but she'd tapped my shoulder in the middle of a rowdy bar in downtown Detroit and said with balls as big as Oberon's, "I hear you shoot people for pay."

How could I have said no to that?

"Your other plans are coming along well?" I asked, nodding to her get-up.

Jemma's smile widened, and my gut twinged with a little jab of the jealousy I'd thought I had reined in. "Very well, I think. Officer Moriarty of the Freising Police Department is much admired."

I'd seen the coy glances and flirty touches she used to work her wiles when she needed to. It wasn't as if, given the choice, I'd have traded places with any of those men. I got the real Jemma Moriarty, without pretense or artifice: focused, brilliant, and brutal. And in all that brilliance, she'd seen fit to rely on me above anyone else in her vast schemes.

No, being her right-hand man was the real honor.

She swept the replica engraving off the table and slipped it into a concealed compartment in her suitcase. "Was Corbin satisfied with his payment? I didn't expect the blows to land quite that hard."

I thought of the big Irish guy I'd handed off an envelope to this evening and chuckled. "He whinged a bit about having walking-stick bruises, but he looked very happy with the cash. He just made more in a day than I'd bet he usually does in a month. That's worth a few bruises. The good doctor has some spirit to him, does he?"

"Oh, he does," Jemma said, in a tone that told me exactly which of her marks she'd been with tonight. "His reaction to that little bit of theater was very enlightening. He's well on the hook now."

"How does our timeline look from here onward, Mori?"

That nickname brought a slight softness to her smile. I could have called her "Jemma" these days—she'd switched from "Moran" to "Sebastian" to "Bash" quickly enough the closer we'd worked together—but part of me liked having a name for her that was only mine.

"I expect we're only a few days from putting the heist into motion," she said. "They'll want to wrap things up for my sake before I have to go 'home' from the conference.

You should get those rooms booked in Algiers—the second passport names."

"Right," I said, making a mental note. "And the flights?"

She shook her head. "I'll handle those. We'll want to take the first one out of here once I've got the prize. By the time they realize what idiots they've been and start looking for me, there won't be a trace left behind."

I gave her a teasing salute. "Your worthy deeds do claim no less than what you stand for."

Normally Jemma would have ribbed me about the bastardized quote, but her gaze had gone momentarily distant. She might not even have registered more than the gist of the words.

It took a lot to distract this woman. There were complexities to this latest scheme I didn't fully understand—stakes that for whatever reason she was keeping to herself. All she'd given me was a warning, a week ago. *In about a month, I might just… vanish. And if that happens, I won't be coming back. I'm only telling you because I need you to promise me something. Don't go looking for me, Bash. If I'm gone, I'm gone.*

She'd spoken as coolly and matter-of-factly as she normally did, but it wasn't like Jemma to talk fatalistically. She was a master at turning an impossible situation around to her favor. I'd only ever seen her falter once, years ago. She hadn't mentioned the possibility of her disappearing again, but the memory still left me uneasy.

I wouldn't pry. That wasn't how we operated. That wasn't how *I* operated. The fact that I cared about her at all, let alone as much as I did, still socked me in the gut with surprise sometimes.

I'd thought I'd been happy living out a life of random crimes for hire before I met her. No, I'd thought I couldn't be meant for more than that. But I was something more now. I might be joking when I called her "Majesty," but she ruled the world we moved through with the power of a queen, and fuck if I hadn't somehow become the dark knight who stood beside the throne and made sure the unworthy bowed down. Without her, I'd just be that guy who shot people for pay again.

So, if there was a way I could keep her out of that fatalistic place and be the rock-solid foundation beneath her if her balance got momentarily shaky, I'd lay down at her feet in an instant.

"Is there anything else you need me to put in place?" I asked.

Jemma's gaze snapped back to me, as alert as ever now. "I wouldn't be surprised if I need you to give another nudge or two during the conference. I can pass on those details online. And it's time to put that worm in the police chief's ear like we talked about. Otherwise, keep on as we discussed."

"Then I shouldn't keep you from your beauty rest," I said.

Jemma snorted at that comment and got up from the table as I did. I was just turning toward the window when an odd fluttering of light washed over the wall beside the bathroom door. It shivered and jerked like a body seizing —and then it flickered away.

When I glanced at Jemma, she had her gaze firmly on me, a hint of defiance in the set of her chin. I knew better than to ask any questions about the odd sight. The strangeness had popped up here and there across the time I'd worked for her, and she clearly didn't like it but didn't think it was worth bothering with. If she ever thought I could do something useful about it, she'd tell me more then.

"There is one other thing," she said abruptly. "I'd imagine our friend Richter suspects I've followed him to London. He'll have people on the lookout for me in case I reach out to the local element—word will have gotten around by now. Let's remind him of the dangers of meddling with my business."

I grinned, the implicit order perfectly clear. My work with Jemma was always steady and never dull. "A job I'm happy to do."

She shot a smile back at me, fierce in its warmth. "Thank you, Bash."

I went from Jemma's room to my own in a much smaller and shabbier hotel where no one asked very many questions and the cleaning staff had loads of respect for the Do Not Disturb sign. My ninth floor view looked out over the few buildings between this one and Jemma's, giving me a clear line of sight to her window if she needed to signal me surreptitiously.

It was a quick change: Bright orange rugby shirt, matching cap, contacts that turned my light green eyes a deep indigo. Give people parts of you to stare at and they won't remember the bits that could actually identify you the next day. The jersey had the extra benefit of easily concealing the holster I slid into my jeans against my hip.

Suitably prepared, I headed for the narrower, grittier streets of London's underbelly. Often the trick to getting what you want is making people think you're giving them what *they* want, a con I'd seen Jemma pull off more times than I could count. I might not be able to manage it with the same degree of polish, but I could put on a good front when I wanted to.

Along the way, I dialed up the police's media line on a burner phone. "Hello," I said in a brisk British accent I'd picked up from listening to a grifter in New York City. "I'm calling from the Telegraph. Can anyone there comment on what I'm hearing about a Stefan Richter suing Scotland Yard for their interference with his business affairs? I understand he opened a similar case against the Paris PD."

"I—ah—we don't have any official statement on that," the woman on the other end said, sounding bewildered. "I'm sure if there's anything to report, we'll share a press release shortly."

She hung up, presumably off to pass on word to the chief that someone believed a guy named Richter might be going to sue them. One of tonight's jobs done, one more to go.

In the first bar, I squeezed between the crowded stools and ordered a beer. As the bartender slid it across the counter, I leaned in and let my voice fall into a rolling Welsh accent courtesy of the owner of a different bar I'd spent a lot of time at some years back.

"I heard someone's asking after a woman just arrived in town, putting out feelers about a big venture. I've got information if you know who I should talk to."

"Can't help you there, mate," the bartender said.

I waited about twenty minutes, gulping the cool beer and tuning out the barrage of voices around me, just in case. Then I moved on.

In the third bar, I hit pay dirt. The bartender's eyes twitched. "I might have heard something about that," he said. "Stick around, and maybe the guy will turn up."

After he served a couple more customers, he stepped off to the side with his phone. I nursed the Jack and Coke I'd ordered like I wasn't in any hurry. It was maybe half an hour before I caught the bartender tipping his head in my direction for the benefit of someone who'd just come in the door.

A burly guy with a drooping jaw stopped by the bar and then pushed through the swarm of patrons to the spot where I was standing. He held up his own glass. "Cheers."

"Cheers," I replied, and clinked my glass to his. "What's the occasion?"

"You have information about a woman who's assembling a crew?"

"Who wants to know?"

The guy fixed me with a hard look. "My boss, who's got a generous reward for anyone who can point him in the right direction. Do you know something or not?"

I held up my hands. "Hey, give me a break. This isn't my usual scene. I'm just looking to make ends meet. It sounds like I ended up in the right place." I glanced at the people milling around us and tugged on my hat. "Should we take this outside? She's got a meeting place all set up for tomorrow—I can show you it."

The guy grunted and threw back the rest of his drink. "Come on then."

Perfect. He lumbered toward the back of the bar, and I followed, letting my wrist brush against the concealed holster at my hip. While I was a rifle man by preference, a pistol worked just fine when circumstances called for it. My army superiors had called me the best distant shot in the forces, but they'd have hesitated to face off against me at short range too. I wouldn't be surprised if that'd contributed to the hurry with which they'd dishonorably discharged me.

Life didn't work the way Shakespeare and his type wrote it. They seemed to think no matter what else was going on, by the end of the drama everyone would have paid for their mistakes and flaws in systematic fashion. I watched those films for a laugh. It was fucking absurd how brutally fair they were.

In the life I knew, shitty people got away with shittier things the whole day long. But here and there, I could give them the shitty end they deserved. It might not be justice, but the act couldn't be more satisfying, especially when it served Jemma's unwavering sense of purpose.

We stepped out into the dank alley. I motioned to the guy, noting the pockets of noise and silence, judging the distance to the river. "It's just a few blocks over. She roped in a friend of mine. I didn't like the sound of it."

The guy guffawed. "Yeah, this crazy bint is a real piece of work, from what I hear."

I smiled tightly. In a few minutes, he'd be a piece of work—bloody artwork splattered all over a brick wall. And now I was going to enjoy it even more.

Jemma

In the car on the way to the gallery, I wound my hair into a loose braid. John must have caught a glimpse through the rearview mirror, even though he *should* have been keeping his eyes on the road.

"Felt the need to mix things up?" he said with a teasing lilt.

"I have the feeling I'm going to want it out of my face," I said, which wasn't exactly a lie. The larger truth, though, was the red waves could be rather attention-getting when allowed to flow freely. I didn't want anyone at the gallery taking particular note of me today.

I smoothed my hands over the skirt of my dress, feeling Garrett's gaze following the motion. It was a modest enough knee-length A-line, navy with a subtle quatrefoil pattern in a paler blue—the sort of thing Officer Moriarty would wear when trying to blend in with an arty crowd while casing a joint for evidence—but it was a lot more feminine than anything the trio had seen me in since the reception. Both Garrett's and John's eyes had shot to me the moment I'd stepped into the lobby to meet them for this field trip.

John roared through an intersection just before the light turned red and whipped us around a corner. He found a parking spot down the street from the building that was hosting Richter's exhibition. The gallery took up the whole other half of the block.

I studied the buildings as we walked over, noting the sleekness of the gallery's black marble-plated face and the narrow alley between it and the neighboring shoe shop. The edge of a fire escape leading to the apartment over the shop protruded from its rear.

"Those are our people," Garrett said with a subtle tilt of his head toward a tan sedan parked at the opposite corner. "Well, my people. The gallery put in a request to the department that we monitor the building the entire time the special exhibit is on—so obviously that order came via Richter."

The bigwig was stepping up his game from Munich. I prepared myself as we came up to the door.

Just like in Munich, Richter had demanded the highest level of security inside the gallery for his precious relics. I stood so the security camera just inside the door only caught the back of my head while the guard by the ticket booth pawed through my purse. More cameras were perched near the ceiling farther inside. I trod carefully between their lines of sight.

Reaching the two rooms that housed Richter's collection required a journey through the main gallery space, up a flight of stairs, and past a thick door with a keypad that clearly required a code for entry outside of visiting hours. Fixtures for motion detectors clung to the beige walls. From the warning lines laid on the floor around the display cases, I assumed pressure pads would set off an alarm if anyone stepped closer than Richter found comfortable.

Oh, he'd thought of just about anything. But I *would* have gotten the better of him in Munich if I'd had a little more time, if that pathetic excuse for an alarm hacker hadn't turned rat. Now Richter was up against not just me but Sherlock Holmes and company. We'd see how he enjoyed that challenge.

I meandered through the room, drawing a diagram of it in my head, letting my gaze skim over the displays on the wall as if I wasn't looking for anything in particular. I'd caught the gleam of gold from a case in the middle of the room. My heart thumped as I wandered closer to it.

I already knew what I was looking at. What I really needed was for the trio to see and to realize the significance, but the impact wouldn't land the same way unless they came on it themselves. I'd only nudge them if I had to.

Sherlock was examining the contents of each case with brisk efficiency, referencing the manifest he'd gotten his hands on by means he hadn't bothered to tell the rest of us. He indicated a bronze shield, a Grecian vase, and a statue lifted from this or that ancient temple, with John nodding along beside him. Then he turned toward the case I'd been working my way over to.

"It appears he organized his shipping containers to match the display layout," he murmured. "All four of these items were in that crate. Any of these are small enough that he could have carried them in a decent sized pocket."

"Sherlock." John came to an abrupt stop by the opposite end of the case. My pulse skipped a beat. *Yes.* He was staring through the glass.

"What is it?" the detective asked, his attention snapping to his friend. I moved to join them as if curious.

John pointed at a jade Buddha figurine about the height and width of his hand, carved up from a thick rectangular base. His arm trembled for a second, but he looked more giddy than anxious.

"The pattern along the base," he said. "Those ridges… I'd need to have it in my hands and to examine the victim's body in person to be sure, but I'd swear they match the head wound perfectly."

"From my memory, you're exactly right." Sherlock clapped the doctor on the back. "Well done, John."

Garrett hustled over, picking up on the momentous vibe. "What's going on?"

"John has found us the murder weapon," Sherlock said, still speaking under his breath. He must be thinking that the security cameras might be picking up sound as well as video.

I focused on the jade figure, schooling my gaze away from the strip of gold gleaming a foot away from it. "Would we be able to prove it? There might be other jade figures with the same construction, right? We don't have any proof that it was *this* one."

"We might, though," John said, excitement rippling through his voice even as he kept it low. "All we need is to find one bit of the victim's DNA on that statue. Obviously he took care to wash it off, but after the way he bashed that man's skull in, with ridges that deep—maybe a few years ago he'd have managed to destroy every usable shred, but now there'd have to be traces that the current techniques could lift, just like your golf shoes."

Thank you, Dr. Tanaka, for priming that epiphany.

"How can we get access to the figurine to lift evidence from it?" I asked. "Will your judgment based on sight be enough to get a warrant?"

Sherlock turned to Garrett. "I believe this is where you can be of great assistance. What can you work out with Scotland Yard? We'd want to move fast—have the warrant here with enough authority to confiscate the piece before Richter catches wind of the problem. He's slipped the police too many times before for us to risk giving him any leeway."

Garrett tore his gaze away from the figurine. "I'll talk to the chief and see what I can get in motion."

John passed him the car keys. "So you can have a private conversation. Just don't go driving off with her."

"That shouldn't be a problem," Garrett muttered, but he hurried out of the room with a spring in his step. Bringing down a man like Richter could make his career.

John frowned as he circled the case. "I wish I could get a better look at the entire bottom. The wound would have been from the edge, but the base made a large part of the mark. If I could see it, I'd be completely sure." A glint I recognized lit in his eyes. "This is a long shot, but… move back."

"John," I said with a nervous twist of my stomach as I eased away. Why did he have to pick right now to indulge his thrill addiction? I had to get him under control. "We don't want to do anything that'll draw attention. Like Sherlock said, if Richter gets any hint we're on to him—"

I'd meant to appeal to his loyalty to his friends and the case. Instead, my effort might have backfired by playing up the danger. John's mouth curved in a little grin. "This has nothing to do with any official business. Just a clumsy cripple whose walking stick slipped."

He turned and lifted his head as if catching sight of something that excited him. Sherlock opened his mouth to speak, but John was already moving. He lurched forward and let his walking stick fly out, sending him stumbling into the display case.

His shoulder hit the platform with a thump. It was so sturdily built the contents didn't so much as tremble.

As John groped for his fallen stick, two security guards barged into the room. I pretended to be fascinated by the vase Sherlock had been looking at earlier.

"Sorry!" John said. "So sorry! I'm still getting used to the stick—it gets away from me sometimes."

"Maybe you should steer clear of art galleries with precious artifacts on display, then, sir," one of the guards said gruffly. I swallowed a smile. That was a valid point, if not exactly presented with the most sensitivity. It sounded as if he'd bought John's lie.

Sherlock drifted past me. "Go out to the car first," he murmured from the side of his mouth. "We'll follow separately after. Better not to make it obvious we're together now that they'll be watching him."

I gazed at the vase for a few seconds longer and then ambled back the way we'd come. It wouldn't do to appear to be in a hurry, either. My slow pace also gave me the opportunity to scope out what looked like a maintenance door on the first floor toward the back, with a sign that said *Employees Only*. I added that to my mental blueprint of the building.

The guards by the front door didn't look twice at me. I strode by them, digging in my purse as an excuse to keep my head low as I passed the camera. On the street, I picked up my pace. My heartbeat sped up too.

I'd set all the pieces of this puzzle on a collision course to snap together, but there was always a small chance one gambit or another wouldn't work, that somewhere wires would be crossed…

Garrett was still on the phone when I opened the door to the backseat. He gave me a pained grimace that took the edge off my nerves. I made a face of sympathy and raised my eyebrows, but he held up his hand to hold off any questions.

"Yes, sir," he said into the phone. "I understand that. But I think considering the circumstances, it's worth taking that risk."

He paused while his chief said something on the other

end. I settled into my seat, keeping an expression of concern on my face while the rest of me relaxed. One step closer.

Sherlock appeared a minute later as Garrett wrapped up the conversation. Garrett jammed the phone in his pocket, and Sherlock twisted around in his seat. "Are we set?"

Garrett's boyish face had turned stormy. "Let's wait until John gets here."

Our Dr. Watson walked into view a couple minutes later. He looked pleased with himself until he dropped into the driver's seat and caught sight of Garrett. "What happened?" he asked.

"The chief won't lift a finger," Garrett spat out. "He said to forget it, just drop it. Not our murder, not our problem. Bloody arsehole."

I widened my eyes. "*Why?* Shouldn't he be jumping at the chance to take down a menace like Richter?"

Garrett made an angry gesture with his hand. "Politics polluting real police work. It can be such a mess down there... He feels it would be too embarrassing for the force if we break apart the exhibit we've already agreed to protect and it turns out we're wrong, and he mentioned the way Richter sued that other police department. I told him both Sherlock and John were sure he was the perpetrator and that statue was the murder weapon, but even that didn't budge him."

My shoulders slumped. "Then Richter is going to get away with this crime too—and this time it's *murder*."

"No," Sherlock said firmly. "We'll come up with another way. Let me think on it."

Yes, think on it plenty. This was the trickiest leap right here. It was more important than ever that they felt they'd come to the idea themselves. They'd never do it if they realized I was trying to push them into it.

I'd left my trail of bread crumbs. They'd followed it right up to the edge of the trap. All I needed was for them to take that final, crucial step inside.

CHAPTER THIRTEEN

Jemma

I knew something was off before I'd even finished opening the door to my hotel room. A cool draft, a hint of a scent in the air—something my senses picked up on a level below consciousness, honed by fourteen years of living in close proximity to the shrouded folk. I eased inside, my body tensed.

There was no sign of Bog itself—no filmy figure floating around, no flashy lighting effects. My gaze swept the room and snagged on the items I'd laid out on top of the dresser. Two of the bottles had fallen over, breaking my Fibonacci sequence.

It could have been the cleaning staff. I eased up to the dresser and peered at the objects strewn there. Something about the clouded sides of the body wash and lotion bottles looked off. I picked up the body wash, and the contents made a soft hissing sound.

My skin prickled. I popped open the cap and tipped the bottle to squeeze a little of the gel out onto my fingers.

Before I could apply any pressure, a stream of fine gritty powder with the body wash's faint floral scent poured from the bottle's opening over my hand. I jerked the bottle upright, but not before a streak of the stuff had spilled onto the carpet.

My fingers curled with the urge to fling the substance off me, but I needed to examine it first. I rubbed a little between my thumb and forefinger.

Bog had turned the gel to dust, scouring all the moisture from it. The same way the shrouded one was looking forward to scouring all the life out of me? A shiver ran through me, and I stiffened my shoulders.

How had Bog even—I wouldn't have thought it was possible—

The doubts slid through my mind, and the powder on my hand quivered before my eyes. The particles melded back together into a pearly blue gel that dribbled across my skin in cool globs.

I exhaled through gritted teeth. Of course. The shrouded folk were limited in their abilities to affect our physical world unless people of this world gave them access. That was why they bothered with people like my parents in the first place. The pain the cultists drew from themselves and others in their rituals, the bodies offered up to the monsters' maws—it all opened a doorway.

Maybe long ago I'd been marked for the slaughter, but the bargain I'd made with Bog had freed me from that, and I wasn't giving it anything until I had to. Without a doorway, the shrouded folk's powers were restricted to illusions. Nothing solid, nothing permanent, no matter how real it felt in the moment.

Which didn't change the fact that now I had body wash all over my hand. Thanks for that, Bog.

With a sigh, I marched into the bathroom to rinse the stuff off—and stopped dead in my tracks.

The shrouded one hadn't been messing only with my Fibonacci sequence. My brush lay on the bathroom counter next to the sink, tendrils of wavy hair woven through the dark bristles. Normally the strands of red showed starkly against the black base of the brush. They still showed starkly right now, but because they'd been bleached pure white.

Fuck the shrouded folk and their misty heads. I strode to the sink, rinsed off my hand, and dried it on the towel. When I glanced at the brush again, my hairs there still gleamed pure white. I scowled at them, willing the illusion to fall away.

Maybe this one wasn't an illusion. The time limit on my contract with Bog was almost up. That might give it enough leeway to work a little magic on this fragment of me.

I touched one of the hairs that curled from the side of the brush, and it disintegrated in an instant. Not just bleached, but drained as dry as I'd thought the body wash had been.

My throat tightened. I snatched up the brush, and the rest of the hairs fragmented into dust as well.

With a jerk of my arm, I hurled the brush against the

wall. It thumped there and clattered onto the tiled floor bristles first. A pattern of white dust flecked the turquoise glaze like ash. No matter how many times I blinked, it didn't fade.

All right. One point to Bog after all.

I walked back into the main room and sat on my bed, but my heart kept thumping at an uneasy rhythm. My trio of investigative geniuses had muttered some more about the police department's cowardice on the way back to the hotel, but no one had settled on any alternate course of action. Garrett had set off to Scotland Yard to speak to someone there in person, which I gathered had been a hopeless errand considering I hadn't gotten any word from him since. John had spent a while frowning at my crime scene photos and becoming even more convinced we'd identified the murder weapon, but scheming wasn't his area of expertise.

No, that talent was Sherlock's, and Mr. Sherlock Holmes had turned depressive and distant by lunchtime. He'd retreated to his room, and I hadn't seen him since.

I'd known it would take time. Making a decision to go this far over the line of legality couldn't be easy for any of them. But all I could feel right now was my time and my chance at escape slipping away from me.

I stood up again and paced the room in an attempt to wear down my nerves. The sugar cube I popped into my mouth seemed to turn sour on my tongue. I went through a series of punches and kicks, thinking over every piece I'd put in play to reach this moment to remind myself that they were all lined up perfectly.

The edgy sensation faded but didn't completely disappear. I stopped by the desk for a minute, torn by indecision, and then decided to hell with it. I'd feel better if I saw where Sherlock was at. I might be able to give him another nudge tonight. There wouldn't be anything odd about dropping in on him to talk after the day we'd had.

His room was two over from John's, right at the end of the hall. The Do Not Disturb sign was dangling from the handle. That was for hotel staff, not me. I knocked on the door lightly but insistently. "Sherlock? It's Jemma."

He took his time, but after several seconds, the door opened. Sherlock peered down at me from his great height, his piercing blue eyes shadowed and his whole demeanor rather sullen. You'd have thought it was his life riding on this "case" and not mine.

"You don't have news," he said, deducing that somehow or other from the once-over he gave me. He crossed his arms over the mouse-brown housecoat he'd put on over his dress shirt and slacks—apparently the hotel-issue bathrobe wasn't good enough for him. "What is it?"

From what John had said, he normally left Sherlock to stew in his thoughts when he got into these moods. That didn't mean I had to take the same tactic. It was ridiculous, really—a grown man older than I was all but sulking in his room because a problem had temporarily eluded his brilliant mind.

He should be better than that.

I motioned him away from the door to let me in. "I figured you've had enough time mulling things over on your own. Let's talk, and maybe we'll get somewhere."

Sherlock's mouth twisted, but he stepped aside and closed the door behind me.

He'd gotten himself a fancier suite than the standard rooms. The floor space was about a third larger than mine, making room for a sort of living room with a couple of armchairs around a sleek coffee table facing a gas fireplace. The fireplace was dark, reflecting his mood. An instrument case lay off to the side. I considered the size and shape.

"You play violin?"

Sherlock made a noise of agreement and sank into the farther of the two armchairs. "It keeps my mind well-tuned," he said, with no noticeable awareness of the pun. "I create my own compositions from time to time."

Of course he did. If I spent more time in his presence, I'd probably discover he baked pastries to rival Hermé, regularly swam the English channel in three hours, and found the time to persuade endangered animals to breed in between all that and his detective-ing.

As I sat in the other chair, he lifted an elegant wooden pipe from a side table and brought it to his lips. I raised my eyebrows at his pensive puff of smoke. "I wasn't aware the hotel allowed smoking."

He waved his hand dismissively. "A pipe is a far cry from cigarettes and cigars. It's a meditation."

From the earthy scent of the smoke, his meditation was Brazilian in origin. At least it was a reminder that he didn't feel many rules applied to him.

"And has your meditating taken you anywhere useful?" I asked, kicking my feet up on the edge of the coffee table, legs crossed for modesty in my dress.

"If it had, I'd hardly still be at it," he said in a sardonic tone. Then he sighed, rubbing his face. The dark brown waves of his hair fell across his high forehead in their usual disarray. "It really is a bitter irony that our efforts are so often hindered rather than helped by the police force employed to solve this city's crimes."

"Well, we know they're not giving us a warrant based on what we've got right now," I said. "So, how else can we make the case against Richter? Hashing it out between the two of us might spark an idea."

Sherlock's expression was doubtful, but he lowered his pipe. "There's no way to determine what was on the photograph that was likely blackmail material. No security cameras covering the area of road it would have shown. I've spoken with a few of our victim's colleagues, and they weren't aware of him carrying any photos or having any interactions with Richter, although he did make a phone call on the day of the murder that seemed to have him quite agitated. The number couldn't be traced. The councilor's behavior is a dead end."

"The shape of the blow—a forensic artist might be able to reconstruct the weapon from that to prove it's a match," I suggested.

Sherlock shook his head. "Only the base, and that base might belong to any number of objects when we can't bring in the one we believe it is for close examination. The only reason we'd assume that statue was the murder weapon is because of our other investigations, which are technically speculative in the eyes of the law."

I tapped the arm of the chair as if in thought. "If we

could prove that the victim met up with Richter, then—
But there wasn't enough evidence on the body to be sure
of the murder site. There must be traces of blood wherever
he was killed. It's almost impossible to fully clean a messy
murder like that unless you've prepared for it, and Richter
obviously acted in the heat of the moment."

"From your report, you had the dogs go out to try to
pick up the victim's scent," Sherlock said. "They didn't
discover any possible sites."

"They didn't. We could start from tracing *Richter's*
movements, since we didn't have him to consider as a
factor before…" I bit my lip. "His collection manager
didn't seem to know where he went when he was away
from the airfield, though. It sounds like he was on his
own. We don't exactly have a plethora of traffic cams in
Freising, but we might get lucky."

"I've already checked that angle. Another dead end.
There is also no documentation connecting the two men. I
determined that the victim dropped in on Cavalier's a few
years ago while visiting London, but even if he saw Richter
then, that's hardly the basis for a murder charge. There was
no outside DNA found on the body. Believe me, I've
looked at this from every angle a dozen times over."

I cocked my head at him. "Are you telling me that this
brute of a man is smarter than the great Sherlock
Holmes?"

"No," Sherlock said immediately, his ego ruffled.
"His wariness simply gets in the way of many of my
usual tactics. I would put out feelers about his
connection to the victim or the blackmail to try to stir

loose a telling response, but given his history, chances are he'll simply pack up his artifacts and leave, and then the one piece of evidence we do have will be completely out of our reach."

I made an irritated sound. "It's so frustrating to have that evidence *right there* and not be able to take it."

"Richter requires more subtlety than the average criminal, but the answer will come to me."

Sherlock said the last statement definitively, as if that were the end of any possible conversation on the subject. Then he settled deeper into his chair, his eyes going distant as he raised his pipe to his lips.

So very helpful. I leaned back in my own chair and found the thick line of my braid pressed uncomfortably against my spine. It wasn't as if I needed to keep my hair tied up any longer. I tugged off the elastic and ran my fingers through the strands to pull them loose across my shoulders.

When I glanced up again, Sherlock's gaze had refocused on me. There was something I couldn't quite pinpoint in his expression, curious but hesitant. I swiped a few stray waves behind my ear. "What?"

"Your relationship with both Garrett and John has become rather intimate in a short time," he said in that matter-of-fact way of his.

Ah. So he wasn't completely out of tune with those sorts of signs. I let the corner of my mouth lift in a slanted smile. "Given that we're all consenting adults, I'm not sure that's at all your concern."

Sherlock opened his mouth and paused for just a half

a second, so briefly I wouldn't have noticed if I hadn't been studying his response. There was that hesitance again.

"I only hope you're taking care to ensure any emotions that arise don't interfere with our work," he said.

Was that really all he was thinking about? A niggling suspicion tingled over my skin. I shifted in my chair, slipping my legs off the coffee table in a way that let my skirt ride a couple inches higher above my knees. "We had sex, not a romance," I said. "There's no reason for any emotions to get involved except enjoyment in the moment."

There. He tried to school his expression impassive, but a flicker passed through it anyway. He *was* curious— curious about what his colleagues had seen in me? About what we'd gotten out of those encounters?

About what he was missing?

A giddy wave tickled through me, washing away any lingering uneasiness after Bog's tricks in my room. From all available evidence and my own observations, I'd believed that Sherlock Holmes was impervious to this particular temptation. It appeared there was a crack in his ascetic persona after all. A crack *I'd* opened up.

I'd hooked his mind—I could hook him right through his passions as well if I played this moment right.

It was a risk. Who could say how a man like Sherlock would respond if I outright shattered his sense of himself as a man without lust? But I needed him caught up in me, I needed him engrossed to the point of obsession, now more than ever.

And I also wanted this. I wanted to find out what I

could experience with a man whose wits might match mine.

That thought sent another little thrill through me. Maybe I had more in common with John than I'd considered, even if our penchant for risk-taking wasn't what he'd meant when he'd mentioned kindred spirits.

"From my observations, human beings are rarely able to separate physical intimacy from tender emotions so neatly," Sherlock said. "And there are simpler ways of gaining bodily satisfaction."

"I suppose," I said, staying right where I was, my gaze holding his. "But it is a rather special sort of gratification. How much direct experience do you have on which to base that kind of judgment?"

"I had a few encounters in my college years. They were a lot of effort for little reward. There was nothing about them I'd recommend."

I smiled fully, just barely holding my lips back from a smirk. "I think you've missed out, then. A good 'encounter' can be incredibly stimulating to the mind as well. You'd have to recommend that."

"If I believed it," Sherlock said in a skeptical tone, but his eyes hadn't left mine. I was sure of the avidness I saw there now.

"So we have a difference of opinion," I said, resting my elbows on the arms of the chair. "What if I could prove it to you?"

Jemma

Sherlock had been sitting nearly motionless before, but now he went completely still. "How would you expect to 'prove it'?"

Oh, he knew. I could see *that* in his face, in the brief bob of his throat.

"I don't think you're really so unaffected," I said, settling more languidly into the plump cushions of my chair. "I bet I could provoke a reaction from you without touching a single place we'd consider overtly sexual. Will you take that wager?"

"A reaction," Sherlock repeated.

"You'll be undeniably hard. And if I win that bet, I get to show you how much more you can feel, without restriction."

A faint smile crossed Sherlock's lips. He really thought

I might not be able to live up to my word. "And if you don't?"

"I will," I said. "But for the sake of argument, what would you want? I've got a connection to a commissioner in Munich, if you want to take on more international consulting. I could write a report praising your talents."

"You'll end whatever you've started with John and Garrett beyond the work," Sherlock said abruptly.

I studied him. Interesting. Did my involvement with them bother him on some level, or did he simply figure that if I couldn't win this bet with him, I must be wrong about whether I was distracting them?

"Deal," I said, and stood up. "No time like the present."

It was rather gratifying simply seeing Sherlock so startled. "Now? I—" He recovered himself quickly. "Do you want me on the bed, then?"

"No," I said before he could do more than start to get up. "Right there will do. But… in the interests of ensuring we can confirm the results of this experiment, I will need you a little less dressed."

His eyes narrowed, but he eased out of his housecoat. "That does seem reasonable."

"Pants too," I said, gesturing. "The rest can stay on. I'll work around it."

He shed his slacks, revealing a pair of striped boxers. As he settled into the chair again, I came around the coffee table.

"Anything else?" he asked, in an impressively even tone.

"You're perfect," I said. "Stay exactly where you are."

I climbed onto the chair, straddling him with my knees on either side of his thighs. Lifting myself up a bit, I was face to face with him as I undid the top buttons on his shirt. This close, the blue of Sherlock's eyes was even more piercing. The earthy smell of his tobacco mingled with a sharp tang of aftershave. He put on such a cool demeanor, but everywhere our bodies touched, his felt blazing hot.

Fuck the risks. I wanted this man too damn much.

And I knew exactly how to get to him.

"It's fascinating how many nerve endings an earlobe has," I murmured, tracing my finger along the shell of his ear. I circled my thumb over the soft flesh at its base and leaned in to nip it between my lips, the smell of him filling my lungs. "Each one of them ready to light up at the right sort of touch."

Sherlock's pulse thumped under my palm where my other hand rested just beneath his shoulder, only speeding up a smidge at my attentions. Not so much an ear man, apparently.

I tipped lower, my breasts just shy of brushing his chest, and kissed one side of his neck while I stroked my fingertips along the other. "The neck too. All that vulnerability tied directly to the brain, ready to go on the alert with pleasure just as much as it can with pain."

"Is this going to be a biology lesson?" Sherlock asked, but he couldn't mask the roughening of his voice. He was plenty sensitive here.

"I thought you might appreciate the scientific

explanation, since you expressed so many doubts," I said, my voice still low, my breath grazing his throat.

"I'm aware of the basics of the physiological process already."

"But most lessons sink in better with an active demonstration, don't you think?" I smiled against his skin and tasted his smoky scent with a flick of my tongue. My fingers glided up to the crook of his jaw and down to his sternum. Sherlock drew in a breath with a slight hitch that set off an ache between my thighs.

"Those tingling nerves are encouraging the blood vessels to dilate all through your mind, urging the blood to flow faster." I kissed my way down to his collarbone, slow and lingering. Then I reached for his arm.

I caressed and then kissed the underside of his wrist as I unbuttoned the cuff of his sleeve and eased it up his arm. My fingers teased over the lean muscles to the inside of his elbow—and paused.

Most people would have taken the faint pink mottling there for normal skin variation. Would John even have noticed it? It didn't speak of an intensive habit—I'd seen what that looked like. But the pale impressions were just a little too regular to be natural discoloration.

I stroked my thumb over the area and looked at Sherlock. His eyes gleamed, a flush starting to seep over his cheeks. He hadn't conceded anything yet, but this moment felt more intimate than any I'd shared with Garrett or John.

He read the question in my eyes. "When the boredom becomes too much between cases, I occasionally take cocaine by injection. I'm extremely careful with my dosing. The energizing and clarifying effect on the mind outweighs any ill effects."

That great mind of his didn't know how to deal with stillness, did it? I touched the side of his face with an unfamiliar twinge in my gut.

"All the better that we're having this… discussion, then," I said. "You can get just as good a high from the right sex with the right partner without burning out fragments of your beautiful brain."

How much less interesting would this world be without at least one man like him in it to challenge me?

Before he could argue against my claim, I turned my attention back to his arm. I traced up and down the sensitive skin with a feathered touch. "Those sparking nerves and that rush of blood heighten the senses, so that each new point of contact comes into sharper focus."

My lips followed my fingers with testing kisses. Sherlock's pulse fluttered, and his body seemed to sink deeper into the chair with ebbing resistance, but I wasn't quite satisfied yet.

I slipped my other hand under his shirt, careful to avoid the area of his boxers and his nipples so he couldn't claim I'd violated the terms of our wager. He might be slender, but compact muscles covered every inch of his frame. He didn't come by his knowledge of the martial arts just through observation. Maybe someday we'd get to spar in a more literal way.

I fanned my fingers against his taut abs, meeting them with tempting softness, and heard Sherlock swallow. His body shifted almost imperceptibly, as if it'd tried to rise to my touch but he'd held it back.

Very good. Neck and stomach. I could work with that.

I let my voice drop even lower. "The more aroused the body becomes, the more oxytocin floods the brain, relaxing and wiping away stress to clear the mind."

Drawing a gentle circle on his palm, I raised his hand to suck his thumb into my mouth. A quiver ran through his legs. I caught his gaze as I rolled my tongue around him and then released him.

"But the real high," I murmured, tipping to kiss his neck again, "comes from the dopamine that's being triggered too, lighting up all the best spots inside your skull—ones no drug is going to reach. And as all those effects come together and build, the high can carry on and on…"

I stroked his abdomen with both hands, switching to a teasing graze of my fingernails and back to feathered caresses as I nibbled along his jaw. Sherlock had barely stirred, but his skin felt twice as hot as it had before. His pulse stuttered against the press of my mouth. I drew every ounce of sensation I could from the side of his neck with lips and tongue and the tips of my teeth. Then I nipped him just above his collarbone.

Sherlock's hips jerked up, flooding my own body with arousal. I had him, as sure as anything. He went still again under me, but there was no mistaking that response or the growing raggedness he couldn't smooth from his breath.

I wasn't in a hurry. I licked the spot where I'd nipped him and sucked on the pulse point above it, just shy of leaving a mark. My hands eased a little higher beneath his shirt. Then I shifted backward to glance down between us. An erection I'd admit was rather impressive tented his striped boxers.

I looked at Sherlock with an arch of my eyebrows. "I trust we can agree on the winner of our bet?"

His cool blue eyes were outright glittering now, sharpened with desire. It sounded as if it took some strain for him to keep his voice steady. "It would be unjust for me to deny it."

A smile curled my lips. "Then this is mine."

I slipped my fingers around his erection through the cotton fabric. Sherlock's eyelids drifted shut. His cock twitched against my palm. Heat and need pooled at my core, but all my focus stayed on his responses. I stroked him from base to head, reveling in the desire that emanated from this one part of his body.

It wasn't good enough, touching him through a barrier. I dipped my hand beneath the waistband and eased his boxers down until I'd completely freed him. His cock rose rigid, almost parallel with his torso, the tip glistening.

I slicked that liquid over his length and leaned in. My other hand slid up to tease my thumb over one of his nipples, earning me a quiver that told me he was sensitive there too. I brought my mouth to the other side of his neck.

With each pump of my fingers around his hardened cock, Sherlock's heart thumped faster. I swiveled my thumb around his nipple and then flicked it right over, kissing every inch of his neck.

His hands stayed braced on the arms of the chair. A prickle of doubt ran through my mind. I didn't want this interlude to end with him feeling mauled rather than indulged. His body might be responding, but if his will still wasn't in it, I hadn't won after all.

I let go of him and pulled back far enough to watch his expression. Sherlock's eyes snapped open.

"I think I've made my point very thoroughly," I said. "If you want me to stop—"

"No," he said—one breathless, determined, perfect syllable—and yanked my mouth to his.

There was at least one thing in the world Sherlock Holmes wasn't an expert at. His kiss was unpracticed and sloppy in its wildness, but so raw with untapped potential that it sent a bolt of pleasure through me anyway. As I cupped his jaw to bring us together at a better angle, my own desire propelled me onward. My hips flexed, pressing my core to the solid member beneath me.

Sherlock groaned and ground into me. Kissing me harder, he jerked up the skirt of my dress to grasp my panties. I wriggled out of them with his impatient tug urging me on.

A tiny alert went off in my mind. But my purse was back by my chair, and I had my own internal means of protection, and Sherlock was both nearly abstinent and the most vigilant person I'd ever met. If I was going to break my rules for any man, it'd be this one.

His hips arched toward me. I gripped his straining

length to position him. He bucked up as I sank down, filling me with a sudden sharp crackling of bliss that brought a gasp from my throat.

If the sex I'd had with Garrett had been urgent, this coming together was outright frantic. Our mouths parted and collided. Sherlock grasped my thigh tightly as he thrust into me hard and fast in pursuit of release. His cock jarred inside me, provoking a jolt of sensation that was more pain than pleasure. Another gasp hitched out of me.

He wasn't so lost in lust that he missed the difference in the sound. He shifted under me, filling me deeper and more smoothly.

"Right there," I mumbled as a fresh flare of pleasure seared through my core. "That's good, that's so—"

He brought my lips crashing into his again. Bliss shivered through me and spiraled higher. He had to be close after all my teasing, but that was okay, because I was almost there too.

We bucked against each other, almost violent in our need. I grazed my fingers down over Sherlock's chest to the dip of his belly again, and that caress propelled him over the edge. A choked sound escaped him as he drove into me even harder than before with a shudder. The feel of him bare inside me, flooding me with heat, sent me careening after him.

The final wave of pleasure shot through me. My body clenched. My mouth skidded across his jaw, my arm bracing against his shoulder as the burst of ecstasy turned my muscles to jelly.

We held like that for a minute or two, me kneeling

over him with my head bent next to his, his hand clamped to my thigh. Our heartbeats slowed together.

"Well," Sherlock said in a voice that was still a little rough. "That experience was certainly… instructive."

I laughed, kissed his cheek, and straightened up. "You're going to have to work on your post-coital sweet-talk if you want to experience it again."

The corner of his mouth quirked up in amusement, but enough intensity lingered in his gaze to tell me that he did hope to repeat this experience. What a shame I might not be here long enough to take him up on that interest any time soon.

"I was under the impression that instructive was your goal," he said. "I suppose you'll go now?"

From any other man, the question would have come across as a cold dismissal, but Sherlock was merely asking me what my usual habits were.

"That's what I'd normally expect to do," I said. "Unless you'd rather I stayed longer?"

He paused, giving the idea genuine consideration as if he wasn't entirely sure of his preferences. Which I guessed he wouldn't be.

"No," he said. "That seems to be where the line between physical gratification and more tender emotions would be inclined to blur."

"Exactly my perspective." I grinned at him. "I appreciate that we're on the same page."

As I recovered my panties, Sherlock tucked himself away and pulled his housecoat back on. He saw me to the door. I stopped there and turned toward him to tap his jaw.

"Now that the rush has cleared our heads, let's see what solutions come to us after we've slept on the problem. We'll talk in the morning."

"Here's to a productive sleep, then," Sherlock said.

Another grin stretched across my face as I headed down the hall. I didn't know yet whether I'd just made the best decision of my life or the worst, but fuck, it had felt good.

CHAPTER FIFTEEN

Sherlock

Throughout my career thus far, I'd traced the threads of each case I pursued with the intention of contributing to justice and the safety of the general public. Personal concern for the client who brought the case to my attention, whether they were law enforcement or ordinary citizen, didn't enter the equation. Clients could lie or be misinformed, after all. The facts had to speak for themselves.

Yet now I found the Richter dilemma gnawed at me not only because of the array of crimes he'd already committed and the many more he'd likely commit in the future, but because of the woman sitting across the breakfast table from me, who was grinning at something John had said while taking a bite of one of those ridiculously sweet pastries. The thought of letting her down niggled at me like a second thorn in my side as a companion to the first born from my lack of progress.

I'd practically insisted that Jemma take me into her confidence on this matter. I'd dragged her away from the conference she'd been invited to as an honor to join me on quests that had gotten us nowhere. Her keen mind had seen a capacity in me that I hadn't known I possessed until last night, and I couldn't bring a murderer to justice with his crime spread out right in front of me.

It was bloody well unacceptable.

The combination of sex and sleep had left me invigorated yet steady in a way I wasn't used to but quite appreciated. Even so, my thoughts hadn't centered on a solution yet. They kept circling around to the stray comment Jemma had made in a moment of frustration about the evidence being so close but out of our grasp.

That was the key my mind kept returning to. The murder weapon was right there for the taking. If we could demonstrate its role in the murder, the police department would have to act. There *had* to be a way we could seize it even without a warrant on our side.

I scooped a spoonful of poached egg into my mouth. The salted yolk traveled stickily down my throat.

Perhaps if we slipped in when the relics were being packed up from the gallery? But last time Richter had been carrying that piece on him. He was particularly protective of it, and he might be even more so now that it could testify to his crime. I couldn't imagine him being careless with it in transit.

Jemma finished her sweet roll with a lick of her fingers. The gesture sent a tickle of sensation over my skin. If our encounter last night had brought my senses into sharper alertness, the effect was especially magnified when it came to her. Every movement she made in my presence echoed through me.

She was still a mystery, really, after all the time we'd spent together. How had she honed her mind to be nearly as incisive and pragmatic as mine was? Why on earth was she wasting her time in some tiny German city? If I could persuade her to consider uprooting, to making a go of it here—imagine how quickly her talents could develop working in tandem with me. Imagine the speed with which we could dispatch the country's, even the world's, most tenacious villains.

It would be a tremendous boon for *her* career, certainly, and a benefit to myself, John, and Scotland Yard as well. I hadn't given her much reason to trust that to be true yet, though, had I?

I swallowed the rest of my egg. Jemma and John were getting up, Garrett already scampering to the side table to pour himself another cup of coffee. I pushed back my chair.

"What are your plans for the morning, Sherlock?" Jemma asked. She smiled at me with the same friendly warmth she always had before, without any indication that the dynamic between us had shifted.

From what she'd said, I supposed it hadn't really. She'd been the same with John and Garrett. I'd only deduced the intimacy they'd shared from how *their* responses to her had subtly but unmistakably changed. John, for example, had suddenly taken up ironing his shirts with considerably more care, a task he hadn't been as attentive with since he'd parted ways with that last girlfriend of his.

"I hadn't settled on any yet," I admitted. I'd been considering returning to the gallery to study the murder weapon some more, but too much attention was likely to put Richter on the alert. After John's stunt there yesterday, we'd have to tread carefully. "Yourself?"

"I figured I might as well take a little more advantage of the conference while I'm here. Maybe one of the speakers will say something that inspires an idea." She glanced at her program booklet. "There's a seminar on criminal psychology this morning that I was looking forward to. In five minutes. I'd better get going!"

"I'll come with you," I said, because inspiration did sometimes work in strange ways. Also because John was clearly planning on tagging along, and the way his hand lingered on Jemma's arm as he encouraged her to lead the way made me wary. My friend and colleague was much more of a romantic than I was or Jemma had shown herself to be. If he'd gotten too caught up in her attentions, I'd like to determine that soon enough to effectively intervene.

The seminar was held in the same room as the first one I'd attended, larger than the others but with a staleness to the air that suggested the ventilation system wasn't working at full capacity. I'd need to give a word to the management about looking into some repairs. We couldn't find seats together, so the four of us—because Garrett had joined our expedition too—ended up spaced out by a row or two in a zigzag pattern near the edge of the rows. I watched Jemma's head and John watching her too as the doctor of psychiatry giving the talk took the podium.

It was not a particularly inspiring lecture. The subject of psychology tended to be rather wishy-washy in general, either common sense observations that anyone with a functioning brain should have been able to deduce or vague conjectures that were either useless or improvable—frequently both. This man's version of criminal psychology appeared to be no different. But the audience gazed at him avidly as he spun out this tale and that one about the mindsets that had led one person or another to commit various crimes, mostly rather mundane cases. Then he opened the discussion to questions, the first couple of which were even more mundane.

Was it worth the perceived rudeness to leave early and take a nice long walk through the city that was a lot more likely to jog some inspiration loose? I'd nearly decided in favor of that idea when Dr. Prashad nodded to someone a few rows behind me. With his attention in my general direction, I delayed.

The voice that spoke up had the lilt of an Australian accent—a somewhat muddy one, as if he'd spend a good deal of time in more than one province. "Is it true that criminals tend to continue down a path toward more severe crimes once they escalate their activities?"

A potentially intriguing concept. I glanced back and spotted a dreadlock-framed face with blue eyes so bright their color was clear even from a distance.

"I'm sorry," the doctor said. "I don't completely understand what you mean. Could you give an example?"

The man ducked his head as if embarrassed. "Sorry. I've just heard it said that if you have, say, a pickpocket, and he ends up getting in on a robbery, assuming he sees he can get away with it, he'll tend to keep on with robberies rather than going back to simple pickpocketing. Criminals tend to behave worse—or the same, I guess—over time, not better. Would you say that's true?"

I swiveled my head back toward the doctor, and my gaze snagged on Jemma's face. She'd looked toward the questioner too, and her mouth had drawn tight, her brow knit. She caught my glance and grimaced before turning to take in Dr. Prashad's answer.

My stomach tightened in turn. From pickpocketing to robbery. From assault to murder. Without listening to what the doctor was saying, I already knew that pattern existed.

Richter had been enough of a menace before. Now he'd learned he could kill a man with his own hands and face no consequences. How many more lives might he ruin in the most literal way if he slipped from our grasp?

A thought rose up with a new concrete certainty: We had to get our hands on that jade statue. We had to *literally* place our hands on it and whisk it to a lab, as soon as we humanly could.

Despite my skepticism of the utility of various laws in

obtaining actual justice, part of me balked for a moment at the thought. I'd never gone to such lengths before… but when had I needed to?

My policy had always been to weigh the potential harm and follow the path that prevented more. No one at all would be harmed in a scheme to steal the statue except Richter—or myself and my colleagues, if I faltered.

So I wouldn't falter. Perhaps I wouldn't normally pursue a matter so boldly, but I wouldn't have believed I could feel what Jemma had brought out in me last night either until I'd been forced to recognize it. How could I truly call myself the world's greatest detective if I was afraid to do what needed to be done, to stretch myself beyond the strategies I found comfortable?

My heart picked up to a brisk but even beat. Yes, this was our solution. I only had to let myself accept it.

The rest of the seminar passed in a blur of voices and a whirl of silent planning. When the audience stood up, I motioned to my colleagues. John hurried to meet me in the aisle. Jemma and Garrett caught up with us in the hall just outside.

"What is it?" Jemma asked, studying my face. She must be able to tell I'd chosen a course of action. My confidence in that course lit me up all through my body. We had so much to do, but we *could* do this.

I would have to lead the way, even though this was Jemma's case. She'd hesitated at my smaller ploys before, still a little too hesitant despite her brilliance. I could take the responsibility on my shoulders, and we'd both win out.

"Scotland Yard won't give us a warrant, so we'll just

have to retrieve the statue by our own means," I said. "Once we can test it and confirm the evidence, any embarrassment or threat of lawsuit will be wiped away. We're going to break into that gallery and take it—simple as that."

CHAPTER SIXTEEN

Jemma

I stopped on the narrower path where the park's trees hid me from view, confirming that my trio was already stationed by the tiered fountain up ahead. It was a typical early spring day in London, damp saturating the breeze that licked over me and a layer of hazy gray cloud blanketing the sky. I tugged my wool jacket close against the cold and pressed my phone to my ear.

"I'm almost there. Have you got eyes on the fountain?"

Bash's low dry voice carried through the speaker. "I'll be watching the whole time, Mori, ready to go if you need me."

"Let's hope there's no redirection required. It'll complicate things—but better to complicate them than to see them fall apart. If I rub my chin, you get in there as fast as you can."

"It shouldn't take me more than thirty seconds," Bash

said. His confidence washed away the remaining chill. I could only imagine how much harder this entire scheme would have been to pull off without him. I'd managed all right during the few years before I'd connected with Bash, but having his help had elevated my reach so very far.

"Good," I said. "We'll talk again soon either way."

I ended the call, switched the phone to audio recording mode, and tucked it into the thin inner pocket I'd added to the jacket specifically for when I wanted to record a conversation. The fabric I'd picked still muffled voices a little, but they were recognizable. Useful if you wanted to double-check your memories later—or if you needed blackmail material down the road.

Having Bash standing by gave me an extra level of security right now. Sherlock had appeared to be determined to carry out his plan, and he'd won his colleagues over, but John and Garrett had shown even more hesitation than I'd allowed myself to. Whether they stayed on board might depend on how this security expert Sherlock knew reacted to his questions—and I was pretty sure I was going to need the entire trio to get us to my goal.

Tucking my hands into my pockets, I strode onto the wide paved path that led between two rows of cylindrical hedges toward the fountain. Dreary as the sky was, the newly grown leaves on the surrounding trees beamed in their fresh shades of green. They weren't going to be subdued by a little cloud cover.

Sherlock spotted me first and acknowledged me with a tip of his head. Garrett nodded too, his shoulders hunched inside his light linen jacket—he'd obviously underestimated the chill. John shot me a flash of a smile as he twirled his walking stick restlessly.

"Where is this guy?" Garrett demanded the second I joined them. "Wasn't he supposed to be here at one?"

"He's got a couple more minutes before he's even slightly late," Sherlock said evenly. "Considering what a last-minute request this was, I won't blame him if he isn't perfectly punctual."

"How can we be sure we can even trust him? You know how suspicious you'll sound with all these questions."

John hummed to himself. "More likely, he'll be wondering whether *he* can trust us."

Sherlock frowned at both of them. "He knows me. He's seen my integrity in action. I wouldn't be reaching out to him if I wasn't confident of his discretion and good faith."

"I trust *Sherlock*," I said in a mild tone. "Isn't that what really matters?"

Garrett scowled but didn't argue, and John looked chagrinned. The comment shut down their doubtful comments and made Sherlock stand even straighter, so that was a win all around.

Sherlock craned his neck. "Here he comes now. Right on time. I agreed to having you all here to ease your minds because of the enormity of the scheme we're putting together, but Neville is used to me working alone. I trust that *you* will let me do the talking and at least put on the appearance of a united front?"

I raised my chin. "Once I say I'm in, I'm in."

"Just pretend I'm not here," Garrett muttered.

John set the end of his walking stick firmly on the ground. "You know I'll stand with you through anything."

The man Sherlock had indicated was skirting a stone planter dotted with small shrubs. He was built rather like a shrub himself, short and portly with a sprig of curly dark hair down the middle of his head. Perhaps he'd sprout flowers later in the springtime too.

"Sherlock," he said with a hint of reverence when he reached us. His gaze slid over the rest of us. "And colleagues." He turned back to Sherlock. "We could have simply met at my office, you know."

"I wanted to avoid any visual record of this meeting, traffic cams and security videos and so on," Sherlock said, as if that were a perfectly normal concern for an everyday meeting. "For your sake at least as much as mine. The subjects I'd like to get your input on are rather... sensitive."

Neville raised his eyebrows. "Well, you've got me intrigued, that's for sure. Go ahead."

Sherlock fished in the pocket of his trench coat and produced a slip of paper. "First, could you tell me whether you know of any ways to break the code on this particular type of lock?"

He held the paper out so Neville could read it without Sherlock actually handing it over. The expert's eyebrows lifted higher. He scratched the corner of his jaw, his forehead furrowing.

"That's a top of the line system," he said. "With the

newest models, you won't find many who could crack it. I could, with the right equipment, of course, but it wouldn't be terribly fast—at least a few minutes. Why do you want to know *that*?"

"It's better if you're not involved beyond the imparting of information and skills," Sherlock said. "And pointing us to the right equipment, unless you can lend me something that wouldn't be traceable. I'd like you to teach me how to use it."

He'd told us this was the plan when we'd discussed the meeting earlier. *This is our case. We can make the decision to take the necessary risks. I want to avoid all possible collateral damage. No one else should have to put their livelihoods on the line.*

"I'd say it's not the sort of thing I could teach very quickly, but I know what your mind is like. I could take you through the paces whenever you want." Neville cocked his head. "Is that all?"

"No." Sherlock flipped the paper around. "I also need to know how one would handle a motion sensor security system of this type. To shut it down, or at least avoid setting it off."

The other man hesitated. I balled my hands in my pockets, holding back the urge to jump in and steer the conversation myself. Sherlock knew this man, and I didn't. I *did* trust him at least as far as knowing what his allies would and wouldn't tolerate. A stranger jumping in might throw off a delicate balance I didn't fully understand.

Even if I did decide intervention was necessary, I'd let Bash handle that.

"It's pretty much impossible to tackle motion sensors of that type once they're running," Neville said slowly. "The only way you can disable them is if you can get at them before they're turned on or if you can cut the power."

"Then it is possible," Sherlock said. "Excellent, excellent."

"Sherlock… I'd really feel more comfortable if you told me what this was all for. I wouldn't even be talking about subjects like this with, well, almost anyone other than you."

"It's for a good cause. The best of causes, really."

Neville gave him a skeptical look. "How good a cause can it be if you can't tell me about it for my own protection?"

I held myself from shifting my weight restlessly. Garrett glanced at John surreptitiously with an expression that seemed to say, *I told you this was a bad idea.*

Sherlock simply gave the security expert a calm smile. "You remember Canterbury, don't you, Neville? I keep my cards close to my chest for a variety of reasons, but you can always be sure there *are* reasons. Consider: Sometimes to foil a criminal you must understand their potential methodology."

Well, that was a bald-faced lie. He was implying that we were trying to stop a break-in rather than plotting to commit one ourselves. Not that I hadn't seen Sherlock lie before, but it'd always been to people he disdained. He considered this man a trusted associate.

There was very little he wouldn't bend in pursuit of

his victory, was there? Lucky for me. How many steps were there between criminal mastermind and crime-fighting consulting detective anyway? The things we could do together if he ever adjusted his morals completely...

His gambit worked. Neville visibly relaxed with a sigh of relief. "Of course. I'm sorry. Caution comes with the line of work, you know—it's difficult to turn that instinct off."

"And that fact does you credit," Sherlock assured him. "I won't keep you from your prior commitments any longer. When would be the soonest we could meet up for a lesson or two? The matter is rather urgent."

"My evening is free."

"Perfect. I'll call you when I have my own plans more settled, and we can arrange an exact time and place."

My hands unclenched. I eased them from my pockets as Neville ambled off.

One more piece of the puzzle was in place. We were getting so close I could almost taste my own victory.

"The motion sensors will require some thought," Sherlock said quietly. "The security company controls them and monitors the whole gallery from an external site. But we can work through one problem at a time."

"I have some experience with pressure sensitive devices," John said. "I can refresh my—"

He cut himself off just as a waft of deeper cold and the scent of parched rot washed over me. My stomach flipped. John's head had jerked up—and Sherlock's and Garrett's followed. I wrenched my own head back to see what they were staring at just above me, but the back of my neck was already prickling like a warning.

Bog floated there, filmy fabric drifting around it even more freely than usual, swaying up and down with an oddly stilted rhythm that jarred in my mind as I took it in. Ice shot down my spine.

My hand darted up in an instinctive gesture to try to ward the shrouded one away. I caught my arm at the last second and yanked it back down. Then my heart lurched for a completely different reason.

I'd caught my hand by my chin. From a distance, Bash might think I'd given him the signal to charge in. Shit.

"What the—" John said hoarsely, and Sherlock's gaze dropped from whatever he could make out above me to my face. Garrett took a step back. I didn't have time to juggle all of their reactions. If Bash rushed in with his ploy now, he could inadvertently throw off everything I'd gained—even more than it was already thrown off thanks to the creature fading away above me.

"Custard!" I snapped out, loud enough to be sure my voice would carry beyond the trees and hedges around us.

The apparently random word at least had the effect of interrupting the bewilderment of the men around me with a different sort of confusion. Sherlock knit his brow, still peering at me. "Custard?"

Bash and I had picked a code word that meant "Abort!" ages ago. In ideal circumstances, I'd have found a way to at least somewhat naturally work it into conversation. There was nothing ideal about this moment.

I swiped at my cheeks as if trying to wipe away a blush

of embarrassment, raising their color as I did. "I just— I saw the weirdest thing— I must have eaten too much custard at lunch. There is an amount of sugar that can mess with your brain."

"*I* saw something too," Garrett said tersely. "I didn't eat any custard—or whatever. We all saw it, didn't we?"

I widened my eyes. "You saw it too? What exactly did you see?"

"It looked," Sherlock said with a frown, "like a ghost out of some sort of horror film. Pale and faded and vaguely humanoid." He swiveled on his feet, taking in the fountain, the path of hedges, the trees, as if trying to determine whether any of them might have been responsible.

Bog hadn't shown itself completely, but the shrouded one had revealed a lot more than a strange wavering of light. My fingers itched for one of my sugar cubes. This felt too familiar. It felt too much like that hopeless flailing sensation years ago when I'd discovered my expected fate. Panic trickled up through my chest.

"That's what I'd have said it looked like too," John said. "All sort of… streamy? Just floating there." He shook his head and touched his temple.

"It was fucking eerie," Garrett said.

Sherlock paced around me, studying the clouds overhead. "It was right above *you*, Jemma. Did you feel anything?"

"No," I said, grasping for some way, any way, to regain control here. I needed Sherlock focused on the gallery heist, not on supernatural beings following me around. I needed Garrett *not* to connect this spectacle to whatever oddity he'd witnessed from Bog in the doorway the other morning.

An idea clicked into place. I grabbed Sherlock's arm. "Maybe we should call off this heist idea. If our nerves are getting to us so much that we're imagining weird spirits—"

His ego kicked in before I had to go any farther. Sherlock Holmes didn't succumb to nerves.

"No," he said firmly. "There's nothing wrong with *us*. It had to be some sort of natural phenomenon. A sliver of sunlight cutting through the clouds at an odd angle, perhaps. We surely wouldn't all have seen the same thing if it hadn't been there."

And the last thing Sherlock would ever believe in was something beyond the world of the concrete and scientific. I'd read enough accounts where he scoffed at the idea of ghosts and spirits to be sure of that, thank all that was holy.

I exhaled slowly as if gathering myself. I'd gotten him back on course. This wasn't a catastrophe.

"You're right," I said. "We were probably all a little tense after this meeting."

"Easy to jump to an eerie interpretation when we're already keyed up," John said, although his expression was still wary.

Garrett motioned toward the path. "I don't know what the hell that was, but at this point I don't care. Can we just get out of here?"

"Yes," Sherlock said. "There's still much to be done."

But he kept frowning as he moved to walk away.

The second my hotel room door clicked shut behind me, I spun on my heel, glaring around the space.

"What the hell was that, Bog?" I said, raising my voice as loud as I dared, hotel walls being what they were. "If you want to give me a message, give it to me directly. Aren't you embarrassed to turn yourself into some kind of schlocky horror carnival trick?"

I hadn't known for sure that the shrouded one had followed me back here, but after the show Bog had just put on, I'd figured it'd want to watch my full reaction. The air near the window shimmered. The pale sunlight seeping through the glass partly solidified into Bog's wavering form.

"You seem very upset, bloodling. How unlike you."

I aimed my glare at the impenetrable mist of Bog's face. "I just can't believe how stupid you're being. How many of your kind's laws did you just break? You have business with *me*, not with anyone else around me."

"And yet your business with them seems so urgent as your days creep toward their end." Bog drifted over the table. "Very strange."

"I should be able to do whatever I want with those last few days, seeing as I still belong to myself for that time."

"I haven't prevented you from doing anything. You move about perfectly freely."

I gritted my teeth. "You know you're disrupting the

human world. Do you really want me to report this to the rest of the shrouded folk? What will they do with you?"

The shrouded one made a sound like a creaky chuckle. "If they realize who you are, it will be just as bad for you as for me. If they don't, nothing they inflict would interfere with contracts already drawn. I doubt we will find out, will we, bloodling? You're in no hurry to place yourself before the ones you were once so desperate to escape."

The words made the back of my neck twitch. "There are ways I can tip them off without them knowing who pointed them in the right direction," I said. "Maybe I'd like to see justice carried out whether or not it affects what I owe you."

"Maybe," Bog said with hollow amusement. "Or maybe you would refuse to take even that chance."

It vanished like a streak of light swallowed up by a shadow, there and then gone. I stood scowling at the place where it'd been for several moments longer.

Maybe you would refuse to take even that chance. Bog was calling my bluff. A finger of cold prodded my stomach.

It *was* a bluff. I'd be worse off if the rest of the shrouded folk turned their attention on me than I was right now.

In the grand scheme of things, Bog was small potatoes. The only reason I'd been able to convince it to make the deal was that it'd never have gotten its maw on a human sacrifice in ten thousand years otherwise. What it'd said was true: If the higher folk found out Bog was the one that'd stolen their prized lamb, they might sever our contract, sure, but only so they could devour me for themselves.

There were certain lines Bog wouldn't cross. If it went too far, the shrouded folk would notice its antics on their own. But what it'd done already was bad enough. How many times could even Sherlock dismiss strange lights and figures he'd never seen before I'd come into his life as a mere coincidence?

There was nothing I could do to stop it. If I'd known a way to contain Bog, I wouldn't have been here in the first place.

CHAPTER SEVENTEEN

Garrett

One of the best things about Thompson was his predictability. He worked the same shift that ended in the mid-afternoon as often as he could get it, and after every shift he went straight to the pub down the road from the station for a beer before he headed home for dinner. He even had a favorite booth.

I spotted him there through the window—alone today, thankfully. Trying to divert more of my colleagues so I could have this conversation would have tied my stomach in twice as many knots.

Sherlock probably would have come in with a subtle ploy, pretending he'd just happened to pop in for a drink and, oh, why not stop by to chat with that coworker who coincidentally was in the same place? Deception wasn't really my style. The fact that I needed to do any at all had prompted those knots in my stomach. Normally Sherlock and John carried out their schemes while I looked the other way, and that suited all three of us just fine.

I pushed past the door into the pub. It wasn't a bad place, really—sure, the booziness in the air mingled with smell of frying oil from their famous wings, and as soon as you moved beyond the front windows it was rather dim, but the amber lighting created a warm atmosphere and the oak tables gleamed with recent polishing. Sprightly folk music played over the wall-mounted speakers.

When I reached his table, Thompson glanced up from the sports magazine he'd been flipping through. "Lestrade!" he said, a grin that looked a little too eager splitting his doughy face. "What brings you here? I thought you were all busy with that fancy conference."

Thompson had already been with the department two years when I'd started on. Three later, I'd become the youngest cop in Scotland Yard to earn detective inspector. Another three after that, Thompson was still on regular constable duty but chomping for the chance.

To be fair, he'd been friendly enough when I'd started. But that friendliness had ramped up several notches as I'd proven myself and then caught Sherlock Holmes' attention enough for me to start working with the consulting detective regularly. One time, I'd spent an hour recounting the not-particularly-sensational events of a two hour dinner at Sherlock and John's shared flat thanks to Thompson's avid questioning.

He played nice right now because he coveted what I had. The second he saw a chance to step in front of me, no doubt he would.

"Duty still calls," I said in a casual tone I had to force. "I've been looking into some things on the side. Do you mind if I join you for a few minutes?"

Thompson drew his elbows in, his gaze sharpening. He wasn't the swiftest bloke on the force, but he wasn't stupid either. And he kept his ear to the ground.

"Sure," he said. As I slid onto the opposite bench, he turned the beer glass in his hands and tilted his head to one side. "I heard you were hassling the chief for a warrant for the Richter exhibition."

"That's actually why I was hoping to talk with you," I said. "You've been assigned to the security detail keeping an eye on the gallery, haven't you?"

"I have." Thompson shifted in his seat, clearly unhappy with the fact. "Seems like Richter is more worried about being the victim of a crime than avoiding being caught for one. What got you all itchy about him?"

"It may not be him at all," I said. Lie number one. "Sherlock Holmes mentioned some concerns related to one of the relics, which are handled by various people, that I was hoping to follow up on. But the chief has to make his decisions as he feels is best." I spread my hands.

The mention of Sherlock automatically perked Thompson up. "This is one of Holmes' theories, is it?" he said. "What's he on the scent of?"

"He hasn't revealed very much yet," I said. Lie number two. "You know how he can be." That much, at least, would usually have been true.

"Well, I don't know much of anything about the stuff

inside the gallery. I've been spending all my time stuck in the car watching the outside of the place."

I grimaced in sympathy that was honest enough. Being staked out like a guard dog on some rich man's whim wasn't a task I'd have wished on anyone.

"I had a few questions about the security set-up—ours, and the private company that's working with the gallery too."

Thompson eyed me. "Why are you still poking around there when the chief turned you down? You'll end up getting yourself in trouble if you keep pushing."

He didn't sound all that distressed about the idea, but he did have a point. I folded my hands together on the top of the table, willing down my growing queasiness.

How had I let Sherlock rope me into this? There were reasons I let him handle the more questionable strategies he liked to employ. If this scheme ended badly, if it came out that I'd helped him obtain confidential police information, I could lose everything.

I'd gone completely barmy, hadn't I?

I was already committed, though, and the words of lie number three tumbled out exactly the way I'd rehearsed them in my head.

"It's mainly to ease Holmes' mind. He wants to be sure there's nothing suspicious about the scheduled activity around the gallery. You know how thoroughly he likes to analyze the details of a scene."

Thompson nodded, relaxing a little. In the past, he'd watched Sherlock spend ten minutes studying an apparently blank wall or a pattern of cigarette ash in an ashtray.

"All right. If it's just between you and him, I can't see how it hurts anything. We've got four shifts scheduled to cover the full twenty-four hours, plus doubling up overnight."

I had the urge to take out my notepad to jot down his answers, but that would make this supposedly friendly conversation feel too much like an interrogation. "What time are the shifts coming and going? Is there a specific spot you're supposed to stay parked?"

"The orders were close but not too close." Thompson ran his finger through the condensation on his glass, drawing the line of the road. "We stay on the opposite side. When it's just the one team, we park at the corner where we can see the entrance but not directly across from it. The second night shift takes the other corner. They're in from ten until six in the morning. The rest of us are doing midnight to eight, eight to four, four to midnight."

"I assume Richter let you know the private security team's schedule as well, so you wouldn't raise a false alarm because of them."

"Aye. He wanted us switching off at different times so there wasn't any moment when both us and them might be distracted in transition. They're doing seven in the morning to three in the afternoon, three to eleven, eleven to seven."

"And they come in the front?"

"Nah," Thompson said. "They go around back down the alley. But we can see the entrance to the alley from where we're parked, to keep an eye on who goes down there. It's easy to tell which is them, even at night. They've got a black van with the company logo stamped on the side in white."

"All right." I leaned back on the bench, a bead of sweat trickling down my back. "Nothing about that sounds like it should raise any concerns. I'll pass the information on to Holmes, but I'd imagine he'll drop that thread of inquiry. Thanks for lending a hand."

"Whatever I can do," Thompson said with a smile. I'd have to remember to figure out some favor to do for him before he called it in a way I didn't like.

I headed out and hailed a taxi—I avoided the hell that was driving in town unless on official business. My stomach churned away as I waited for the car to pull up to the curb.

I'd just baldly lied to a colleague multiple times to aid and abet a crime. Where the hell would I be if I blew up my career? I *loved* this job, jockeying for favor and petty in-fighting and all. I'd hardly had a chance to make a real name for myself without Sherlock's hanging over it.

As I got into the taxi, my phone chimed with a text— the consulting detective himself. *Have spoken to the fellow I know with camera experience. Will meet with you tomorrow, 11am, Fox & Crown.*

Right. Sherlock had grabbed hold of the fact that last year we'd worked a case where I'd had to do a lot of poking around with a shop's security cams. He'd decided in his authoritarian way that my task during our assault on the gallery should be rigging a camera loop. I'd imagine with some pointers from Sherlock's "fellow" I could manage it. Which would put me on the same level as the criminals we'd caught last year.

I shoved the phone into my pocket without answering.

The whole way to the hotel, the driver nattered on about the weather and a rugby game I hadn't watched, barely appearing to notice that I only responded with wordless sounds like "Hmm" and "Ah." My input wasn't required as long as I played my part.

I came into the lobby to find Jemma there waiting for me.

"Hey," she said with a smile, ambling over. "I saw you getting out of the cab while I was passing the window, figured I'd see how your talk went."

Somehow her presence made me feel better and worse at the same time. I found her striking face prettier every time I saw her, and her soft smile brought back the moment in John's car when she'd seemed sorry that our time together was limited. But it *was* limited—she'd be heading back to Germany in a few days now—and damned if she wasn't the first woman I'd met in years who stirred up an attraction that ran this deep.

On top of that, she was also the reason I'd gotten wrapped up in this crazy scheme of Sherlock's in the first place. If she *hadn't* been here, he never would have gotten onto the case and then apparently consumed by it.

The collision of emotions must have shown on my face. Jemma's smile faded. "Not so well?" she said. "Come on, let's grab coffees and you can tell me about it."

I wasn't sure how well coffee would mix with my

unsettled stomach, but I followed her to the regularly refilled pots just inside the dining room anyway. It was kind of amusing watching her stir four spoonfuls of sugar into one mug. I didn't feel quite up to teasing her about it, though. Even the blissful look on her face when she took her first sip didn't quite penetrate my uneasiness.

We ended up in the little lounge room where the four of us had talked the first morning after we'd met her. Jemma sat next to me on the sofa, angled to face me, her knees just a couple inches shy of grazing mine.

How she could look so fucking sexy in loose slacks and a blouse buttoned up to her collarbone, I didn't know. Maybe it was just because I'd seen how much fire she could generate when those clothes came off.

"Did your colleague on the security detail not want to talk?" she asked. "It's all right. I'm sure we can figure out most of it through observation—it'll just take a little longer."

I shook my head. "No, he talked plenty. I got all the answers Sherlock wanted. I just…" I swept my hand over my face and into my hair. "This scheme Sherlock has dreamed up is so much crazier than anything he's even proposed, let alone seen through before. No one has to tell me how brilliant he is, but no one's infallible either. We're putting so much on the line. What if his ego has gotten the better of him, and his reach is exceeding his grasp?"

"I was nervous about it too when he first suggested it," Jemma said. "All right, I'm still a little nervous. But he sounds as though he's considered every angle. If we can't find an answer to every problem in the way, then we simply won't go through with it, right?"

"But I've already stuck my neck out, just digging for information the way I did today." I hated saying the words, especially to her, but the sick feeling inside me propelled them out. "I don't lie to people. I don't plan robberies. That's not—that's not who I want to be, even if it's for a good cause." I'd gone into policing specifically to prove to myself that I could be a person with real principles.

Jemma's expression twitched, her lips pursing tight. For a second I thought she was angry, but then I met her eyes again and saw nothing but sadness there.

"Garrett," she said in a voice that was slightly hoarse, "the last thing I'd want is for you to feel like you've been forced into something you don't agree with. I've felt guilty all along because of how dangerous Richter could be, what with everything he's shown he's willing to do to protect himself and all the crimes before that too. This wasn't your problem. You shouldn't have to take those risks."

The mention of Richter's extensive crimes made my throat tighten. "It's not that I don't want him caught," I started.

"I know. But you've already done so much for me… I'm sure the three of us could handle it on our own if you'd rather step back now. You don't even need to share what you found out from your friend, so you won't be complicit. Sherlock and John will figure out everything quickly enough. I can tell them we're going forward without you, and then you can get those worries off your back."

She was already getting to her feet, all determined compassion. My heart wrenched. Suddenly I was on my feet too, grasping her shoulder, not really sure what I was going to say but only that I needed to say something.

Was that really what I wanted—to watch Sherlock and John stride ahead with this plan, to see it unfold from the sidelines as if I hadn't made a difference anyway, as if I couldn't have contributed anything they couldn't do themselves? If they failed, I'd kick myself for abandoning them. If they succeeded, I'd kick myself for not having the guts to try.

The tricks with the security cameras—Sherlock could teach himself those quickly enough, no doubt. But none of the others could handle the police side of the equation like I could. Without me, there'd be no one to ensure the evidence was even admissible. No one to finesse the situation with the chief. There were all kinds of elements to this operation that *only* I could handle.

This was about a man who'd terrorized countless people across this city and our best chance at bringing him to justice. Wasn't *that* what I'd gotten into this career for, really—to make the world better instead of worse? I should be at the front of the charge, not flailing around like an anxious child. For fuck's sake, John was in, and solving crimes wasn't even technically his job.

"No," I said. "I—I was just talking out loud, getting those doubts out. Maybe I've gotten too caught up in my own head. We're going to bring Richter down, and I'm going to be there to make sure it happens."

Jemma wavered. "Are you definitely okay? I wouldn't—"

"One hundred percent," I said, shoving my queasiness aside and setting my jaw. "I'm in, until the end."

Jemma

"Having fun?" John said, sounding amused.

I nudged the last few torn scraps of hotel notepaper into my Fibonacci sequence on John's desk. "It's something to pass the time," I said, keeping my tone casual as if I wasn't doing anything more meaningful than idle doodling.

The sight of the orderly spiral set my nerves slightly more at ease. I already knew the pattern wouldn't keep Bog out, but those scraps might delay the shrouded one from picking up on where I'd gone if it came looking for me. It couldn't keep too close a watch on me without raising questions with the rest of its kind.

I left the desk and dragged my chair over to where John was sitting at the room's small table. "How far off was Sherlock the last time he texted?"

"He said ten minutes, but he was relying on a taxi, so

it depends some on the traffic." John looked at his phone. "Although I wouldn't be surprised if he walks in exactly at the time predicted. Which would be in about one more minute…"

I dropped into the chair, my ears pricked. I'd only taken a few more breaths when a knock sounded on the door. John chuckled and started to get up, but I waved him down since I could lope over there faster.

Sherlock strode into the hotel room looking wind-blown. I hadn't realized it was possible for his hair to get any more messy than it typically was. He shrugged off his trench coat, obviously having come up straight from the street, tossed it on the bed, and glanced at the three chairs around the table.

"Garrett isn't joining us?"

"He had more police business to look into," I said, taking my seat.

The truth was I hadn't mentioned the meeting to the detective inspector. After Garrett's near defection this afternoon, I suspected it'd be better to give him a breather from heist planning. Let the crime stay illusory and vague in his mind while he focused on the heroic underpinnings. And if he found out that we'd talked without him, chances were that would only feed his competitive desire to prove himself useful to the cause.

He'd looked so distraught when I'd talked to him that I hadn't been sure even my last-ditch gamble to suck him back in would work. The cop had more of a conscience than I'd anticipated. But his need for keep pace with his more daring colleagues had won out. For now.

Despite what I'd said to him, we did need him. He was the key to making the theft legitimate as evidence in the eyes of the police. Sherlock and John would never continue with the scheme without him. I'd known setting this plan in motion wouldn't be easy, but I didn't like walking a line this delicate.

I had to tense my leg to stop my foot from swinging restlessly as Sherlock sat down between John and me. Earlier, I'd groped in my purse for a sugar cube and discovered I'd nearly burned through my entire supply. As much as I tried to squash my emotions down, echoes of the helpless moments from my past gnawed at the edges of my consciousness.

I wasn't going to let this mission fall apart. I was stronger now—so much stronger.

"How did it go?" John asked his friend. "Are you now the city's foremost expert on lock cracking?"

Sherlock made a dismissive noise. "I may be the second highest expert on this particular lock. Neville took me through the paces. I've got the device and the connectors I'll need." He motioned to his coat. "We'll be able to get through the door to Richter's exhibit regardless of the hour."

"We know the hours we're working with now," I said. "Garrett got the full details of the various security schedules."

"Excellent." Sherlock glanced at John. "You were going to brush up on your understanding of pressure sensitivity."

"And I did." John leaned his elbows onto the table. His hazel eyes gleamed with eagerness to show off his knowledge. "As you can imagine, pressure-sensitive alarms are *somewhat* different in nature from the sorts of devices we had to worry about in the field in Iraq."

"Mines," I supplied.

"Yes. But the gist is essentially the same. The device is rigged to spark a chain reaction when a certain amount of weight is applied to it. In a mine field, that reaction results in an explosive blast, thanks to which my hip will never be the same—but at least I wasn't the poor soul who stepped right on the thing. Here, we only need to worry about the alarm system triggering."

"Though that would be equally catastrophic to our goal," Sherlock said.

"True. So, here's what we need to consider." John cast around and grabbed a deck of cards off the bedside table. He waggled it at me. "Always handy to keep around for impromptu entertaining of new friends and also as a prop for demonstrations. Let's say this is our display case."

He slipped several cards from the box and laid four of them together to make a large rectangle on the table in front of him. Then he built a smaller rectangular structure on top of that.

"Pressure here or here will trigger the alarm," he said, pointing to the area around the structure and then to the structure itself. "Where we have some wiggle room is that there's a lower limit to the weight that the device will register. Just as our enemy combatants don't want their mines exploding at a kicked rock or a fallen twig, the gallery doesn't want the alarm sounding because someone breathed too hard on the glass. As far as I can tell, it's incredibly unlikely they'd have set the lower limit at anything less than a few pounds. Ten is fairly standard."

"So, if we're careful, maybe swapping another object out that's close in weight, we should be able to remove the figurine without setting off the alarm," I said. "Getting *to* the display case is no problem. We can touch it without stepping on the pads—they're not that wide. The difficulty is going to be opening up the case to get to the figurine, isn't it?"

"Exactly. Only the base will be rigged, not the glass, but a significant amount of vibration in or pressure on the glass will trigger the system. I did think of a solution to that problem, though. We use heat." John drew his finger along the top of his model and down over the edge to the side. "Take a blowtorch and melt a line to cut out a chunk —along the edge, so we can easily 'fold' the piece out."

"Yes, that'll make handling it much easier," Sherlock said, his eyes distant but in an intent sort of way, probably picturing the actual display case we'd seen in the gallery.

John nodded. "And while one person handles the glass, another can slide an object we estimate to be around the same weight as the piece we're removing onto the top of the case to balance things out. I figure we should be able to make a guess that isn't more than a pound off. We can bring a hunk of jade to balance out the removed statue as well, like Jemma suggested."

"You've covered all the variables. Well done, John!" Sherlock smiled at his friend with genuine appreciation, and John's grin turned giddy at the praise.

My God, lovers in the fervor of a new relationship

high gazed at each other with less adoration. And I was sure now I saw a little wistful hunger in John's expression when Sherlock glanced away.

An idea sparked in the back of my head with an eager quiver. How much passion could I spark in *them* if I guided them to the water's edge? Just the thought made the gnawing restlessness inside me ease back.

I was Jemma Moriarty. I could play the world like Sherlock played his fucking violin. Why not? I'd be giving them what they both might very well want if they'd let themselves admit it.

"Wow," I said with a breathless laugh. "We're almost there." I picked up one of the cards and tapped it thoughtfully against the others as if the idea were only just coming to me. "I don't know about the two of you, but I feel like I need a break from the planning and the worrying. Anyone up for a game of cards? We are new friends, after all."

John stretched his arms behind him and aimed his grin at me. "That sounds like just what I need to end off the day, actually."

"It's not a pastime I generally enjoy," Sherlock started.

I nudged his calf with my foot under the table, arching an eyebrow. "Now when have I heard *that* line before? You've got to know the basic rules of poker. We can play a simple five-card draw. To make things a little more interesting, we can play for dares instead of money."

"Dares?" John said. "That'd be a new one."

"We play it at the station sometimes back home," I improvised. "Kind of like strip poker, except safe for work." I winked at him. "Whoever wins gets to challenge the others to do something—within the same room, and nothing *too* extreme. It's all in good fun."

John laughed. "Somehow I think we'd better not let you win."

I spread my hands. "Well, if you don't think you can handle the heat…"

A sharper glint had lit in Sherlock's eyes at my nudge. Perfect. "All right. A few rounds won't hurt anything."

"Such an avid vote of enthusiasm," John teased. "I'll give it a shot. No bets and no folding, if we're not playing for money?"

"Exactly," I said. "We check our hands, exchange cards as we see fit, and then we discover who's made the right gamble. I'll deal first?"

John slid the deck toward me. I made a show of shuffling carefully. I couldn't guide the results of the hand completely, of course, since it was up to them whether they exchanged cards. But I could set one or another of us up in a good position with a bit of quick finger-work.

To start, it'd be better to let one of them win to warm them up to the game. And Sherlock clearly needed more warming. The cards flew between my hands. I tossed five each out across the table.

Despite his disinterest, Sherlock naturally had an excellent poker face. He looked at his hand in studied concentration, giving no sign of what he made of its contents. John let out a chuckle that might have been pleased or self-deprecating. From his swipe at his bright hair, I guessed the latter.

"One," Sherlock said blandly, discarding.

"Confident, aren't you," John remarked as I flicked a new card to his friend. "Ah… I'll take three."

"Two," I said, just to mix things up since I wasn't going to win anyway. I ended up with a rather nice three of a kind in nines. Not quite good enough to match Sherlock's three queens, though. John groaned as he laid down a hand with only a pair of sixes.

"What's the damage?" he asked Sherlock.

"Let me think." Sherlock steepled his forefingers against his mouth. "Ah. I'll have you both sample my pu-erh tea. I picked up a fresh bag while I was out." He pointed at John when the other man opened his mouth to protest. "You haven't given it a proper try yet."

He got up to fiddle with the tea kettle that came with the room. In a few minutes, he was setting down steaming cups of dark brown liquid in front of us, each only halfway full.

"No point in wasting it on the two of you if you don't enjoy it," he said. "But I expect you to drink everything I gave you."

An astringent scent carried on the steam. I let more heat rise off and then took a sip.

I'd tried pu-erh before, but there were quite a few variations. Sherlock favored one that leaned bitter and earthy, rather like his tobacco. He watched me as if daring me to try to pop a sugar cube in. I restrained myself, draining the cup slowly and steadily, but it did give me an idea for my first "dare." I was going to need to work up to the real challenge.

John set his cup down with a smack of his lips. "Yep, still not on the pu-erh train."

Sherlock looked satisfied anyway. "I suppose that means I can continue not to worry about you raiding it from the cabinet like you do my Colombian coffee."

"All right, let's get on with the next round," I said, clapping my hands.

Sherlock dealt, and I smiled inwardly when I lifted my cards. This was going to take a little luck but…

"One," I said, and then I had a flush.

"And I thought I was doing pretty well this time," John muttered, setting down a straight. Sherlock had nothing to speak of.

"You like to hassle me about my sugar habit," I said. "So you can both suck on a sugar cube." I handed over a couple from my remaining supply. A task both short and sweet, most literally. I took one myself to clear the bitterness of the tea from my mouth.

"You know," John said after he'd rolled it around with his tongue a few times, "I can see how this could grow on me."

"You would," Sherlock said fondly. "I'll stick to my tea."

I would have won again in the third round with a high straight of my own, but I swapped out a few cards and ended up with only a pair so as not to rush things. John crowed over his three aces.

"You," he said, with a pointed look at Sherlock, "have to listen to that new Burstback song you keep whingeing about. And actually listen to it, not just assume it must be awful." He glanced at me. "Obviously you'll listen to it too. If you're as snobby about music as he is, maybe it'll do you some good too."

"Play away," I said as Sherlock brought a hand to his agonized face.

The song that spilled from the speaker of John's phone was a bouncy pop anthem that wound into a more complex harmony made up of multiple guitars, a harp, and a rich cello. I got plenty of entertainment simply from tracing the different melodies. Sherlock's expression had mellowed by the time the melody wound down.

"Well," he said, which John seemed to consider a victory in itself.

All right, it was time to get things moving along. I dealt myself a nice full house and then kicked off my shoes.

"Since we aren't at work and we can get a tad racy, I would like a good foot rub," I announced. "Both at the same time. Five minutes, shall we say?"

John shook his head in amusement. He came around to sit on the edge of the bed and lifted one of my feet without argument. Sherlock went to work on the other.

John approached the task with the anatomical awareness I should have expected from a doctor, finding just the right angles to work the tension out of my arch, and Sherlock focused on a pressure point I hadn't known existed but that seemed to release a taut line that had stretched right up to my ribs. By the time my five minutes were up, I was quite pleased with my choice.

I'd been prepared to lose a couple rounds before I got

the chance I'd been waiting for, but Sherlock's deal placed four tens in my hand. I certainly couldn't argue with that. And neither could the other two when they laid down their lesser offerings.

"Let's see," I said, drumming my fingers together. "I know. Kiss."

John blinked at me. I saw an inkling of understanding in his eyes, but he still asked, "Kiss *you*?"

I kept my voice perfectly calm, as if there were nothing at all unusual about what I was suggesting. "No. Kiss each other."

Sherlock had stiffened. John hesitated. A flush crept up his neck past the collar of his shirt.

"Is the idea really that horrifying?" I said. "I didn't ask for tongue." As enticing as that might be to watch. "You've shared a living space for two years; I'd imagine innumerable body parts have contacted other body parts without anyone going into fits."

"Not those particular body parts," Sherlock said, but his tone was more dry than defiant. The most obvious resistance had gone out of his posture. He glanced at John. "Would it make you terribly uncomfortable to indulge her?"

John's jaw worked as if he were grappling with the words. "Not if it wouldn't for you," he managed after a moment. He aimed for casual and didn't quite hit the mark, but the possibility that he might be excited by the prospect was clearly so far outside Sherlock's range of considerations that the detective didn't pick up on it.

Sherlock appeared to analyze their positions relative to

the table and opted to stand up. John got up too. Even his cheeks were a bit ruddy now. I settled into my chair to watch, folding my hands on my lap.

Sherlock stepped toward John slowly enough. Then he leaned in faster than lightning and touched his lips to the other man's so briefly I'd have missed it if I'd blinked. He reached for his chair as if he figured that was the end of it, leaving John frozen in place.

"Hey!" I said. "I did say *kiss*, not barely perceptible peck. You didn't let us get away with one sip of your awful tea. Hold on right there." I hopped to my feet. "I'm sure you can do better than that. Let's see what we can produce with a little inspiration."

"Jemma," Sherlock said, like the start of an argument. I cut him off with the brush of my fingertips over the slanted trail down his neck where I'd determined his skin was most sensitive. All that came out then was a soft hitch of breath. I grasped the top of his shirt and tugged him back toward John.

The doctor was watching me with an expression that was almost pleading. Did he even know what he was pleading me for?

I tugged him closer too, staying partly between them. My hand glided down John's chest. I stroked Sherlock's neck again. My knuckles skimmed over John's belt and grazed his already hardening cock. He swallowed audibly.

I slipped my other hand down over Sherlock's body, tweaking my thumb across one of his nipples, fanning my fingers against his stomach the way I had yesterday. His only enjoyable sexual experience. I'd pretty much written the book on how to turn this man on. I let the heel of my hand reach his waistband and held it there without dipping lower. He needed a lighter touch.

"All right," I said in a low voice. "Let's try that again. Kiss."

Something had made up John's mind during my intervention. He didn't wait for Sherlock's cue. He reached for the other man, his hand settling on the same part of Sherlock's neck where he'd watched me caress him, and planted one on him.

I eased farther out of the way, my fingers stroking over both their sides. Sherlock hesitated, a shiver running through his body. Then he tilted his head just a smidge, leaning into the kiss.

Fuck, they looked gorgeous, bright- and dark-headed in the stark hotel light, John pressing the kiss a little more deeply at Sherlock's response, both of them giving themselves over to the moment. The sight sent heat flaring between my thighs. John raised his other hand as if to cup Sherlock's face completely, and—

Sherlock jerked back, his legs trembling for a second before he caught his balance.

"Well," he said, not quite meeting either of our gazes. "I think that's rather enough entertainment for one evening, considering the business ahead of us. I do have lock-breaking skills to practice."

He snatched his coat off the bed and fled the room in a rush of hastily summoned composure.

I winced inwardly. That hadn't exactly been the result I'd been hoping for. But then, had I really believed

Sherlock would happily leap into making out with his long-time, utterly platonic friend with a few minutes of encouragement? I was smarter than that.

I hadn't been thinking with my smarts. I'd run with the idea to try to chase away the restless anxiety that had been nibbling at me. Now that uncomfortable sensation had returned. What if I'd just screwed up the dynamic I'd cultivated so carefully—the dynamic I needed for this scheme to work? Fuck.

John wet his lips, his hands having dropped awkwardly to his sides. He looked elated and gutted and startled all at once. Despite my frustration with myself, a little twinge of sympathy ran through me.

I could at least salvage things with him.

"I'm sorry," I said. "That wasn't— I shouldn't have pushed it that far. Maybe I shouldn't have suggested it at all."

"It's all right," John said raggedly. "It's not even really your fault. I mean, it wasn't as if we couldn't have called it off at any point." He gestured toward the door. "He'll be all right too, I'm sure. Sherlock deals with personal issues in a very predictable way. Come tomorrow morning, it might as well have never happened."

I studied his face. "Is that how *you'd* prefer to handle it?"

"I…" He couldn't seem to find the answer.

This poor sweet ridiculous man. I crossed my arms over my chest. "You really had no idea you wanted to do that, did you?"

"What? No. I—" His gaze jerked to me. "Did *you* know?"

The corner of my mouth quirked up even though my gut was still tight. "I saw a few signs. Call it an educated guess."

"Bloody hell. You're as bad as Sherlock with the mind-reading."

My lips stretched into a full smile. "Maybe that's why you wanted to kiss me too."

John laughed, and for the first time since Sherlock's departure, the tension ebbed from his stance. "Oh, no. You're something else altogether, Jemma the Jewel."

He dipped his head, and I bobbed up on my toes to meet him for a kiss that was nothing but enthusiastic on both sides. A trace of sweetness from the sugar cube lingered in his mouth, and I caught a smoky flavor that might have been Sherlock's. A thrill shot through me at the impression of kissing them both at the same time.

Any desire I'd been feeling had dampened with Sherlock's abrupt departure, though. I eased back with a softer smile to ease the rejection if John had hoped for more.

"I think we should all probably get some rest. We're going to want to be as alert as possible if we're going to pull off this plan."

John nodded with no hint of disappointment. I gave him one more quick kiss before heading out.

I shouldn't have let myself get carried away like that. From here on, no matter how precarious my situation seemed, I had to keep control of myself.

CHAPTER NINETEEN

Jemma

I was doing crunches at the base of my bed when the smell of desiccated rot quivered through the early morning sunlight. Resisting the urge to wrinkle my nose and the even stronger urge to snap around and find out what the asshole shrouded one wanted now, I finished my set of fifty reps. My abdominal muscles emanated a satisfying burn as I stretched them. Then I sat up and swiveled to look.

In the corner over the table, Bog was wafting its gauzy tendrils of fabric like a squid made out of spider-silk. I'd rather have talked to a squid.

"You know, I'm starting to think you're a little obsessed with me," I said.

The shrouded one ignored the remark. "You have been attempting to divert me," it said with a rasp in its distant voice that sounded almost angry. "Did you think I would not notice? Those wards will never be truly effective."

"I wouldn't bother with them if you'd leave me alone. While my life is still mine, I don't think it's unreasonable for me to aim for a little privacy."

Bog's body shuddered. "You're lucky you've had any extra time at all beyond the fate you were named for, bloodling. I'd like to hear gratitude, not complaints."

It wanted *gratitude*? I'd happily take a hunk of gratitude and shove it up Bog's ass. If the shrouded one even had an ass. It was kind of hard to tell.

In any case, I sure as hell wasn't in the mood to be lectured about my attitude from a creature who intended to shred apart my soul in less than a month's time.

I shrugged, pushing that irritation deep down inside. "A deal is a deal. You agreed to ten years. That's what I'm supposed to get."

"No part of that agreement forbade me from following your activities."

I ignored the growing itch of my contract mark. "And no part of it forbade *me* from making following me less comfortable for you."

The strips of Bog's covering swelled, its presence expanding until it looked twice as large as before. The mist where a face should have been clotted and churned.

"There is one fellow bloodling you've associated with for a long time. The darker male with little hair and many guns."

It didn't take a leap to realize the shrouded one meant

Bash. My fingers started to curl into the thick carpeting before I caught them. "What about him?"

"I simply thought you should keep him in mind. Because if you do anything particularly stupid to hinder your association with *me*, there are ways I can appear to him. I can convince him that he can save you by giving up his own life. And then I will claim both of you."

Fear hit me in an icy wave. Would Bash really sacrifice himself if he thought it would save my life? We understood each other, we trusted each other, but it wasn't as if we ever talked about feelings of a tender sort.

I couldn't deny that he'd put his life on the line plenty of times over the seven years since I'd first hired him, though. Or that I knew he would again, the moment I asked him, without a second's hesitation. That was *why* I trusted him.

I didn't want to take Bash down with me. I'd done everything I could to keep him out of this part of my existence. If I failed, then the empire I'd been building, the money I'd amassed—it would all be his and deserved. That was the plan. That was the way it was supposed to happen.

How fucking *dare* Bog threaten to destroy the only person I gave a damn about who wasn't already gone.

The chill of my fear crackled into cold sharp rage. I held that in too, my hands braced against the floor beneath me, my heart thumping hard in my chest.

"I do business with the man," I said evenly. "We're hardly best buddies. If that threat is supposed to have me shaking in my boots, I apologize." I pushed myself to my feet. "Feel free to stop by if you come up with something better. I have to go get some breakfast."

I pulled a sweater on over my workout tee, not wanting to change in front of the shrouded one, and walked out the door without a backward glance.

The truth was my stomach was too full of that acrid mix of fear and rage for there to be any room for hunger. In an ideal world, I'd have found a punching bag on which to let out a lethal amount of force ten times over. But the hotel fitness center was a yuppie paradise of treadmills and exercise bikes in gleaming rows, and I'd probably burn through a few breakfast pastries' worth of calories just fuming on my way down.

If that fiend touched one particle of Bash's being—if it so much as whispered a word in my accomplice's ear—I'd find some way to tear *it* to shreds while I was going down its gullet. Just let it try me.

I hadn't slept all that well. The morning was still early, so not many of the conference goers had drifted into the hotel dining room yet. The pastry table waited for me, fully stocked with a fresh assortment—and Sherlock stood farther down the buffet line, decisively dropping a slab of French toast onto his plate.

He didn't look any worse for wear after our entertainment-turned-awkwardness last night. Well, perhaps a little. He held his shoulders a tad stiffly as he turned toward the tables, and I caught a nick from shaving on his jaw just beneath his ear. He'd never had anything but a steady hand with his razor before, from what I'd seen.

John hadn't arrived yet, or Garret either. That might be another sign in itself. Sherlock would know his roommate's usual morning habits. Was this the detective's usual breakfast time and he'd only delayed before for John's sake, or had his sleep been disturbed like mine?

I headed over to join him at the table he picked, keeping my expression blasé as I watched him. He gave me a mild smile and a nod as if it were a perfectly normal morning. Well, John *had* said Sherlock would simply erase the uncomfortable moment from his version of history.

"I see your tastes remain the same," he said, raising his eyebrows at my plate.

I might have gone slightly overboard with conveyances of sugar glaze. I considered my plate as I sat down. "I realize now my eyes may have been bigger than my stomach."

"I suppose the conference organizers would prefer we took too much rather than go the slightest bit unsatisfied. Have you had trouble this morning?"

I was starting to feel exhausted from how much emotion I'd had to squash down in the last half hour. Damn him and his perceptive eyes. I could already guess what he'd tell me if I asked how he knew—I'd normally have brushed my hair and dressed with more care before coming down for breakfast. He could tell I'd left the room in a hurry, driven out of my usual habits.

No point in denying it. I'd just have to give him an excuse he'd believe. He certainly wouldn't have been able to wrap his head around the truth. Let's see if I couldn't spin this slip in my favor.

"Not really trouble," I said. "I got woken up by a call from the front desk that a package had been delivered for me, and with everything that's been buzzing in my head and being half asleep, I thought it might be something to do with the case and rushed right down."

I shook my head at myself and tugged at the sleeve of my sweater. "It was just this—my mom sent one of my old sweaters express because I mentioned how chilly it was here. Sweet, but I'd rather have a bunch of crime scene photos."

"A sentiment I can respect," Sherlock said. His gaze lingered on my face, and I'd have been surprised if he couldn't read signs there that I hadn't slept well even before the supposed phone call, but he didn't say anything about that. Because mentioning sleep, I guessed, would bring us too close to the other nighttime activities we'd been engaged in.

"Once I was down here, I figured I might as well eat." I tugged my hands inside the woolen sleeves as I hugged myself. "I'd just like the whole thing with Richter to be over. Have you seen Garrett—or John? We have so much more planning to do."

Sherlock held himself with admirable composure, but his eyes twitched at John's name. "I'd imagine they're still in bed," he said, his voice impassive. "I prefer to rise early, myself."

He gripped his fork and knife and sawed off a piece of French toast with a fair bit more force than it really required. Oh, yes, he was working very hard at willing last night away.

I didn't have much of a conscience left, if I'd ever had one. The upbringing I'd had wasn't structured to teach anything like empathy. Still, my stomach prickled with a faint sensation that might have been guilt. I appreciated Sherlock's unwavering intellect, and it appeared I'd shaken it. At the very least, that effect hadn't been my intention.

But it was what I had, so I might as well use it. Feeling unsettled, a man like him would commit twice as fast with twice as much determination to any task that would allow him to train all his focus on something concrete and separate from his emotions.

He wanted distractions. I'd point him toward one that would benefit me too.

"It seems like the most important factor we haven't really touched on is the motion sensors," I said, keeping my voice low in awareness of the other conference attendees breakfasting around us. "I've considered every angle, keeping in mind the elements we've already worked out and the layout of the place, and I can't see any way we could contrive to meddle with them before the security team turns them on at closing time."

"We'll have to let them go on and then interrupt their power supply before blocking them," Sherlock agreed.

"We can't turn them off directly from inside the gallery, right? You said you'd determined they're controlled from the security company's external site. I suppose we could cut off all the power to the building to give us time… but I have to think the police surveillance would immediately become suspicious. Can even you figure a way around that problem?"

Sherlock's posture straightened at the subtle dig at his ego. "There will be a way," he said. "I'll need to refresh my memory of the electrical layout around the gallery. Talk to me again later today and see if I don't have an answer for you."

He smiled, his pale blue eyes bright with the prospect of a challenge and his demeanor instantly more relaxed. I'd done him some good too.

If we pulled off this heist, it'd save Bash from the shrouded one as much as it would me. As soon as I could slip clear of Bog, it wouldn't know where to look for Bash either.

Invigorated by the work ahead, Sherlock polished off the rest of his breakfast in the time it took me to chew through one chocolate-filled croissant. The moment he'd left the dining room, I pulled out the phone I used for Bash.

He picked up after one ring, sounding ready for action. "What's the word, Majesty?"

The playful nickname made my lips twist. He had no idea how great a threat now hung over his head as well as mine. Not just one life but two might hang on this scheme's success—and on it succeeding soon.

I could cut him loose, couldn't I? Tell him I didn't need his services right now after all, transfer him the funds for a lovely, distant vacation, and order him to leave. Remove him from Bog's line of sight.

Only, if I was honest with myself, I wasn't entirely sure Bash *would* leave. He'd find the abrupt change odd— he'd suspect something else was wrong. Every instinct told me that he'd stick around surreptitiously, checking up on me.

The shrouded one would still find him. And taking on this challenge without him, I'd be so much more likely to fail, screwing over us both.

No, the only way through that I could tolerate was forward.

"Slight change in plan," I said. "The wiring gambit we talked about? I'll need you in place within the hour."

CHAPTER TWENTY

John

Driving made it easy to avoid uncomfortable subjects. I could completely occupy myself with navigating traffic while Sherlock flipped through textbooks about electrical systems on his phone. If we weren't talking about anything at all, of course we weren't talking about the fact that I'd been about ten seconds shy of slipping him tongue last night, even if at moments it felt as if I was thinking about it so loudly he should have been able to hear every word.

It probably would have been *easier* if Sherlock had gone off on this quest alone or with Garrett—or, hell, the Scarlet Pimpernel, as long as it wasn't me—but then he would have been admitting failure. Admitting that our kiss last night had mattered, somehow or other. The only way he knew how to make everything fine was to act as if everything *were* fine and assume all the things would sort themselves out in accordance with his will.

To be fair, I'd seen that strategy work several times in the past. He'd just never been erasing something that had happened with me.

The biggest trouble was, I was pretty sure the kiss did matter, at least to me. But I had the feeling trying to discuss that possibility with him might cause a meltdown of reality that wouldn't end well for either of us. Which was probably why I'd buried all hint of my apparent desire under several layers of plausible deniability until Jemma had yanked it blazing to the surface a little more than twelve hours ago.

If only those emotions had come with a manual on what the hell to do with them now that I'd admitted they existed.

"Park behind the blue sedan," Sherlock said, still so absorbed in his phone I didn't know how he'd managed to identify the open spot. "We'll walk the rest of the way."

I pulled in where he'd requested and checked my false beard. We hadn't gone for heavy disguises, just enough that the police wouldn't mark us as Holmes and Watson from a distance and that any internal security who noticed us passing by wouldn't connect us to recent visitors, one particularly clumsy.

Sherlock borrowed my walking stick and started tapping it ahead of him as though he were blind. My hand itched for the familiar surface as I ambled along beside him.

I could steady out my gait completely if I walked

slowly enough, and the effort only provoked a slight prickling in my hip, but the walking stick had become about more than just balance. It was a weapon and sometimes a disguise in itself. No one expected much threat from a man who couldn't even walk without help.

While I was this close to him, Sherlock's pale eyes showed through the dim panes of his sunglasses. He used those to hide the darting of his gaze up the utility poles we passed and along the thick black wires that ran between them. Now and then, he murmured verbal notations into his phone.

I tugged my own gaze away from the furtive movements of his lips. I definitely shouldn't be looking at them.

"We'll circle the place," he said as we came up on the corner past the gallery. "If there's a trick we can employ, we're not likely to manage it in full view of the police. We just need to be sure we take into account the proper connections. Ah, there's the line directly into the building."

The cable ran by above our heads, just a few feet around the corner. "No chance we're messing with that unnoticed," I remarked.

"Indeed."

We rambled past the back of the gallery along the alley and then looped around to take in the adjacent road. Sherlock hummed to himself thoughtfully but didn't bother to mention any of his thoughts to me.

He stopped at the far end of the road, gazing up at the utility pole next to him and then frowning at the sidewalk.

"John," he said abruptly. "As a doctor, you'd have a reasonably accurate idea of the chances of pregnancy from a single unprotected encounter?"

Of all the personal questions he could have asked me, *that* was what he was going with? It wasn't a surprise that he'd deduced that something had happened between Jemma and me, but I'd have expected him to give me some credit for common sense. Did he have a reason for trying to imply I was careless, or was he just being irritatingly obtuse? If he'd made some observation that had worried him, he'd obviously been mistaken.

"Approximately zero, considering it was actually protected twice over," I said tersely. "We used a condom, and she has an IUD. I won't be procreating any time soon."

Sherlock's frown faded. "She told you about the IUD?"

Of all the ridiculous— He didn't know when to stop dogging a subject, did he?

I crossed my arms over my chest. "No. There are simply ways of noticing when one is intimate with a partner in particular ways. You'd think, considering that I *am* a doctor, and you..."

My agitation dwindled at the clear relief that washed over his expression. The phrasing of the questions and certain moments last night clicked together in my head.

God help me, was he asking for *himself*?

Watching the way Jemma had touched him last night, I'd assumed she'd been riffing off her general experience of what men responded to. It could actually had been the specific experience of having touched *him* before. It just hadn't occurred to me—for fuck's sake, the man sneered at the faintest whiff of romance or passions of the heart. He treated his body like a machine built for the sole purpose of carrying his brain around. When had *that* happened? *How* had that happened?

The idea that Sherlock might have had sex with Jemma was actually more boggling in itself than the possibility that he'd forgotten to take precautions. He could be rather… oblivious when it came to topics that didn't generally affect him. I'd once commented to him about whether we might ever see another man travel to the moon, and he'd expressed surprise at hearing any had gone there before.

It'd be pretty difficult to develop certain practical habits if you weren't practicing the act that went with them.

The image flashed through my mind of Jemma pressed up against Sherlock's tall frame, her lips on his, the sugared sweetness of her mouth and the bitter tartness his had held mingling together—and just like that, I was half hard.

Conveniently, Sherlock appeared to be just as thrown by the conversation as I'd been. He switched subjects at top speed with a jerk of the walking stick.

"It was rather strange, that vision we all had at the park yesterday, wasn't it?"

I blinked at him, needing a second to catch up. "The figure that seemed to appear over Jemma? Yes, I'd say so. I've never seen an effect of the light like that before."

"Two days before that, quite a few people in the dining room noticed other odd light effects," he said.

"Which also appeared near her. And Garrett had an odd reaction Saturday morning while we were talking with her —he looked startled and said he'd thought he'd seen something in the doorway, 'a trick of the light'."

"Where are you going with this?" I asked. "Do you think she created those effects somehow?" I guessed it would be possible with a small but powerful projector that Jemma could have carried on her without us seeing it, but... "Why on Earth would she do that?"

"I don't know." Sherlock flexed his hand on the head of the walking stick as his gaze strayed into the distance. "In fact, every indication I've seen from her behavior would lead me to conclude that she wasn't at all pleased by the fact that they occurred. I started thinking about the repeated occurrences while I was doing my electrical research, and recalling each event, she's always been in quite a hurry to dismiss the strangeness and move on to other subjects."

Thinking back, I had to agree. "And it wouldn't make much sense for her to produce an effect she didn't want anyone to see."

"Precisely. Yet I can't shake the feeling that there's some connection between her and them." He paused. "I'd never seen light behave as it did in the dining room the other day either. Had you?"

I shook my head. "There was something unnerving about it, in a way I can't put into words. I'd remember if I'd experienced that before."

"Agreed. It seems too great a coincidence for us to have witnessed two such unique events—perhaps three, in

Garrett's case—all within a week of meeting her and always in her presence. But, as you said, what could be the purpose? And why would she want to divert our attention from the very place she'd drawn it to?"

"Could it be someone else targeting her?" I said. "A strange intimidation tactic?"

He rubbed his mouth. "I considered that. It might have been the case with the instances in the hotel. But for an impression so precise and bright to appear directly over her the way it did in the park—the source would have to be quite close. We were in the middle of the broad courtyard around the fountain. I haven't been able to conceive of how it could have been done from farther afield."

"It must have been generated somehow or other," I said. "Unless you're going to tell me you think she's being haunted by a literal ghost, in which case I'll have to ask who you are and what you've done with my good friend Sherlock."

Sherlock's grim expression relaxed a little with a dry chuckle. "No, I'm not quite that far gone yet. I simply feel there's more to this matter than I can pin down, and that is not an ideal position to be in when we're planning a move this bold."

My mind leapt to last night, to Jemma's pained expression as she'd apologized for the dared kiss and the gentle humor with which she'd encouraged me to acknowledge my desire. She'd deciphered more about me than I'd realized about myself in the space of a week. Had she gotten to know all three of us that well that quickly? I hadn't seen any hint of maliciousness in her interest. If anything, she'd tried to rein us in from our riskier ideas in pursuing her case.

"Whatever's going on, I'd have trouble believing she wants to hurt us," I said.

"But harm can come as a secondary consequence as easily as the main goal." Sherlock tapped the walking stick against the sidewalk. "I'll speak with her and see what I can draw out before we see this plan through. We need to be sure of exactly what's at stake."

As we started along the road again, my heart sank. "Do you think we'll need to call the operation off?" I'd picked up a blowtorch this morning, and excitement had flickered through me when I'd pictured applying it to the display case. To snatch that statue right from under Richter's nose… "Richter needs to be caught at *something*. He's gotten away with too much already. We can't let him slip through our fingers when we're so close."

Sherlock's eyes gleamed behind the dark panes of his sunglasses. "We won't. One way or another, I intend to see him behind bars. The exhibit is scheduled to stay open until the end of next week. We have room to ensure our plans cover every possibility."

He was as eager to carry off this heist as I was, and damn if that enthusiasm didn't bring out everything that was most attractive in his face. I'd always loved seeing him caught up in a case. When had that enjoyment become more than friendly?

I honestly had no idea.

Sherlock waved the walking stick toward the buildings

farther away from the gallery. "Hmm. What's that fellow over there up to?"

A man in a maintenance worker uniform, his neon yellow vest catching all of the midday light, was perched near the top of a utility pole down the road. Beside him, a dark cable dangled toward the sidewalk. He adjusted something on the metal outcroppings and then reeled that cable up slowly. It swayed back and forth against the pole as he formed it into a thick loop.

When I looked at Sherlock again, his lips had curled into a satisfied smile I recognized at once. My pulse beat faster. "What?"

"You never know where you'll find inspiration," he murmured. "What if we don't cut the power, John? What if we set up the police to do it for us?"

CHAPTER TWENTY-ONE

Jemma

The hotel lobby had the perfect little nook near the front windows where a stand of fake ferns hid me from the room, and the tint on the glass made me invisible to those outside. I'd been sitting there for a few hours, catching up on business through my tablet and setting new contracts into motion as if I could be sure of being around when they were fulfilled. Finally, John's silver Ford pulled up to the parking garage entrance.

Bash had texted to let me know that the doctor and Sherlock had left the gallery area a while back. They must have gotten started on whatever new strategies they'd thought up right away. I slung my purse over my shoulder and slipped across the room to one of the columns near the lobby elevators.

The savory buttery smell of shepherd's pie was already drifting from the dining room where the dinner buffet was about to open. Chances were good they'd come by this way.

I positioned myself where I couldn't see the elevator doors and no one coming off could see me, but I could hear just fine. The doors rasped open to Sherlock's voice in mid-sentence. "…should be quick enough to assemble," he was saying.

"It's good that it gets dark early at this time of year," John said. "At least we have a decent window in which to set things up."

They passed my column on the way to the dining room, their voices fading away alongside the tap of John's walking stick. I counted to ten in my head and then pushed off to follow them.

I'd nearly made it to the dining room doorway when the lobby door squeaked. I glanced over my shoulder out of habit and froze.

The man who strode in had a face so distinctive I recognized it in an instant. His rounded jaw jutted forward like that of an anglerfish, his ruddy skin gone leathery with too much sun over too much time. He'd combed and parted his white-blond hair neatly, and he'd decked out his bulky frame in a button-up shirt and dark jeans that didn't look totally out of place in this establishment, but I'd have marked him as a predator at a glance even if I hadn't tangled with him briefly before.

Anglerfish was one of the thugs Stefan Richter kept on his payroll. He'd come after me when the heist in Munich had gone sour. After a brief scuffle, I'd gotten away easily enough, and I'd been wearing a black wig and a lot more make-up, but he might still recognize *me*.

I crept back to the line of columns until I was close enough to the front desk to listen in. Anglerfish waited stiffly as the clerk helped the woman who'd already been in line. Then he marched over.

"I need to leave a message for John Watson—he's staying here."

"Just a second." The clerk tapped at her computer keyboard. "Yes, of course. What's the message you'd like to leave?"

"Let's see… Oh, hold on, I see him right over there. I'll go talk to him myself. Sorry for the trouble."

"Not at all," the clerk said blandly.

Anglerfish hustled away. As soon as the clerk was occupied with someone else, he headed out the door.

I darted across the lobby and ducked into my hidden nook. On the street outside, the thug crossed the road and got into the passenger seat of a car parked farther down the block. I watched for a few minutes, but the lights didn't come on.

Whoever else was in there, they were just sitting, watching the hotel like I was watching them. They must have followed Sherlock and John back here but only suspected who they were trailing. Now they'd gotten confirmation.

All the intimidated witnesses, all the destroyed evidence that stopped Richter's cases from going to trial— guys like these carried out that work. Richter wouldn't like a prominent detective and his partner hanging around his precious exhibit, whether or not he had any idea they were working with me. I wasn't sure if his thugs would dare take on Sherlock himself, but I wouldn't put it past them to try to put a whole lot of fear into John.

My throat tightened. I had practical reasons to want to keep all of my trio safe—the heist plan might fall apart if John was too injured to participate. But the thought of him being battered and bruised made me tense for other reasons as well.

He was only doing his job, and I could admit I was starting to believe he was a lot more earnest about it than most of the crime-fighters I'd encountered, even if he got off on the thrill too. There were a whole lot of people who deserved to be roughed up more than John Watson did.

My phone pinged with an incoming text. Garrett was asking whether I was coming to have dinner or at least dessert. I hesitated over the screen for a minute before answering.

Got some information from a friend back home that I'm following up on. Will check in with you all if it leads somewhere.

If Richter's men were planning on making a move, I wanted to know about it immediately.

I didn't see anyone stir inside or around the car for close to an hour. The sky darkened outside, the streetlamps glowing more starkly. I was debating alternate tactics when an all too familiar tapping reached my ears.

John was heading toward the front door, not in any great hurry but with a purposeful stride. Where the hell was he going on his own and on foot? Didn't he know there could be paid mercenaries waiting around to corner him in some dark alley?

No, that possibility clearly hadn't occurred to him.

I had only a couple seconds to grapple with my options. I could have reached out to Bash, but in the absence of other instructions from me, he'd have gone back to his hotel room. Even at his fastest, he couldn't make it here in time to follow John.

That left me. Fuck. Maybe if John had company, the thugs wouldn't hassle him in the first place, and Anglerfish wouldn't get close enough to have a chance at connecting me to the woman he'd chased through München Hauptbahnhof station.

I slipped between the ferns. "John!" I said as I caught up. "Are you heading out too? Good timing."

John blinked at me and then smiled. He held the door open. "Is your lead taking you anywhere useful?"

I made a face. "No, it ended up being a dead end, at least for now. Richter owns a large property in the councilor's district, so I'm thinking the blackmail might have been to pressure him into some decision regarding that, but I haven't found a clear link between the two of them there either."

"Well, it would give us a motive. Where are you off to, then?"

"I ran out of sugar cubes. Again. I figured I should buy my own stock before depleting the hotel's supply any more. What about you?"

John chuckled as we fell into step together on our way

down the street, but he hesitated for a beat. "Just picking up some more tobacco for Sherlock."

Had he felt awkward admitting that? I raised an eyebrow at him as we passed Anglerfish's car and crossed the street. "Do you normally run his personal errands for him?"

"Only when it benefits me as well as him," John said, still smiling. "I noticed the tin is getting low, and Sherlock's too deep in planning mode to pay much attention. Halfway through the night, I expect he'll finish it off and then be irritable that more didn't magically appear. You really don't want to see him irritable. So, I'm making the magic happen." He waggled his fingers.

Car doors thumped softly behind us—two of them. From the sound, I guessed both Anglerfish and whoever had been in the driver's seat had gotten out. Their footsteps rasped against the sidewalk after us, no faster than we were walking. For now, they were just seeing where we went.

Waiting for a chance to attack.

My heart thumped, but I didn't let anxiety color my voice. "You really take care of him—Sherlock—don't you?"

"Oh, well, it's mutual, so I don't think it's so bad. Sometimes he notices when I've pushed myself too hard before I do and gets me to rest. He'll even play actual classical pieces on his violin to help me relax instead of insisting on his rather experimental compositions. There was one time he shot a guy who would have killed me. Little things like that."

His tone was light, but I caught just a hint of hesitation in it again. He looked at me with unusual intentness. A tingling of suspicion ran down my spine.

He'd spent a lot of time alone with Sherlock this afternoon. It was possible they'd compared notes about their experiences since meeting me and noticed something that had made them wary. Not incredibly so, or I didn't think we'd be having this conversation at all, but John wasn't quite as easy with me as he had been.

Maybe I should have intervened to reduce that alone time. I hadn't wanted to interrupt whatever schemes they were laying down. Well, I couldn't do anything about the past, but I could keep him distracted from speculating about me right now.

"I should be able to grab my sweet stuff in here," I said, pointing to a convenience shop up ahead, and then, as John followed me in under the bright lights, "Did you talk to Sherlock about last night?"

A faint flush crept over John's face. "No," he said. "You must have seen how he was this morning. He'd rather set it aside and move forward. I don't think there's any way I can bring it up without seeming 'dramatic' about it, and there's not much he hates more than unnecessary dramatics."

One man came into the shop behind us and sauntered down the aisle next to ours. I caught a glimpse of him between the shelves: not Anglerfish but of similar stock, built like a truck with a forehead nearly as square as a windshield. A really friendly-looking guy. No doubt they only wanted to chat.

I grabbed a box of sugar cubes off the shelf and headed to the counter. "I have trouble picturing you being all that dramatic about it. But I've learned my lesson about meddling in whatever's going on between you two."

John was quiet while I paid. I scanned the street surreptitiously on our way out and spotted Anglerfish mostly obscured by cars on the other side of the street, a few down from us. The bell over the shop door sounded when we were several paces on our way—our other tail rejoining the chase.

"How did you do it?" John said, his gaze fixed on the street ahead. "Get him to… open up to that kind of experience?"

Ah, so he'd figured out that much. I suspected that had been deduction on his part more so than Sherlock admitting it. And now he wanted me to act as couples therapist? Dear lord.

I might as well be honest. "It was just sex. Purely physical, like a very enjoyable workout. I don't think I could give you any tips you could use. He can't be the same with you because he likes you."

John snorted. "And you're trying to tell me he *doesn't* like you?"

"He hardly *knows* me," I said. "He finds me intriguing. It's not the same thing. Your lives are entwined—you have a deep, life-saving, tobacco-fetching kind of loyalty. I doubt that kind of caring about another human being comes very easily to Sherlock in the first place, from what I've seen of him. It'd probably be even harder for him to detach those feelings from physical intimacy than it is for most people."

All the more reason why I'd been right to avoid that kind of complication between me and Bash, come to think of it.

"The intimacy wouldn't necessarily have to be *detached.*" John paused. "But that's why your approach wouldn't work."

"I don't know. You could just talk to him about it and see what he says, dramatics or not."

"Yeah." He let out a sigh. "I should probably figure out exactly what I'd want out of that conversation first. I'm pretty sure I wouldn't want to actually *date* the guy. He's too… Sherlock. But maybe, if we stayed the way we are and just added in kissing and… whatever else, now and then—I don't know."

His befuddlement over the situation was kind of adorable. "Well, I don't get the impression he's going anywhere, so I'd imagine you have plenty of time to figure it out."

"Very true."

He led the way around the corner to a tobacco shop a couple blocks down. Truck-guy followed us in again. John poked through the offerings with practiced speed and made his purchase. We were partway back to the corner when he leaned close to my ear.

"As you may have already realized, we have extra company on our errand."

All his time in Sherlock's presence had clearly honed his own instincts. I nodded without glancing back.

John gave his walking stick a little twirl. "In situations like this I generally prefer to set up the ambush myself and turn the tables rather than waiting to see how my opponent would like to play things."

"What did you have in mind?" I asked. I couldn't say I'd complain about giving our followers some incentive to back off.

"Oh, maybe a shortcut down a darkened alley." He shot me a grin and caught my elbow to draw me with him down an alley that had presented itself. "The two of us against one—I don't think we have anything to worry about."

Against *one*? "John," I started with a lurch of my stomach. Before I could correct him in warning, the thugs charged into the narrow shadowed space after us.

They both barreled right at John. He was their real target, after all. I tossed myself into Anglerfish's path with a faked stumble, letting a gasp of surprise slip from my lips. Then I jammed my elbow as hard as I could into his gut.

You might think that it'd be easier to fight a massive dude from a distance, but I'd found with my particular skillset of speed and focused strength, I worked best when I was close enough to land my blows with maximum impact—especially in a space like this where there wasn't much room to maneuver anyway.

I slipped Anglerfish's attempt to catch me in a hold and socked him in the throat while kneeing him in the balls. He grunted but kept swinging.

He was going to regret that. I dodged to the left, and

he grabbed my hair, yanking hard enough to send pain splintering through my scalp. For a second, he snapped my head around to face him. Our gazes locked, and then I was stabbing my fingers into his eyes.

With a choked sound, his grip loosened. I pulled free and slammed his legs out from under him with a sweep of my foot, adding a blow to his spine as he toppled. His head smacked the pavement, and he sprawled there in a half-conscious daze.

I spun around. John had been doing a decent job of holding his own against Truck-guy. The beefier man was favoring one foot, and a walking-stick shaped welt decorated his cheek. Apparently deciding he needed an extra advantage, the thug whipped out a knife.

That was hardly playing fair.

Before I could jump in, John lashed out with his stick and knocked the blade right out of the guy's hand. I snatched it up before it even hit the ground. Truck-guy glanced from John with his stick to me brandishing the knife and appeared to decide he'd had enough. He shoved past me on his way out of the alley.

John caught my arm to steady me. "Are you all right?" he asked.

He clearly was. His eyes were sparkling, elation emanating from every inch of his body. He'd enjoyed that fight for his life.

John Watson was an adorable sick fuck, and I liked it.

"I'm fine," I said, and nodded to Anglerfish, who'd found the wherewithal to roll onto his back. "Let's get out of here before they decide to make another go of it." As much as John might have enjoyed that, *I* wanted to get him back to the hotel in one piece.

John walked the rest of the way back at an energized pace. He burst into the lounge room, where apparently he and the rest of the trio had planned to meet. The moment Sherlock and Garrett ambled in several minutes later, he launched into an account of our adventure. I hung back by the door, watching the other two watch him.

"I don't know if we can even be sure they're Richter's people," he finished. "It's not as if we haven't pissed off plenty of other criminals and their associates."

"But most likely Richter," Sherlock said grimly. "They might have noticed us by the gallery today. I should have been more careful."

John waved his concern off. "If it is him, it'll be my own fault for that stunt trying to shake the display case."

Sherlock's gaze slid to me, and there was definitely a cooler edge to his penetrating stare than I'd felt before. "You're lucky Jemma happened to be with you."

Did he think I might have prompted the ambush somehow? Or just that I'd suspected it might happen?

Before I had to answer, Garrett's phone chimed. He woke up the screen and peered at it. A frustrated sound escaped him.

"What?" Sherlock said, his attention diverted.

"I set up alerts for any news about Richter," he said. "The gallery's just sent around a press release—he's pulling the exhibit early. Which means it's all getting packed up Saturday evening after closing."

The bottom of my stomach dropped out. It was

Thursday. I didn't have to ask to know it was already too late for us to put any plan into action tonight.

Unless the men in front of me were ready and committed to go tomorrow, all this work had been for nothing. My last chance would slip right through my fingers.

I sank onto the sofa and tipped my face into my hands, not needing much imagination to appear distraught. "He must suspect something's in the works—how can we be ready in time? He's beaten us. Outsmarted us."

It was a shove more than a nudge, but it hit the mark. Sherlock's mouth twisted. "He hasn't. John and I hashed out the final necessary element this afternoon. We have all the pieces we need."

I glanced at him through my fingers. "Are you sure? If something goes wrong—"

"It won't," Sherlock said firmly. "We're bringing down that bastard once and for all." His gaze twitched toward John, and I realized my shove hadn't been the only thing that had pushed him. For all his cool composure, he was furious about the attack on his friend.

Thank you, Richter, for playing right into my hands, even if you had to fuck things up along the way.

Sherlock's coolness toward me hadn't slipped my mind. I had the feeling it would be wise for me to avoid giving him the chance to ask many questions before our pending heist.

"If we're going tomorrow, I'm going to practice the swaps some more," I said, getting up. "The last thing I want is to be the weak link. You know how to get a hold of me if you need anything else—don't hesitate."

Sherlock looked as though he might have protested, but John launched into an eager question about some plan involving a sign, and I ducked out unhindered. On my way down the hall to my room, I sent Bash a quick text.

We're a go for tomorrow night, but the situation is already dicey. Keep costume and stay ready.

Adrenaline quivered through my nerves as I slid the keycard into my door. In a little more than twenty four hours, I'd have achieved either my greatest victory or my most epic failure—and the balance between the two had never felt more precarious.

CHAPTER TWENTY-TWO

Jemma

Light was searing into my eyes from everywhere around me, and an icy chill jabbed into my skin. I spun around, my arms flailing, my throat closing against a swell of panic, my pulse thumping so hard the beat shuddered through my whole body. My fingers brushed a delicate shoulder.

"Jemma!" Olivia's thin voice wavered through the glaring light. I caught a glimpse of her face, the skin even paler than usual beneath her freckles. Her strawberry blonde hair whirled around her. Then the stark shine yanked her away from me and swallowed her up.

"No!" I threw myself after her, lashing out at the glow so forcefully the joints in my arms cracked.

My body jerked forward, my eyes popped open, and I found myself sitting up in the hotel bed in my pitch-black room, sweat-damp and shaking. My pulse raced on through my veins.

A dream. A horrible fucking dream.

I dragged in a rough breath, and a stench that was all too real flooded my lungs. Cloying and metallic with a sour undertone, it coated my mouth with the impression that I'd bitten my tongue raw.

My chest constricted. I groped for the bedside lamp.

The glazed bulb came on with a click, and all I could see was red.

Blood drenched the bed from head to foot, punctuated by chunks of gristle and severed bits of human flesh: a finger, an ear, a hunk of hair with scalp still attached. It drenched *me*. That wasn't sweat but blood seeping all down the front of my nightshirt, drying cool on my skin from hands to armpits as if I'd dunked them in a barrel of gore.

The surge of scarlet had washed over the entire room. Blood spattered the floor, the furniture, the mirror, the walls. An arm lay beside the desk, wrist wrapped in a heavy watch I recognized. Over there, a booted foot. And there on the dresser, hair slicked ruddy to the sides of her face and lips parted over crimson-stained teeth, Olivia's head stared at me with gouged out eyes.

A scream ripped out of my throat. My arm swung instinctively and smacked into the lamp. The impact sent pain spiking up from my wrist as the lamp flew off the bedside table. It smashed onto the floor, and the light snapped out.

Everything was dark again. The bloody stench congealed deeper into my lungs.

What had I done? What could I do? Oh, fuck, fuck, fuck.

My stomach knotted tight. My mind balked at even thinking about the scene that had been laid out in front of me. I sat there frozen, willing myself to move but not quite managing it.

Footsteps hustled down the hall outside. A sharp knock rang through the door, and a woman's voice came with it. "Hello? Is everything all right in there?"

I choked on a horrified laugh that almost turned into vomit. My head was still numb, but my body finally got the message to get moving. I peeled off the wet covers and crawled out of the bed. Walked across the soaked carpet, tuning out the faint squelching sounds beneath my feet, to the bathroom door where the carnage stopped. Wrenched on the bathrobe to cover myself.

Was there any blood on my face? I couldn't tell. I didn't dare touch it to try to find out, my hands were so smeared. I tucked them inside my sleeves as I eased open the door just a few inches.

The bright hall light left me blinking. A woman in the hotel uniform of white dress shirt and forest-green vest and slacks was standing just outside, her mouth set in a tight frown.

One clear thought pierced through the mess of my mind: I had to get her out of here. I couldn't let her see what I'd done.

"One of the other guests reported hearing some

sounds of distress from your room," the woman said. "Is something wrong?"

"No," I said quickly, ducking my head. "I get nightmares every now and then—it's a PTSD thing—I'm so sorry I disturbed anyone. It shouldn't happen again. They don't—they don't come that often."

My halting embarrassment and the mention of a mental condition were enough to diffuse the woman's inquiry. She backed up a step. "My apologies. You understand, we have to check when there's a report…"

"Of course," I said. "You're just doing your job. I really thought I was past this." I let out a weak chuckle.

She had no idea what to say to that at all. "I hope the rest of your night is more restful," she managed, and hightailed it out of there.

I pushed the door shut and flipped the door guard over to prevent any sudden intrusions. Then I turned around, gripping the cuffs of the bathrobe. The numbers on the digital clock gleamed through the darkness—it was just after midnight.

My night wasn't going to be restful at all. I had to deal with this, clean it up, something, somehow.

Bracing myself, I flicked the switch for the main light. It washed over the same gruesome scene I'd been met with before. My bare feet had left bloody footprints across the carpet from the bathroom to the door; my fingers had streaked the doorknob. So much fucking blood. And the bits and pieces—the head on the dresser—

My stomach clenched. I wasn't going to let myself look at that again, not yet.

Where did I even begin?

I wavered at the edge of the chaos, my mind freezing up again. My eyelids were heavy with exhaustion. This didn't even make *sense*, did it? How could I have— These people were—

Across the room, the window pane I'd left a crack open rasped up. My heart stuttered. I started forward and then stalled as Bash's muscular form eased past the blind.

I'd told him to "keep costume." He had on his wig with the dreadlocks and those shockingly blue contacts that drew a person's gaze straight to his eyes. He stepped onto the bloody carpet without any hint of disgust or horror, *his* gaze fixed on me.

"Are you okay, Mori?" he asked, worry coloring his tone as he took in my expression. "I saw a light flash and go out—it looked like some kind of struggle."

My voice came out hoarse. "I… It's everywhere. I don't know what happened. I don't know how to get rid of it."

Bash's forehead furrowed. He glanced around me, and I winced inwardly in anticipation of his reaction. But he only looked confused.

"What do you have to get rid of?"

Understanding sank through the muddle of shock and panic in my head.

He couldn't see it. It wasn't really there. None of it— the blood, the body parts. It was a hallucination to outdo any hallucination I'd experienced before.

Of course it was. That arm and that watch belonged to a Chicago mobster whose death I'd ordered months ago.

That booted foot belonged to a deceased loan shark who'd tried to screw me over. And Olivia…

Bog had collected mementos from my memories and strewn the wreckage around me. The shrouded one had probably provoked that horrible dream too, the asshole.

I inhaled slowly and deeply, but the butcher-shop stench stayed just as thick. The red splattered all around me didn't fade.

Bog had put a hell of a lot of power into this illusion. I'd have taken a little satisfaction knowing the shrouded one must have exhausted itself so much I'd have a temporary reprieve from its presence if I hadn't wanted so much to erase *this* evidence of its presence from my senses. I rubbed my eyes, but that didn't help either.

"Mori?" Bash said again. What the hell would he be making of his boss apparently losing her mind?

"It's okay," I said, as convincingly as I could manage. Olivia's gouged face stared at me from the corner of my vision. I took a step forward to put it out of my line of sight, but I could still *feel* it, even though it wasn't even there. "There's no real trouble. I just have to sort this out."

"Sort *what* out?"

How could I explain it to him when I could hardly explain it to myself? I drew my spine straighter, but I couldn't quite stop a tremor from running through my limbs.

This wasn't how I wanted him seeing me. He couldn't do anything here anyway.

"I'll take care of it," I said. "Don't worry about it. You should go."

Bash's mouth twisted. With a jerk and a couple quick flicks of his hands, he'd tossed his wig on the table and popped out the contacts so he looked only like himself. He crossed the room and grasped my shoulders, his natural light green eyes fixed on mine.

"I'm not leaving you when something's obviously wrong. It's my job to protect *you*, not the other way around."

"Bash…"

I meant to protest, but as I stared back at him, the heat of his hands soaking through the cotton fabric of the bathrobe, the imaginary stink retreated. The scarlet splashes around us hazed.

He was real. He was pushing the horror back. My hands rose of their own accord to clasp his arms, to increase that contact.

His grip on my shoulders tightened, his gaze searching my face. "What do you need? Whatever it is, I'll get it. I'll tear apart the world if I have to. Just say the word."

I believed him. A devotion I'd suspected but never let myself assume thrummed through his voice. It woke up an ache in my chest, an echo of all the moments when I'd wanted but not let myself have, not let myself see, not let myself feel.

If I had my way, we'd get to tear down the worst horrors in this world together, Bash and me—if my fucked up past didn't tear him to pieces first. He didn't even understand what he was up against.

I closed my eyes, but the image of Olivia's mutilated

head swam up, merging with her frightened face from my dream. I swallowed hard.

"It's my fault," I said. "It was all my fault."

Bash's hands shifted from my shoulders to the sides of my face. The firm but gentle pressure of his fingers drove more of the carnage away, replacing the stench with the smell of gun oil and the tang of his natural musk. When I opened my eyes, all I could see was him.

"I don't know what you're caught up in, Jemma, but I know whatever it is, you're fighting it as hard as you can," he said. "Because that's what you've always done for as long as I've known you."

I couldn't remember if I'd ever heard my first name in that low smooth voice. It turned the ache inside me into an eager pang that spread low in my belly.

"You know me," I said.

His lips formed a tight but definite smile. "I do."

"And you're still here even though you know what I am. A liar. A villain. A murderer."

"Who do you think you're talking to?" Bash said. "I wouldn't have you any other way."

He sounded so certain, so full of faith in me. The fervent sensation inside me swelled through my chest. In that moment, it felt more powerful than anything I'd ever experienced, stronger than the guilt and the fear that never quite stopped nipping at my heels, stronger than anything the shrouded folk had ever thrown at me.

I wanted to grab hold of the sensation with both hands and hang on tight. I wanted to wrap it around Bash too to shield us both. But I didn't know how. I didn't know what to do with myself or this rush of emotion.

My fingers curled into the front of his shirt. I brought him to me the only way that seemed right, with my mouth pressing hard against his.

Bash's breath caught, and then he kissed me back with so much intensity my head spun. I tugged him even closer, melding my body to his, and kissed him just as fiercely, as if I could conduct the rush of power into him just by touching him.

There were too many layers of clothing between us. I dislodged the buttons down the front of his shirt and let go of him just long enough to yank the belt of my bathrobe loose. Both shirt and robe fell to the floor without us needing to break the kiss. I trailed my fingers down Bash's sculpted chest, following every curve of muscle, every dip and ridge of a combat scar.

"Mori." Bash's mouth slid from my lips to brand the corner of my jaw, the side of my neck. He held himself back for a second with an effort that tensed the muscles beneath my hands. "You were upset."

"That's gone," I said, willing the words to be true. "It's all right. I needed *you*."

He brought his mouth back to mine, tender and insistent all at once. I jerked open the fly of his jeans. He snatched out his wallet before kicking them off and dropped it onto the bed. Which would be an excellent place for us to find ourselves too.

I pushed him around and onto his back on the

mattress. As he eased himself farther up, I climbed over him and straddled his hips while I reclaimed his lips.

Bash propped himself up on one elbow to meet my kiss even more avidly. His free hand teased up my thigh and under my sleep shirt. His thumb traced the hem of my panties, and I couldn't stop myself from grinding into the erection that was stretching his boxer-briefs.

He growled, his teeth nicking my lower lip with a perfect jolt of painful pleasure. Then he was rolling us over to pin me beneath him. His mouth traveled over my throat.

"I don't want to rush this," he muttered against my skin, "but all I can think about is getting inside you."

A breathless laugh escaped me. "So why aren't you there?"

He gave another growl and wrenched at my panties. I yanked his boxer-briefs down too. He paused to grab a packet from his wallet, stroking my clit at the same time so I wasn't left unattended. I squirmed against his touch, wanting more, wanting him everywhere.

He eased up over me again, slicking the condom over his jutting cock. I took advantage of his momentary distraction to flip us with a strategic heave, landing back on top of him. His sound of protest was lost in a groan as I sank onto his erection.

His thick length filled me, stretched me, sparking pleasure all through my core. I took him in completely and lifted up with a flex of my hips, leaning forward in search of the best angle. He rocked up to meet me, and bliss quivered through me. Mmm, right there would do fine.

No amount of training would have put me on par with Bash's corded soldier's body. He could have taken back control if he'd wanted to, but he let me set the rhythm, caressing my breasts and my thighs, his mouth curving into that quiet little smile when I gasped.

I dug my fingers into the bedspread beside him and tugged his head up with my other hand. As I kissed him, pleasure hummed from my core all the way to the top of my head. It raced farther with each pump of my hips until it shot through me in a crackling wave of ecstasy.

I bowed over Bash as my orgasm crashed through me, and he looped his arm around my waist. With one careful but powerful motion, his cock still hard inside me, he rolled me beneath him again.

Raising my hips up to meet him, he thrust into me so hard the burn sent my release soaring even higher. My head tipped back against the sheets. A cry of pleasure broke from my lips. Bash's chest hitched, and his rhythm broke apart with the groan of his own peak.

In the hazy afterglow, Bash tucked me against him, my back to his front, his breath on my shoulder and his hand on my belly. I tucked my arm over his instinctively. The stress of the horrors before we'd come together and the intensity of our collision had left me drained.

A vague sense of uneasiness crept up over me, but before it could sink in its claws, exhaustion dragged me down into sleep.

CHAPTER TWENTY-THREE

Bash

I woke to a softer light than I'd been used to the last several nights, the patter of bare feet on carpet, and the swish of Jemma's hair. She'd pulled the red waves back into a ponytail for her training. Right now she was repeating a kick-cross-hook-roundhouse combo that I could easily imagine toppling her imaginary opponent. Her breath sounded steady enough, but from the gleam of sweat on the back of her neck, she'd been at it for a while.

She held so much controlled but ruthless power in that slender body. I could have watched her work it for hours. Whatever had shaken her yesterday, she'd bashed its head in and thrown it out the window.

That same woman had softened enough to come apart under me last night, to curl up against me and fall asleep. But as much as I'd enjoyed that, I had to say I enjoyed this side of her even better.

She was seeing her mission through today, with her trio of dupes that she'd wrapped around her finger. I'd be waiting on the sidelines, but it'd still be quite the show.

I sat up, reaching for the right wry quote to make her roll her eyes at me, and she whirled at the movement. The look on her face—jaw tight, eyes clouded—stopped me. Her shoulders tensed and then came down as she consciously willed herself to relax.

"Bash," she said, evenly enough. "We should talk."

"Talk away," I said, but my stomach had sunk. She was upset.

She sucked in a sharp breath, somehow looking fiercer than most of the soldiers I'd faced off against even in her loose sleepshirt and leggings. "This can't happen again. I'm sorry I let it happen at all. Last night—I didn't rein myself in when I should have. I hope we can move forward as we were."

Did she really think I'd abandon the seven years of work we'd done together because she didn't want to fuck again? A prickle of jealousy might have run through part of my mind thinking about the other men she'd recently slept with without expressing any of the same qualms, but I'd taken this leap knowing who she was. It wasn't as if I'd have even wanted a grand romance. I'd be here for her however she needed me.

It'd just seemed for a moment there that she did need me that way. To hold her, to adore her, to make her cry out with bliss.

"If I overstepped at all," I started cautiously.

"No," Jemma said quickly. "You were—You did everything right. It's on me."

She closed her eyes for a second as if gathering herself and crossed her arms over her chest. Then she looked straight at me with a determined expression.

"The thing is, I use sex as a tool to maneuver people for whatever ends. I've *only* ever used it as a tool—and if I happen to get off, great. I don't know if I can turn off that mindset and just be with someone honestly. And I never want to find myself using you like that. You mean too much to me to risk it. All right?"

Whatever niggling jealousy I'd felt disintegrated with those words. We didn't talk about the various ways our relationship had warped far beyond simple employer and employee across the years. I never acknowledged that there wasn't anyone I felt closer to in the world, and she'd never indicated it was the same for her. Until now.

Maybe she saw the acknowledgment as payback for the devotion I'd admitted last night, but I could tell from her tone and her eyes that she meant it. I'd take that over another hot-and-heavy session any day.

"Of course it's all right," I said. "If that's how you feel, then nothing has to change from how it was at this time yesterday. I'll have your back like I always have, we'll topple the assholes who think they run the show, and it'll be great."

She relaxed completely then, with a small but relieved smile that—damn it—made me want to kiss her. I'd gotten awfully good at roping in those urges, though. So what if it might be a little harder now that I knew what I was missing? I'd hone my self-discipline even more.

Apparently it did need a little more honing, because I couldn't help adding, "But I meant it when I said it's not your job to protect me."

The corner of her mouth twitched as if she'd caught it from turning into a frown. "Then don't think of my decision as being for your protection. Think of it as being for mine. I don't have much conscience to go around—I'd like to keep any weight off it that I can."

She turned and knelt down beside her suitcase. Her agile fingers unearthed a plastic envelope from a hidden compartment I'd never seen her open before. "That's also why I think it's time I told you a little bit more about what I'm—what *we're*—doing here."

She sat down on the edge of the bed, and I eased over to join her, keeping the sheet spread over my lap. Carefully, she opened the envelope and slid out a faded photograph, the edges creased.

The picture showed two young girls sitting side by side on a wrought-iron bench with a ratty shrub looming behind them. The older girl couldn't have been more than nine or ten, but I could easily recognize her as Jemma. She'd had the same penetrating gaze and thick red hair back then, her face and limbs just as pale and angular in the sack-like dress she was wearing. Her arm was slung around the younger girl, who was equally pale and skinny, but with softer eyes and hair somewhere between blonde and red.

"They didn't take many pictures," Jemma said. "This

is the only one I got to call mine." She slid her thumb along the bottom of the photo to rest beneath the younger girl. "This was my little sister, Olivia. Four years younger. The only thing that mattered to me other than —other than living up to expectations was taking care of her."

Her use of the past tense hadn't escaped me. "What kind of expectations?" I asked instead, because that seemed like a safer question.

"That part isn't important," Jemma said in a tone that told me we weren't touching on that subject at all. "The gist of it is, we were trapped in a place run by a sort of monsters. Monsters that sometimes ate kids when they got to be a certain age. I got out of there the only way I could find how, and I did everything I could to be ready to come back and get her out too…"

I knew something about growing up with a monster, but I could tell she didn't mean quite the same thing I would have. She paused for a second, but when she spoke again, her voice was just as steady as before. "Do you remember the mountain village you came with me to in Utah?"

Six years ago. I couldn't see how I'd ever forget it, even though she'd left me behind for whatever quest she'd been on, staked out partway along the path. She'd made it back to me hours later clutching a swelling wrist to her stomach, her eyes as glazed and face as drained of color as a corpse.

I'd seen that vacant hopeless look on men who'd just glanced down and seen that a blast had taken their lower half straight off. It'd never bothered me half as much on my fellow soldiers as it had on her.

"I remember it was bad," I said.

"Well, yes." Her fingers pinched the photograph. "That was where they'd moved to. Our family and the monsters. She should have had almost another year before they'd have taken her, but—the one that wanted me, it must have been pissed off that I slipped out of its grasp. So it took her early. She was already gone. I didn't make it back in time."

My mind leapt to my siblings—to hustling them out of our parents' house and hitchhiking across three states to the grandparents we'd never met. Promising my grandmother that I'd go back home, that they wouldn't have to deal with some thirteen-year-old delinquent as long as they took in the little ones.

It'd hurt, leaving my brother and sister behind, going years before I saw them again, and I'd known they were safe. I'd known I'd gotten them out.

How agonizing would it have been if I'd lost them along the way?

It's my fault, Jemma had said last night, looking like she'd seen a ghost.

"You did everything you could," I said. "I *know*. I was there with you helping you prepare. You were practically still a kid yourself, Mori."

"I was eighteen."

"And already pulling off more than anyone I knew three times that age. You had to balance being ready enough to really save her with getting there in time." I remembered my own childhood tightrope walk with a twist of my gut. "Was there any way you could have tackled the 'monsters' if you'd gone there earlier, before they took her?"

Her jaw worked. "I don't know," she said. "At least I could have tried. But that's not the point. That's the past. Since then, I've had to— To get out, I made a deal with one of the monsters. I bought myself ten years. That time's almost up. What we're doing here, it'll help me break that tie so I'm free of it. I just need to do that, and then I'm going to destroy all of them, with all the means I have. If I have to burn down the rest of the world in the process, I don't really care—but I don't want you getting burned. That's not what you signed up for."

"I signed up to kick all the ass you need kicking and to pitch in whatever other ways I can," I said. "If some of those asses belong to some kind of monsters, it doesn't really matter to me. The lines of work I've been in, there's always a chance of getting burned. It comes with the business."

"This isn't like any business you've ever been involved with before. These things are… worse."

I held her gaze. "I don't fucking care. Okay? If there's something I need to know to help me stay ahead of them, by all means tell me, but I'm not going to run."

She looked away for a moment and then glanced back at me, her eyes fiercer than before. "They can't touch you, not really. All you need to remember is not to make any deals. Even if you think it could save me. It won't. If I'm gone, then I'm gone."

"Fair enough," I said with a nod.

The answer appeared to reassure her. She slipped the photo back into its envelope and tucked it away in her suitcase. "If everything goes well tonight, I'll have that worry off my back."

"Have your detectives come up with a solid plan?" I asked. "You sounded a little concerned in your last text."

"Oh, that. I think we can pull it off. Garrett's determination, John's optimism, and Sherlock's genius make a pretty potent combination, exactly as I expected. No, the problem is more that the damned genius seems like he might be forming suspicions I'd rather not have to tackle. But with the heist moving forward this quickly, I think I can dodge them."

Her tone had softened with something like fondness as she'd mentioned the three men's names. Not an emotion I was used to hearing from her.

"You're starting to like them," I said.

"What?" Her head jerked up, and she blinked at me. Then she laughed. "I don't like people. It's not my style."

I raised my eyebrows at her. "Oh, really."

"You're an exception. They're…" She waved her hand vaguely. "I don't know. They're interesting. That's not the same thing."

Jemma didn't tend to care about things she didn't find interesting anyway. I leaned back on my hands, watching her with curiosity. "What's interesting? You didn't think they'd be as good as they act, but you've discovered they actually are?" What were the chances of that?

Her gaze went distant for a second, with a hint of

longing that woke up my earlier jealousy despite everything she'd just shared with me.

"No," she said with a crooked smile. "Although they might be. It's more that I'm starting to see how much they might be like me."

CHAPTER TWENTY-FOUR

Jemma

"He's just getting the check," Bash said over the phone. "The way service has been going in there, I'd say we're waiting another ten minutes."

"Great. Just enough time to finish my coffee." Stretching out my legs beneath the little glass-topped table I was sitting at in a café around the corner from Richter's chosen lunch spot, I plopped another sugar cube into the mug for good measure. Then I took a gulp of the bittersweet liquid. The bitter side woke up my brain a little more, and the sweet side smoothed out my nerves. My head still felt slightly fuzzy from two nights of disturbed sleep in a row, but I could work around that.

Bash shifted on the other end of the line with a rustle of his down jacket. "Shouldn't you let me handle this? Richter knows you—or at least he knows about you."

"It's a two person job. I don't trust anyone else with it. If you do your part right, he won't even notice I'm there."

"When we were working out the London plan ahead of time, you said we weren't going to need a sample."

Bash's tone was mild, but there was a hint of a question in it. I wet my lips.

"I always knew we might want to doctor the real figurine. That's why I had you take the sample from our departed friend in Freising. This way the trio will get what they wanted, no embarrassment, no need to worry too much about my role in the whole thing. Now that I've seen them in action, I got thinking that if I leave them in the lurch, they won't let it go. I'd rather not have to deal with vengeful criminal investigators on my tail."

Bash hummed to himself. The sound might have been skeptical, or maybe I was reading too much into it.

My answer had been pretty much the whole truth. Since arriving here, I hadn't really thought about where I'd be leaving Sherlock, John, and Garrett at the end of my plan. I'd been too focused on getting us to that end and trusting that I'd worked everything out. The jade figurine they'd end up with didn't have the slightest trace of DNA on it, because it wasn't a murder weapon. The real murder weapon was an excellent copy that Bash had since tossed in the Pullinger Weiher lake.

When I'd decided on that outcome, I'd had a laugh to myself imagining the three most brilliant crime-fighters in London fumbling to explain themselves after the proof didn't present itself as expected. Now the thought had become less satisfying. I *wasn't* a monster like Bog, spreading misery for the pleasure of it. All of my plans had a purpose.

Whatever their flaws, the three men did by all appearances care about bringing Richter to justice. And there was plenty of justice that Richter was due. On the balance, it now seemed more prudent to throw him under the bus rather than them.

Which meant I needed a little piece of him to plant.

"The waiter has brought the check," Bash reported. "Target getting his coat on. I'm moving into position now."

"Same here." I got up. "After this, I'll see you tonight."

"Everything's ready to go."

"Perfect." I paused. "Thank you, Bash."

"I am made of faith and service, Majesty," Bash said in his wry Shakespeare-quoting voice.

The comment settled my nerves more than the sugar had. When I'd first woken up this morning nestled against him, I'd been afraid that I'd completely fucked up the one good sure thing I had in my life by, well, fucking him. But he'd taken my concerns in stride. He'd listened to my story about Olivia and the shrouded folk without badgering me with questions I didn't know how to answer yet. Exactly as I should have expected him to.

I'd yet to see anything really shake Sebastian Moran. It was too bad that was such a turn-on as well as being an excellent quality in a right-hand man.

It was so absurd that he'd suggested I was starting to care about my trio of investigators. It didn't matter how appealing they could each be in their own ways—they were a means to an end. When I slipped out of their lives, when they realized I'd used them, they'd be glad to see the back of me. Bash was my constant, my rock in the rapids.

Although if he ever did leave, I could go it without him too. I had to remember that.

I left a fiver on the table and tugged my hood up over my hair as I headed out. We'd gotten another damp dim day, but at least it wasn't outright raining like it had been this morning. I dodged the shallow puddles on the sidewalk.

When I turned the corner, Bash came into view at the other end of the block. He walked with a brisk stride, the collar of his puffy jacket pushed to the bottoms of his ears. I picked up my pace to be ready for the interception and curled my fingers around the little scalpel inside my sleeve. He tipped his chin in a slight nod before he started jogging.

Richter strode out the restaurant door—a tall, broad-shouldered man with eyes sunk as deep as his nose protruded out. Bash ran right into him, their shoulders colliding.

"Hey, watch it!" Richter shouted as he swayed backward.

I ducked past the two of them with a flick of my scalpel. There and then gone, so shallow and swift a scratch that Richter wouldn't see it had happened until he was sitting in his car. A papercut he hadn't noticed at the time, he'd have to guess.

A tiny splatter of blood was all I needed.

I dropped the blade into the baggie in my pocket and

hurried on down the street. "Watch where *you're* going," Bash was saying in a belligerent voice. As soon as I'd slipped around the next corner, he'd back off and end the distraction.

A few paces down the nearest cross-street, I waved over a cab and hopped in. My pulse thumped at an eager tempo as I gave the driver the name of the hotel.

I'd done it. The last piece was in place. Now all that mattered was making sure tonight didn't fall apart before it happened.

The trio had made plans to hole up in Sherlock's room for most of the day, hashing out the final details. I stopped by my room to drop off my illicit acquisition and pick up the morning's purchases before heading upstairs.

John answered my knock. He ushered me in, excitement beaming from every inch of him like lights on a Christmas tree. Clearly I didn't have to worry about *him* getting the last-minute jitters. Last-minute boners was more likely.

"You're absolutely sure they won't get hurt?" Garrett was saying to Sherlock where they were bent over the table looking at a diagram Sherlock had drawn.

"The last thing I want to do is electrocute a member of our precious Scotland Yard," Sherlock replied. "I've studied the matter thoroughly."

"Only you would consider a twenty-four hour education to be 'thorough'," Garrett retorted, but with half a smile. He glanced up, and his smile touched both sides of his mouth while also becoming more hesitant. "And here's our Firecracker. How did the shopping go?"

I tossed a couple bags onto the bed from the errands I'd run while Bash had tracked Richter to a convenient location. "Four blue jackets, to your exact specifications. I bought them each at different stores so no one would think a batch purchase was odd."

"Exactly what I should have suggested," Sherlock said with a snap of his fingers.

"I think you sent me to do it so you wouldn't need to figure out all the necessary suggestions." I winked at him and dropped onto the edge of the bed next to my loot. "Where are we at?"

"All things considered, I believe we're remarkably well-prepared. I got the call that the van was ready about an hour ago." His gaze lingered on me for a beat too long to be totally relaxed. He motioned to John. "Did you want to get in a little more practice with the blowtorch? We have that spare pane."

All right. I had two potential stumbling blocks left in front of me. No need to get fancy. I could tackle them one at a time.

"There's a disturbing lack of coffee in this room," I said. "I feel I can best contribute by getting some of the good stuff from downstairs. Garrett, help me carry?"

It was a bit of a weak excuse, but I'd wanted it to be. I wanted him to pick up on the fact that I was angling for a conversation.

"Sure," he said with an expression somewhere between curious and wary, and followed me out.

I waited until we'd almost reached the elevators. "How are you doing with all of this?"

Garrett shrugged, but his shoulders tensed. "It's fine. The plan is coming together. Sherlock is… He's Sherlock, but not really all that much more so than usual. I'll just be glad when we're done."

The elevator arrived with a chime. I gripped Garrett's arm gently as we stepped on and turned to face him.

"I hope you know how much I appreciate the way all three of you have taken on this case as if it's your own— you especially. You have so much on the line. I don't see that kind of courage or commitment to justice very often."

I really did appreciate those qualities in him, whatever had stirred them to the surface in this particular situation. He was helping save my life, even if he didn't know it. A little honesty helped sell the words.

The tension in Garrett's body ebbed. "That's why I picked this job," he said. "So I could contribute something good to the world while other people are doing their best to destroy it."

"Evil doers beware," I said in a teasing tone. My fingers trailed over his wrist. He gazed into my eyes and grasped my hand abruptly, leaning in at the same moment. His mouth caught mine with all the determination he'd had that first night.

A second later, the elevator chimed at the ground floor. Garrett pulled back as the doors slid open with a curse under his breath. "Elevators," he muttered.

As we headed toward the dining room, I twined my fingers with his and let my voice dip low. "I'm here until Sunday. Maybe tomorrow, after the farewell dinner, we could… celebrate a very successful conference, just the two of us?"

A smile that was nothing but pleased crossed Garrett's face. I'd picked him for my last night here. He'd won twice over.

"I'd like that," he said, his gaze lingering on my face. "And if you ever happen to be in the city again…"

Or maybe he simply enjoyed being around me.

I shoved that thought away. He enjoyed the woman I'd shown him, a woman I'd catered to his tastes. That was the whole point, after all.

"Let's hope I have the opportunity," I said.

Now I had two secure on the line, with one still in danger of wriggling off the hook.

By the time we returned with the coffee mugs, my third fish had apparently decided to take matters into his own, er, fins.

"Sorry to send you off again," Sherlock said, aiming his piercing gaze at Garrett, "but John would like to work with a structure as close to the actual display case as we can find. He won't be able to carry it alone, and I need to get the emblems on." He tapped the jacket he'd spread on the table. "Will you lend him a hand?"

"As long as I can bring my coffee with me," the detective inspector said, looking pleased to have something else to do to distract him from the looming heist. John met him at the door with a clap to his back, and then Sherlock and I were alone.

My first instinct was to toss out an excuse and get the hell out of there, but I stood my ground. If he was going to insist on working through whatever was nagging at him, it was better that we did it now rather than half an hour before go-time.

I ambled over to the table and nodded at the thin metal contraption in the corner. "So, that's going to cut the power for us?"

"Assuming we set the cable up properly, but I don't expect that'll be too difficult." Sherlock placed the replica of the security company's badge he'd had some associate manufacture on the jacket's breast and raised the hotel iron with a faint hiss of steam. "Jemma," he added, looking at the task in front of him rather than at me, "can you think of anyone who would have known you were heading out to Regent's Park the other day?"

He asked in an off-hand way, but my skin prickled with the importance of the question. This was his first feint. He was feeling me out.

And his main concern was Bog's brief haunting by the fountain. Damned shrouded one.

Sherlock must be trying to put together the pieces of how that hazy figure could have appeared. I couldn't blame him for not being convinced it was yet another trick of the light. Either I'd created it or someone else had. So I'd give him an imaginary someone else.

"It's possible," I said slowly, as if thinking back to that afternoon. "When I requested at reception for them to have a taxi there for me, the concierge asked where I was off to, and I told him the truth. I didn't want to risk him hearing me direct the cabbie and wondering why I lied.

There might have been someone else in the lobby close enough to overhear."

"Did you see anyone lingering near the fountain courtyard when you came to meet us?"

I frowned. "No. I checked as I approached to make sure no one looked to be close enough to overhear us, and I kept an eye out through the whole conversation." I let my eyes widen. He knew I was smart enough to follow his thread by now. "This isn't about our plans. You think someone might have followed us there and… created that weird lit-up figure we all saw?"

"The thought had crossed my mind," Sherlock said calmly. "Considering the number of events in close succession. Have you experienced strange light effects like that or the one in the dining room before?"

I shook my head. "No. It *is* strange. But it seems even stranger to think someone would be doing it on purpose. What possible reason could they have?"

"That was where I was hoping you might enlighten the rest of us. You have a quick mind, and you know your situation better than any of us could." He set aside the first jacket and laid out the second.

I sank into the chair opposite him and brought my hand to my mouth in thought. I needed a story he'd accept that wouldn't incriminate me or make him too nervous about my involvement in the heist tonight. It wasn't hard to think of one. All I had to do was remember why I'd picked this trio in the first place.

"I'm not sure if there's anything specific to me," I said. "I came on my own, and I'd be surprised if there's anyone here who already knew me. But an awful lot of people here know *you*, and presumably John and Garrett in relation to you. If I were going to pick a most likely possibility, I'd say one of the other attendees has seen how closely I've ended up associating with the three of you, and they tried to disrupt that closeness out of jealousy. I find the idea pretty far-fetched, though."

A waft of steam rose off the iron as Sherlock finished the second jacket. Heat tickled over my skin. He set the iron down and rubbed his chin. "It is," he said. "But the explanation would fit with human nature of a certain sort. I'd hardly assume that every individual here is of the most stable emotional makeup."

He was buying the ploy. With a little more of a nudge, we'd be back on solid ground.

I wet my lips. "You don't think someone like that could compromise our plans tonight, do you? I'd swear no one could have been close enough to overhear us, especially with the sound of the fountain—that was why you picked that spot, wasn't it?"

"Indeed. And I've been extremely careful while arranging our supplies." He paused and raised his head to meet my gaze. "I'd hoped I could have said the same of you."

A chill quivered through my chest. I wasn't sure what he was talking about now. "Of course I've been careful," I said. "I haven't mentioned the gallery or Richter in public. I kept an eye out during every errand I've run. I want to see him caught and brought to justice at least as much as any of you do."

"Then why did you arrange to cross paths with him today?"

Shit. I held my face impassive, my mind whirling. How could he know about that one brief instant? Did he know what I'd done beyond simply "cross paths" with Richter?

His street-kid squad. There might have been a homeless teen I hadn't noticed tucked away at the edge of some alley. The informer couldn't have been close then—no one had heard my conversation with Bash or seen the scalpel. All they could know was that I'd gotten close to Richter.

"Did you have me followed?" I demanded with what felt like appropriately righteous indignation.

"For good reason, it seems," Sherlock said. "Although no, you weren't followed per say. I simply put out the word to certain parties to keep an eye out if they saw you on the streets, to see if anyone *else* was following. Why would you risk drawing Richter's attention when we're so close to our goal?"

His eyes stayed fixed on me, analyzing every particle of my response. I folded my hands together on the table.

My poker face was at least as good as his. I could navigate this unexpected storm.

"I kept my hood up and my head low so he wouldn't get a good look at me, which would only matter if he's seen me in the German news reports about the investigation. I just wanted to see *him*, once—to get a proper measure of him. When you three break the case and have him in custody, Freising will probably pass it over to your jurisdiction. I'll be heading home. I might not get any other chance to even look at the man I've been chasing for three weeks."

"So you let ego guide you."

He was one to talk about ego. I drew myself up straighter. "I thought it was possible I might notice something about him that would help tonight as well. But maybe that was ego too."

It was ego Sherlock could relate to better. He was still frowning, though. I'd given him the best possible answers, but he wasn't happy with them. It couldn't sit well with him that he'd misjudged the situation. Any second now, he was going to suggest they could go through with the heist without me, that it was safer that way.

I had to head him off at the pass with something that made him even more uneasy. I tossed out the trick I'd been holding in my back pocket.

"Are you trying to suggest that I should back out of helping tonight? If I really thought our plans were at all compromised, I swear to you I would. This whole effort has been built on my work—I should at least *be* there— I've been practicing for the switch-offs." I sucked in a breath. "If this is really because of the other night and the dare thing, I'm so sorry. I got a little carried away—the last thing I wanted was to offend you. I hope you won't dismiss my contributions over that."

Sherlock's posture stiffened as the jab landed. Mine relaxed a smidge in turn. Whatever gods there were, let that be enough.

He opened and closed his mouth a few times before he

worked words out of it. Funny how mentioning the dared kiss opened John up but shut Sherlock down.

"I've put that incident completely out of my mind," he said finally in an equally stiff voice. "And I can assure you that I would never let some sort of petty retaliation guide my decisions. *I* apologize if I've given the impression that was my intent. I agree, I've seen no indication that our plans are compromised. We're more likely to succeed with you than without. I'd only ask, steer clear of our target for the rest of the day?" He managed a small smile.

My lips quirked upward in return. "I can make that promise without any trouble at all. Here's to bringing the bastard down."

Both Richter and the shrouded one who'd better not come any closer to ruining my plans.

CHAPTER TWENTY-FIVE

Jemma

"That should do it," the kid said, looking up from the receiver box he'd been fiddling with in the back of the van. He couldn't have been more than thirteen, his hair cut ragged and his too-small jacket going threadbare at the elbows, but apparently he knew radios—or at least certain tricks you could play with radios—better than anyone else Sherlock knew. "You'll catch the call from that frequency, and the other place will be blocked. All you've got to do is answer."

Right now the box was only emitting a static crackle, but Sherlock looked satisfied with that. "Your assistance is greatly appreciated," he said, and handed over a few tenners.

From his seat at the front, Garrett watched the kid scamper out the back. "Are you sure we can trust him not to shoot his mouth off?" he asked when Sherlock had closed the doors.

"He doesn't know enough to have much to say," Sherlock said. "But yes, I'm sure. I'm a rather good judge of character."

I had to catch my lips from twitching into a grin. A giddying combination of excitement and anxiety jittered through my nerves. I curled my fingers around the cuffs of my security guard jacket sleeves, itching for a sugar cube, but I'd left everything with Bash except the absolute essentials.

"There isn't much time left for anyone to interrupt us anyway," I said.

John glanced at his watch. He'd taken the driver's seat, naturally. "With the way we placed the spikes in the driveway, if they're on schedule they should be calling in the delay in just a couple minutes."

Sherlock held up his hand, cloaked in the same flexible leather gloves we all wore, and hunched over the receiver. "Quiet, then."

We sat there, braced in the dark of the van with only the thin light of the streetlamps seeping through the tinted windows, listening to the wavering static. I leaned into the firmly padded seat and clasped my hands together on my lap. My heartbeat counted out the seconds until a blunt voice broke from the hiss.

"Team Three, we're having a little van trouble. Can you hold off departure? Over."

Sherlock grasped the mic. "We hear you, Team One,"

he said in a brusque tone. "We can hold. How long do you expect to need? Over."

"I'm hoping no more than half an hour. We'll call in on thirty if it looks like longer. Over."

Sherlock motioned to me. I already had my hand on the door handle. I darted out and yanked off the black sheet that had been covering the copied logo. John started the engine as I hopped back in.

"Half an hour," he said with a breathless laugh.

"If we do this right, we'll only need three quarters of that," Sherlock said.

The van lurched forward and roared along the city streets. We'd parked in waiting only a few blocks from the gallery. I pulled the scratchy curls of the light brown wig Sherlock had offered me over my head and adjusted my prescription-less glasses on my nose.

Sherlock had gone darker, with a unibrow and a beard to match the team leader of the real security detail. John's blond locks were tucked under a chestnut fringe with a coordinating moustache. Garrett had gone coppery auburn.

"Time to make the call?" the detective inspector asked, holding up his phone.

Sherlock paused until we'd turned the corner toward the gallery's back alley. "Now."

We cruised into the alley past the police surveillance, looking for all the world like the team they'd been expecting. Garrett brought the phone to his ear. He pitched his voice higher with a distressed strain.

"Yes, I'd like to report a hate poster I just saw. It's truly horrible—I can't imagine if my children saw the picture they've printed on it. I wrote down the exact post. Can you get someone out there to take it down as soon as possible? I thought I saw a police car already nearby."

As he gave the details to the dispatcher, John parked beside the matching van that Team Three had arrived in. He slung his duffel bag over his shoulder. Garrett flashed a grin at me as he hung up the phone. For all his hesitations, he couldn't help enjoying getting one up on his Scotland Yard colleagues.

And I couldn't help returning his grin. Yeah, I might miss that competitive determination a little after this was done. Who knew if I'd ever see it again?

Sherlock leapt out of the van first. He keyed in the passcode another of his young allies had spied out for us, and we strode behind him into the gallery's back rooms before spreading out as if beginning our patrol. Only Sherlock passed the departing team with a salute that partly hid his face.

"Quiet night, as usual," the other team leader said. "Try not to get bored out of your minds."

Then they were gone, and the gallery was ours.

Garrett hustled off to loop the camera feeds pointed at the Richter exhibit. The rest of us waited for his signal and then hurried to the exhibit's doors. John handed Sherlock the code-breaking device from his bag.

He had to get this done and get us into the exhibit room before the power cut out. Otherwise we'd lose our chance to stimmy the motion detectors.

Sherlock opened up the side of the keypad and fiddled

with the wires. Garrett pinged us that he'd gotten in place standing watch by the back door. Numbers flickered on the device's screen. I resisted the urge to shift on my feet.

A tendril of scent crept into my nose: a dry sour smell like old rot. My heartbeat stuttered. I glanced around surreptitiously, but my eyes couldn't make out even a glimmer of the shrouded one in the darkened gallery room. That reassurance didn't stop my chest from constricting.

Bog was here. Too weakened from the massive hallucination he'd wrapped me in yesterday night to make much of an appearance, maybe, but the fact that he'd followed me this far from the hotel through the mortal world meant he'd gotten some strength back. If he recovered enough before we were finished…

I couldn't afford to let that fear distract me.

Sherlock peered at the device's screen as several more seconds slipped by. Finally, the numbers froze on a code. I held my breath as he tapped it in. With a sigh, the steel door slid open.

We'd only just crossed the threshold when the security lights blinked out. "Quick, now!" Sherlock said, flicking on an electric lantern and setting it in the middle of the floor.

We all had squares of the thick black material in our jacket pockets, designed to block the sensor functions so they wouldn't pick up the heat of our bodies. John boosted me up to fix one and then another over the devices high on the walls, keeping his weight on his good leg. Sherlock managed to reach them on his own with his great height. We moved through both rooms, covering all of them.

A sliver of my attention lingered on the glass case that held my prize. A tingle raced over my skin. So fucking close now. I could almost feel it in my hand, feel the relief of its release.

But Bog's scent trailed after me too. A glimmering streak of movement caught my eye in a corner. My head jerked around, but at the same moment, the lights gleamed back on, dimmer than before. The building had a backup generator someone off-site had turned on.

John drew the blowtorch from his bag. Nothing that generator was powering could tip the security team off now as long as we handled the display case just right. He braced himself in front of the section where the jade figurine lay, his shoulders loose but the muscles in his forearms tensed, exactly like when he'd practiced.

He'd insisted that he be the one to carry out this part of the heist since he was the one who'd suggested it. His eyes glinted with anticipation, but his jaw had tightened.

For him, taking on this task wasn't just about pulling off this one heist, was it? It was about proving he could play an equal part despite his lingering injury in everything he and Sherlock did together.

The spurt of the torch's fire made his eyes spark even brighter. I readied myself with the chunk of glass we were going to use to offset the removed weight, watching him and the line of flame. A thin pang of emotion fluttered through my chest.

I was going to miss his earnest recklessness too, just

a bit.

Heat grazed my face. John drew the lines of the rectangle again and again, a sheen of sweat forming on his forehead. Then he stopped, set the blowtorch aside, and nodded to me.

He tugged, and the edge of the case gave. As he tipped that chunk out, I slid my piece onto the top of the case at exactly the same speed. Then I slipped closer beside him, a piece of jade in one hand, a fake golden etching tucked inside my other sleeve. Fixed to my baby finger, I held a metal pick coated in two different sets of blood, just out of view.

I moved even faster than I had in practice. One hunk of jade swapped for another, two quick swipes of the pick inside the grooves, flicking the pick back into the nook in my sleeve as I handed the figurine to John. Sherlock stepped closer to him, his face lit with eagerness now. As I turned, I dipped my other hand into the case behind my back to complete the second switch.

My fingers closed around a cool gold surface marked with lines etched with mathematical precision and speckled jewels perfect in their symmetry. Joy trembled up my sternum as I tucked my real reward away as quickly as I'd taken it. The shrouded one's smell touched my nose a little more strongly, and the lights overhead wavered faintly, but the men were too absorbed in their score to think it was anything other than a fault of the generator.

The relic I'd needed was mine. Bog's tricks, the trio's smarts—none of it had stopped me. All I had left to do was complete my escape.

John eased the piece of the display case back into place while I removed the extra weight. We gathered our things in a concentrated flurry of movement and hustled to the back door where Garrett was waiting.

"Call it in," Sherlock said. We all shed our wigs and security uniform jackets and stuffed them into John's duffel bag. He handed the bag to me. I was the only one unneeded for the last part of their plan; I was the ideal person to dispose of the evidence. Which worked out perfectly for me.

As Garrett pulled out his phone, I raised my hand in friendly farewell and set off around the van.

"Jemma," Sherlock called after me, keeping his voice low. I stopped just past the van with a hitch of my pulse and turned as he caught up with me. Had he noticed part of my larger ploy or caught on to Bog's attempts at signaling them? Did he suspect something?

He reached toward my face and eased off the glasses that had been part of my disguise. "You were in such a hurry you forgot about removing these," he said.

He didn't miss much even in the middle of the craziest scheme he'd ever gotten wrapped up in. I gazed into his sharp blue eyes and wondered once more what it might be like to work *with* a man with a mind like that instead of against him.

I was never going to know.

"You pulled it off," I said. "It was brilliant. I guess I got too focused on making sure the rest goes off without a hitch."

"There's always a necessary balance between caution

and speed," he said, so perfectly Sherlock that an unexpected urge rose up inside me despite my sense of the time slipping away. Then a waft of Bog's scent filled my nose, giving me the perfect excuse to indulge myself. Just as another streak of light shuddered into being above us, I bobbed up on my toes and brushed my lips to Sherlock's.

When I released him a second later, Bog's final effort had faded. "Thank you," I said, meaning it for far more than he could guess right now.

Sherlock blinked at me, momentarily startled—not a look I saw on him often. My throat tightened, but his hesitation gave me just enough opening to pat his arm and lope away.

John had left his car at the other end of the alley for me to use. I dropped the fob he'd given me on the pavement just behind one of the front wheels, where I expected Sherlock would spot it easily enough in the morning, and headed in the opposite direction from what we'd planned.

The farther I got from the gallery, the faster I picked up my pace. The desiccated shrouded folk scent licked after me, growing thicker by the moment. When I switched to breathing through my nose, it coated my mouth.

I came up on the shadowy spot of bank I'd picked, the darkly glinting waters of the Thames ready to meet me. The weight of the piece of glass should be enough to sink the bag, but I stuffed in a few large rocks for good measure while retrieving a couple items from my jacket. Then I hurled the whole lot as far as I could over the depths. The bag hit the surface with a splash and dropped like a stone.

I couldn't wait any longer, not with Bog hovering nearby trying every play it could. I dug into the pouch I'd fastened under my sweatpants and drew out the three other etched golden shapes I'd collected over the last year.

As I tugged down my pants, another wave of the shrouded one stink washed over me. A glow crackled through the air. I fumbled with the pieces. They fit together, end to end, around my mid-thigh like a metal cuff. Bog's light seared brighter as it closed around me, the mark on the back of my neck burned—and I clicked the last section, the one that had once belonged to Richter, into place.

The supernatural glow vanished into the night, and the burning faded away. A quiver of energy raced over my skin from the cuff. It lingered there, a gentle tickle that brought a choked but ecstatic laugh to my lips.

Bog couldn't find me now, couldn't reach me now. Not one of its shrouded one skills could penetrate the cloak this relic gave me. I'd just bought myself my freedom.

With a smile stretching my lips, I tugged my pants back up and loped off toward the spot where Bash would be waiting to drive us to the airport. In a few short hours, I'd be far away from here. Far from anywhere Bog knew to look for me, and far from the three men who'd helped me in more ways than they knew.

They might not have known how final that farewell was at the time, but I'd even gotten to wave my trio good-bye.

CHAPTER TWENTY-SIX

Sherlock

Sometimes I enjoyed taking the lead with an interrogation, but often it was more instructive to stand back and watch the questioning play out, studying the suspect's reactions. Especially today.

On the other side of the one-way glass, Garrett leaned his hands onto the interrogation room table. Richter sat across from him, his hands in cuffs, his long-nosed face held at a haughty angle.

"If you didn't have anything to do with the murder, then how did your DNA and the victim's end up on an object you own that's a perfect match for the killing blow?" Garrett said, his voice turned slightly tinny by the speaker system. "Please, let's hear your explanation."

He might not have as incisive a mind as some, but our little detective inspector made up for it in tenacity. Richter scowled at him. His lawyer in the chair beside him, a stout mole-faced man, started to raise a protest, but Richer waved him quiet. When he replied, he sounded just as certain as he had before.

"I don't know. Maybe you planted it there. Maybe *she* did. I didn't even know this councilor who apparently died, and that statue was packed away in its crate for hours before the plane took off."

Garrett raised his eyebrows. "Who's this 'she'?"

"I don't know that either," Richter snapped. "There's a woman who's been trying to steal one of my pieces since my last exhibit—and not that jade one. I haven't had a chance to sit down and chat about it with her. Why do you think I had so much security set up?"

Beside me, John shifted his weight to lean on his walking stick. "I suppose some criminals will do whatever they can to displace the blame."

"I'm not so sure that's what's happening here." I wrinkled my nose against the lingering odor of sweat and stale coffee in the room—and against what my instincts were telling me. "His body language suggests he's telling the truth."

John stared at me. "What? You don't think he's our murderer, after all this?"

"I'm still forming my impressions. Watch, and see what you make of him."

Richter had switched to a different tactic. He was nodding to his lawyer, who shuffled his papers. "Your evidence will be inadmissible in court regardless of the details. My client can attest that you or a Sherlock Holmes broke into the gallery and stole the artifact from its display case, eliminating the correct chain of custody completely."

Garrett chuckled. We'd worked out our story together, and I'd heard him give it to his colleagues more than once since last night without missing a beat.

"You're going to have a hard time swinging that as your defense." He fixed his gaze on Richter. "Sure, the gallery was robbed. You're lucky my esteemed colleague Mr. Holmes happened to be passing through the area and noticed the warning signs. He alerted the police, but the robbers fled before we arrived. They dropped the statue they'd stolen, so we took it back to the lab for testing, and it was a total surprise when it matched up with an unsolved crime all the way over in Germany. Pretty ballsy, leaving your murder weapon out in plain view, I've got to say."

Richter glanced toward us—toward what to him would look like a mirror. He was familiar enough with police investigations to be aware someone was on the other side. If he'd expected an interruption declaring Garrett's story untrue and releasing him from custody, he was disappointed. His posture deflated, but he jerked his chin up even higher.

"I'd like to consult with my lawyer before I answer any further questions."

John tapped his stick against the linoleum floor. "We should ask him about Jemma. If one of his men was watching the area around the gallery and spotted her leaving, who knows what they've done to her. We shouldn't have let her go alone."

The concern in his voice snagged sharp as a hook on something inside me. It dredged up a flash of memory: her sly smile, sitting at the table in John's hotel room. A hand on my—

I shoved that fragment back into the compartment I was keeping sealed tight. It wasn't important and certainly didn't bear any relevance to our current situation.

"If Richter caught her, we wouldn't be having this conversation, because he'd have all the evidence *he* needs," I said. But perhaps Jemma had seen reason to fear for her safety and had gone to ground. She hadn't returned to her hotel room last night. We hadn't received a single text or call. The more hours passed, the more her disappearance weighed on my gut.

I knew how sharp *she* was. Surely she'd have found some way to contact us?

If she wanted to, that was.

One of Garrett's colleagues ambled past us. "Did you hear the latest about his victim?" he remarked, nodding to Richter through the window.

"His victim?" I repeated.

"Yeah." He worked his jaw as if chewing on something. "This morning, someone raised a complaint out in Germany that this city councilor abused him as a kid when he was part of a youth program. Seems like a few have come forward now. Maybe this knob here did us a favor twice over, taking that guy out of commission and then getting caught for it."

John frowned as the officer sauntered off. "Richter's older than the councilor, and he has no children. This couldn't be revenge. Do you think he might have been a partner in the abuse? That would be blackmail worthy."

The threads of suspicion that had been unfurling in my mind tightened into a starker image. "I think our councilor died in part because no one would end up sorry to have seen him gone."

Before John could ask what I meant, Garrett emerged from the interrogation room. "What a piece of work Richter is," he said. "But we've got him. He hasn't produced an alibi, and with the circumstantial evidence alongside the DNA and his history—I doubt he'll even get bail."

"I'd like to take another look at the gallery," I said.

The detective investigator gave me a puzzled look. "Right now?" he said, in a milder tone than I expect he'd have used if there hadn't been officers around who might overhear.

"If they can spare you. Or if you can arrange official permission for us to enter the crime scene without accompaniment."

"No, if you're tracking down an additional lead, I want to be there for it too." He ducked out of the room to speak to one of his superiors and returned a few minutes later. "All right, let's go."

This once, Garrett drove in his official duty vehicle, leaving John to tap his walking stick restlessly in the back seat.

"What's this about?" Garrett said as soon as we'd pulled out of the parking lot. "What the hell could you possibly want to look at there now?"

"Richter is claiming that someone was targeting his gallery," I said. "Trying to steal a different one of his artifacts. Indulge my curiosity."

The gallery's entrances were taped off, with no one inside other than one officer ensuring the crime scene remained secure. She exchanged a nod with Garrett. We walked straight to the rooms that housed Richter's special exhibit.

I studied the area around the display case that had held the jade statue and then stepped closer. With the pressure alarms off, I could come right up to the glass.

The cut piece of the case had been removed, along with the piece of uncarved jade we'd used to balance the statue's weight. My gaze came to rest on an object farther down the display: a rectangular strip of etched gold set with tiny gemstones.

My heart sank as I studied it. "I'm going to take a closer look at this," I said to Garrett, pointing to it and then pulling on my gloves.

"What does that have to do with anything?" he muttered, but he didn't try to stop me.

I eased the piece out and turned it to catch the light. My thumb rubbed one corner. I lowered it with a grimace.

"This is a fake. Plated gold—cheaply done, even. Richter couldn't have missed the signs. It's been switched since he last saw this display."

John went still. Garrett's eyes widened. "What?" the smaller man said.

"I think we'd better discuss this matter in more detail in private."

My thoughts whipped through my head as we headed back to the car. I sank into the passenger seat and got out my phone. As before, when I dialed the number Jemma had given me days ago, the phone on the other end rang and rang. No voicemail. No indication of its owner. Just a blank.

"What's going on?" Garrett demanded. "Who are you calling?"

"I'm not sure," I said slowly.

"Sherlock thinks Richter might be telling the truth," John put in. "He might not have been involved in the murder."

"*What?* But we have all the pieces—all the evidence leads to him."

"Where did we get most of that evidence?" I said. "Or at least the start of the trail, like that scrap of photograph?"

"From Jemma," Garrett said. "What does that have to do with anything? Of course she—"

"Did you ever confirm with the Freising police that they have an officer on staff by the name of Jemma Moriarty?"

He hesitated. "Well, no—she was worried there'd be repercussions for her if they thought she'd asked the London police to get involed. I made it sound as if we stumbled on the case ourselves. But there was an article about her in the internet, with a photograph and everything. Some award she'd won. You said you'd seen it too."

There'd been a few mentions of Jemma in articles I'd

had to translate from German. "See if you can find it now," I suggested.

Garrett took out his phone and typed in a search. I watched him, nearly certain of the results, as he scanned his screen. He clicked through to another page and then another before raising his head. "It's gone. Hold on. Maybe I only searched her name, not the city too, and that's how it came up."

He typed again and paused. Then he handed his phone to me, the color starting to drain from his face.

The top search result for simply "Jemma Moriarty" was a profile for a math tutor based in Oxford. Her credentials included an impressive list of publications and honors, but none of them had anything to do with policing or criminal investigation. The photo on the page showed a meek woman with pale auburn hair pulled back in a loose bun, her lips so pale they nearly blended into the rest of her face, her eyes obscured by thick rimmed glasses.

I'd trained myself in the art of facial recognition. I could draw the features of the Jemma I'd known over this woman's cheekbones, the angle of her nose, the depth of her eyes, the slant of her neck. But I knew at the same time that no one at the conference would believe this woman was the one who'd toppled a gunman in our midst nine days ago.

John confirmed it. "That can't be her," he said, peering over the back of my seat.

"It is," I said quietly. "The articles we found before were a ploy."

"But—why—"

"She wanted to steal that trinket from Richter?" Garrett filled in. "*She's* the woman he's talking about? How much could that little thing be worth that she'd go to those lengths…" He trailed off, looking even more sick than before.

"She fooled all of us," I said with a strange mix of revulsion and admiration.

How had I let myself be led astray? How quick a mind must she have to have managed it?

I thought I'd seen a woman on the verge of greatness, close to matching my skills. She'd just given a demonstration in how to run circles around me. It was close to being both the most shameful and the most stimulating thing that had ever happened in my life.

Most importantly, where the hell had she gone now?

"All of that subterfuge, all of the pieces she must have set up to get us into the gallery…" John rubbed his face. "I agree with Garrett. I can't see the point of risking all that if it was only about that one piece."

"Unless that piece had some value we're unaware of," I said.

"If she set up Richter," Garrett said slowly, "then who murdered the Freising councilor?"

I glanced at him pointedly. "How could she have set up the details so perfectly to point us—and only us— toward him if she didn't have a hand in it?"

We were all quiet for a moment. "He was a child molester," John pointed out in a rough voice. "But it is still murder. What do we do now?"

That was the question I'd been turning over in the

back of my head from my first inklings of the truth. I exhaled and flexed my hands. "Before I give my opinion on that, I'd like to talk to a few people at our hotel while the conference is still running."

Garrett started the engine. "She lied about everything," he said.

"Possibly. At the very least, she lied about a lot." My mind darted back to that moment just before she'd left last night, when she'd given me a quick kiss and thanked me.

I'd have sworn as readily that she'd meant those two words as I'd have sworn that Richter's indignation was legitimate.

At the hotel, we marched up to the front desk. Garrett flashed his badge. "Official business," he said. "We need to know what information you have on file for one of the guests, who may be involved in a major crime."

The clerk blanched. "Which guest, sir?"

"A Jemma Moriarty," I said. "She was staying in room 247."

The clerk brought up the record on her computer and frowned. "Do you mean Jena Morisarti? That's the name we have for that room." She turned the screen so I could see the spelling.

I almost laughed. How neatly Jemma had played that gambit. If we'd overheard the staff calling her "Miss Morisarti," we'd have thought we'd misheard or they'd simply mispronounced her name. But it meant there was no record of any Moriarty, including the Oxford math tutor, staying here this week.

"Perhaps we were mistaken," I said. "Thank you for your assistance."

Dinner was being served. I walked into the dining room and spotted the Glasgow commissioner Jemma had saved at a nearby table. John and Garrett trailed behind me as I sidled over.

"I'm sorry to bother you, ma'am," I said. "I just had a quick question. Did you get the name of the young lady who subdued your attacker during the welcome reception?"

The older woman brightened at the memory. "Yes, of course. Jemina Moriety. What a promising officer. She does Dover credit."

The other two and I exchanged a look. Another name, another story. How many had she used throughout the conference?

Had any of them been real?

We retreated to the lounge room where we'd spent quite a few hours of the conference in discussion—most of it with the woman we'd known as Jemma. Garrett paced for a few seconds and then threw himself down onto one of the chairs. John leaned against the arm of the sofa.

"I ask again," Garrett said. "What now? Do we throw out the entire case against Richter?"

I paused. "No," I said. "I think… whatever her many crimes, Miss Moriarty—or Morisarti, or Moriety, as the case may be—has given us a gift. We *know* Richter was a terror. We have a solid case where we never did before. A sentence for murder won't cover half his previous transgressions. No one has to know what we do."

John nodded. Garrett gnawed at his lip, but I could tell he wasn't against the idea, even if it didn't entirely sit right with him.

"It's still justice," John said to him. "Just arrived at in a pretty convoluted way."

"And we could be wrong about Jemma," Garrett put in. "It's possible we're conjuring this entire conspiracy, and he really *did* murder that man."

I'd have placed the chances of that at approximately one in a million at this point, but I couldn't see the benefit in saying as much.

"What do we do about Jemma?" John said, his gaze on me.

"We couldn't charge her with anything even if we wanted to," I said. "We can't explain how we know she took that relic without admitting our own crime. We can't even prove the woman we knew *exists*. At least, not yet."

Garrett perked up. "Not yet?" he prompted.

Despite my tangled emotions, a smile crossed my face. I knew what I was up against now. The game was afoot.

I leaned forward, resting my hands on the top of the sofa. "There are a few answers I'd like to obtain before I settle the matter completely. Wouldn't you say the same?"

CHAPTER TWENTY-SEVEN

Six weeks later

Jemma

"Forget Shakespeare," I said, pointing my fork at Bash's plate. "*That* is an absolute tragedy."

He lifted his eyes from his coffee to consider the quarter of pancake that he'd abandoned under its dollop of whipped cream and drizzle of syrup. It was the only surviving piece of the room service breakfast I'd ordered for us after he'd stopped by to discuss the day's plans. His gaze rose farther to meet mine.

"Are you asking permission to steal it?" he asked with a hint of a smirk.

"Only if you're not going to eat it. It would be a horrible waste, is all I'm saying."

He pushed the plate toward me. "By all means, Majesty."

I wrinkled my nose at him for a split-second before scooping the fluffy creamy goodness into my mouth. Okay, now back to business. After I licked the traces of syrup from my fork.

Bash made a not very convincing show of restraining an eyeroll, but his smile had that fond quirk to it that would have stirred up other sorts of hungers if I'd let it.

"When we're done here," I said, "I promise we'll go to Italy next, and you can eat the most authentic pizza in existence every day while I see what I can make of the mob."

"I look forward to it." Bash flipped the page of one of the national papers. "I'm not seeing any useful articles today, as per usual."

"We might as well keep looking, just in case." I skimmed a little farther through my tablet's map of Croatia. "There are too many fucking mountains in this country. None of the feelers you've put out have turned up anything?"

"Not so far," Bash said.

I grimaced. I was starting to think I was going to have to climb to each peak and circle around it for good measure just to find the place I needed. "Why don't we give a helicopter rental another try? We can cover a couple of the slopes. Even if these people are hiding, they can't cover a whole village perfectly."

"If that's what you'd like to do, I can arrange it," Bash said. "Which part of the country?"

"Hmm… How about up here?" I swirled my finger over the northwestern edge of the map.

He nodded and pulled out his phone to look into making arrangements. I tossed my napkin onto the table and got up to stretch my legs.

When we'd picked up this trail a couple weeks ago, I'd known this process might take a while, and it was a lot easier with Bog's threats so distant. But damn, a careful search of an entire country could be mind-numbing.

One of my phones rang—one of the urgent business lines. I scooped it out of my purse and yanked it to my ear.

"Hello?"

"Ms. Matthams?" a reedy voice said, using the name I'd signed into the hotel with.

"Jakov," I said with a skip of my pulse. I'd learned a thing or two during my stint in London, one of which was the usefulness of employing the local youth. Although in my case I'd gone a step above street kids and slipped some cash to the needier looking porters who worked in the lobby. "What have you got for me?"

"Well," the young man said, his accented English slightly muffled as if he'd huddled away in a corner, "you said to call you if anyone came in asking about a woman and showing photos. An old man did a few minutes ago. The people at the front desk didn't say anything, but I followed him a little ways outside, and he met up with two other men, younger guys, like you said might happen. So I called."

A jolt of adrenaline tingled through my veins. "Thank you, Jakov," I said. "You did wonderfully. I'll leave an envelope for you with the front desk when I come down."

"Thank you very much, Ms. Matthams!"

When I turned around, Bash was on his phone. I made a slicing gesture, and he ended the call.

"What?" he asked, cocking his head.

I tapped my phone against my palm. The corner of my mouth curled up. "Change of plans. We have company."

Eva Chase lives in Canada with her family. She loves stories both swoony and supernatural, and strong women and the men who appreciate them. Along with the Moriarty's Men series, she is the author of the Looking Glass Curse trilogy, the Their Dark Valkyrie series, the Witch's Consorts series, the Dragon Shifter's Mates series, the Demons of Fame Romance series, the Legends Reborn trilogy, and the Alpha Project Psychic Romance series.

Connect with Eva online:
www.evachase.com
eva@evachase.com

www.ingramcontent.com/pod-product-compliance
Lightning Source LLC
Chambersburg PA
CBHW061323190726
48288CB00002B/633